Confessions

OF A SIDE DUDE

Lamar's Story

EDWARD LOHR

FOREWORD

I'm sure I don't have to tell you how difficult our journey here can be, from the constant pressures to perform to the demands of who and how to be. It can all become a bit much, and like you, I've thrown my hands up more times than I can count.

Coming from where I do, no one gives you anything and more often than not, instruction is hindsight and you're left with the 1 thing that makes each breath worth it: Hope.

Such a simple thing. Such a difficult task.

The pursuit of hope has left many a man broken, scarred, and spent with many more never even seeing the day of fulfillment.

In this novel, I played around with the idea of what if... What if you were given a blank canvas and told that today is the beginning of the rest of your life? What would you do with it?

Would you dare to dream? Would you finally leap to see if you could truly fly?

I don't propose to have any of the answers. All I have is hope and my mind's eye to explore these very questions.

So then, with all these instigators, I present to you, my story.

Happy Reading!!!

Yours truly,

Edward

Contents

Chapter 1

August 3, 2017. Miami was hot and humid as usual as Lamar made his way down towards Bayside to meet up with his best friend, Julia. They had been friends since they were 10, and 19 years later, not much had changed.

Julia had gone on to Miami-Dade College and graduated with an Associates in Nursing then landed a job at Jackson Memorial Hospital. She'd worked hard while continuing her education and in the past year, landed the position of Head Charge Nurse in the ER department. Lamar, on the other hand, had traveled a slightly different path.

When he was 17, he started working at a Lounge and Bar called Ed's and being exposed to entrepreneurship at such an early age, he decided to become his own boss so much so that he attended Miami-Dade College and studied Business Management with a focus on Entrepreneurship Operations and Accounting. Over the 9 years that he was under the guidance of the Lopez's, he blossomed into an amazing Assistant Manager, and when the owners were retiring, they offered to sell the business to him. That was 3 years ago. Since then, as owner, he'd done some renovations and added on a few new features such as Open Mic Night and Family Night.

Business had really taken off, so much so that he'd had to hire an Assistant Manager who eventually became his General Manager.

As Lamar finally pulled into the parking lot under the Bayside Metro Mover station, he smiled in anticipation of seeing his friend. With the two of them often being so caught up in adulting, they didn't really have a chance to see each other, so they'd made a pact that they'd meet up every Thursday at an alternately chosen location for lunch and a catch up.

After finding a spot, Lamar turned his car off, grabbed his keys and phone, and hopped out of his 2017 Nissan Altima. He waited for the sign for him to cross over Biscayne and then made his way towards Bubba Gump Shrimp.

As Lamar made his way towards the entrance, he spotted Julia standing there in her scrubs with her phone glued to her ear. The sight of her smile brought an even bigger smile to his face. She'd been a huge support in his life as he navigated his way through often stormy seas. She would never know the depth of his gratitude just for her being there and not judging him.

As he neared her, she must have caught him out of the side of her eye because she turned towards him with a smile and her index finger lifted while she finished her conversation. When she was off the phone, Julia embraced Lamar in a big bear hug and planted a kiss on his right cheek. Arms intertwined, they made their way into Bubba's.

They made small talk as they waited to be seated and were quickly caught up on each other's day. They stood there for about 10 minutes before being ushered over to an available table and given menus.

While they looked through the menus, their server came back with water and lemons and asked, "Ready to order yet?"

"Yeah," they both responded at the same time.

"How about two Grilled Seafood Trios along with 2 Strawberry Mango Chillers?" Lamar said.

"Let's get that," Julia responded.

They thanked the server and continued their conversation.

"So how you been?" Julia asked as she sipped her water and leaned back to take in her friend.

"I've been well, honestly," Lamar began as he paused to take a sip of water. "Business has been amazing and my family is decent enough. I'm also really getting into this single life." Lamar laughed as Julia nodded in agreement. With their busy schedules, neither one of them had time to date and often joked about who would be single the longest.

"Baby, I'm with you when you're right," Julia started, "So I've noticed over the past month that you've seemed really preoccupied. What are you not telling me?"

Laughing to himself as he never could keep anything from her ever-watchful eye, Lamar answered, "Well, I was going to wait until it was official, but I've been in talks with my attorney about a property up in Carol City."

Julia excitedly reached out to squeeze Lamar's forearm. "Are you serious?"

"I am." Lamar began just as their server was rounding the corner with their meal and drinks. They waited a moment while their server situated their plates and glasses before them, thanked her, and then Lamar continued. "About 6 months ago, I mentioned to my attorney that I was interested in expanding my portfolio and was particularly interested in Real Estate." Lamar paused as he took a sip of his drink before continuing, "...and last Saturday while at a networking, she came across a lead. She says that it's a 65 unit building that, though needs some work, provides the perfect opportunity for not only equity but also for quality, affordable housing."

Lamar recalled the conditions of the homes he'd lived in when he was younger until his mom was able to get housing assistance. That substandard type of living had impacted him so much so that Lamar had vowed to himself that when he was able to do so, he would see to it that children coming up after him had an opportunity to experience a nice, comfortable home, whether a house or an apartment, where they could feel safe from the world.

"I'm so freakin' excited for you!" Julia exclaimed as she again reached across the table and squeezed Lamar's forearm.

Lamar laughed. "I really appreciate you for believing in me. I don't think I'd have made it this far without you pushing me."

The two of them sat there momentarily, basked in their friendship, before saying grace and digging into their food. The rest of their lunch was spent going over things at work, their families, and how they needed to plan a vacation to get away from it all for a bit.

After they finished their meal, they again thanked their server, left her a handsome tip and made their way, arm in arm, back to where Lamar's car was parked.

"Oh, before I forget..." Julia began, "my cousin Devon recently relocated to Miami and is having a housewarming party tomorrow night. I told him I would love to come and that I would be bringing a friend," Julia said as they stopped at the crosswalk to look both ways. "Interested?"

Smiling, Lamar replied, "Apparently I am." Lamar laughed as they neared his car.

"I knew you would be." Julia laughed as she leaned in to give Lamar a hug. "Be at my house around 7pm. Devon will be picking us up around 7:30pm."

"Cool beans," Lamar replied as he hugged Julia back tightly and kissed her on the cheek. "Any plans for the rest of the day?"

"Nothing major. I'm going to do a little shopping and then go see my mom," Julia replied as Lamar remote-started his car to get his AC going.

"Well, enjoy the rest of your day, and I will see you tomorrow," Lamar said as Julia began making her way towards Metro Mover's station entrance.

"Thanks, babe. You do the same and you be safe out there. Love you!" she called as she made her way into the station.

After watching Julia make it upstairs to the train platform, he hopped into his car and made his way back into traffic, and headed towards Ed's.

Chapter 2

Lamar was on autopilot as he drove towards NW 27th Ave from 20th St where he then made a right and made his way towards Opa-Locka, where his lounge was located. He was lost in his thoughts as he drew near to his establishment. He thought back on how his mom had relocated to Miami from Bristol, PA, in an attempt to get her life together. She'd battled addiction for a good portion of her life and as she saw her babies growing, she'd committed to fighting harder for her family.

With renewed strength and determination, his mom reached out to one of her cousins in Miami and was invited down to get a fresh start. She'd then taken the initiative to sign up for rehab, and through her sponsor, she signed up for housing and eventually landed a job working for the housing authority. Lamar couldn't have been prouder of her for taking back control of her life and made sure to often tell her so.

After pulling into the parking lot of Ed's, Lamar sat in the car for a few moments, still lost in his thoughts, when his phone rang, jarring him back into reality. He looked down and saw that it was his GM, Angela.

"Hey, lady. I just pulled in. What's up?" Lamar asked as he turned his car off and made to get out.

"Oh, nothing major. I just wanted to check in with you to let you know that we're a go for tonight and that you should be receiving the summary sheet momentarily."

Lamar blessed the day he met her and remembered it vividly. Ed's often hosted open mic nights to support and promote local and not-so-local artists. It had been 3 years prior, and Angela had just come off stage to standing ovations after sharing her story about how she escaped an abusive relationship. Lamar made sure to introduce himself, thank her for her vulnerability and courage, and gave her a hug. Maybe a week later, during another open mic night, Angela was there sitting out in the crowd appreciating all the talent who'd graced the stage. As she looked around in quiet contentment, she noticed Lamar running all over the place while still trying to greet everyone.

Smiling, Angela made her way over to him and, upon recognizing who she was, smiled, gave her a quick hug, and asked, "Is everything ok?"

"That's what I wanted to ask you," Angela responded. "You look like you're juggling so many things."

Lamar had chuckled. "Just a little short-staffed and so I've had to take on more responsibility tonight."

"Are you hiring?"

"I'm definitely in the market for some help but don't really have time to interview anyone."

Angela looked around, taking in the crowd. "I'd love to come on board and assist."

"For real? Tell you what, get back to me tomorrow and let's talk about what you bring to the table."

"Perfect! You'll be seeing me tomorrow." True to her word, she called, and from then, it had been history.

He loved how she'd quickly grown to be his right hand in all things Ed's. She was loyal, honest and had a mean eye for detail.

As Lamar returned to the present, he moved across the parking lot and entered the lounge, smiling at the progress he'd made in his life. He spoke to the few team members he encountered as he approached Angela's office.

After checking in with her and comparing notes in preparation for the night, he shared, "I'll be back later. And oh, I won't be here tomorrow night. I have a housewarming party to get to."

"That's cool. I got you. Everything here is under control, as per usual." They shared a quick fist bump before Lamar left and made his way home to get ready for the evening.

Chapter 3

It was around 9am when Lamar woke up the next day. Last night had been amazing with the steady flow of patrons and a generally relaxed atmosphere. He'd returned a couple hours later after freshening up at home, and got busy, greeting and serving his guests. He made announcements about a soon to come VIP experience where guests would not only receive their choice of meal from an exclusive menu, but they'd be provided with their choice of bottle service and transportation to and from Ed's. At that, the crowd roared and cheered in appreciation, and everyone wanted to know when it would launch. Lamar let everyone know to follow their social media and to sign up for notifications on Ed's website because that was where they would be able to request the service.

As he rolled out of bed to head towards the bathroom, he was again hit with how successful his business was becoming and to think of where he'd come from and what he'd been through. Even though he never really verbalized it, it was hard to forget the violence and pain he'd felt prior to his family relocating to the city. He was reminded that, in this moment, he was truly living his best life and that there was no longer anything that could keep him from reaching his goals.

He performed his morning routine, which consisted of a nice cool shower to fully wake and then grooming. He then threw on some boxers and a tee shirt, grabbed his phone, and made his way towards the kitchen. As he walked through his 3/2.5 home he took note, for the 1st time, at the lack of thought put into his décor. Sure, he had some really nice furniture along with a few expensive electronics, but he'd done nothing with his walls and the in-between spaces. He also noted that he'd still not researched who could install the seawater aquarium he'd wanted since he was a kid.

As he made it into the kitchen, he beelined towards his Keurig, where he popped in a green teacup and made mental notes to begin working on accenting his house over the weekend.

While waiting for his tea to brew, he grabbed a yogurt out of the fridge along with some granola and fresh berries. He set the items on the kitchen island and then went to grab a bowl out of the cabinet along with a spoon from the drawer beneath. After he'd finished mixing everything together, his tea had finished brewing.

He placed the remaining yogurt, berries, and granola back into the fridge, grabbed his tea, and made himself comfortable at the island. He dipped his head in a quick prayer and then began enjoying his meal.

He checked his emails as he alternated between spoonsful of food and sips of tea. As he scrolled through, he was notified that he'd just received a new one. Upon viewing the sender, he opened it immediately. In the email, his attorney informed him she wanted to meet with him around 1pm that afternoon to go over their offer before submitting. She also wanted to go over the paperwork that was to establish the LLC for managing the apartment complex. He excitedly responded that 1pm would be fine, and he continued scrolling through emails in search of responses from a few vendors with whom he'd been looking to do business. He made notes to himself of the vendors that had yet to respond and then logged onto bedbathbeyond.com to hand-pick gifts to be given to the 1st 100 VIP guests for the newest addition to Ed's services. He then sent over his notes and his shopping cart info to Angela so that she could finalize the purchases and reach out to the vendors he'd not heard from.

Satisfied with his checklist, he finished the last bite and sip of his breakfast and then cleared the island. He started up the dishwasher and then made his way into the guest bedroom that had been set up as a gym. He tuned into 99Jamz, turned the volume up and began his workout routine.

It was around 10:45am when Lamar finished up. He turned off the stereo and made his way back into his bathroom where he took a hot shower and rinsed off with cool water. After getting out of the shower, he took his time preparing himself and getting dressed before heading out to hop in his car and make his way towards his attorney's office.

Chapter 4

Lamar decided that since he didn't have any plans on coming back out until later that evening, he would go ahead and stop by a liquor store to grab a bottle for the party that night. It was around 12:50pm by the time he pulled into the parking lot of his attorney's office off NE 183rd St and 23rd Ave.

Seeing as he still had some time to spare before meeting his lawyer, he decided to sit in silence for a few moments to gather his thoughts. After about 5 minutes, he decided to text his mom, Ms. Santi, his brother, and his sister. After getting those texts sent off, he then grabbed the water he'd purchased while at the liquor store since he left his water jug at home and made his way into his attorney's office building.

He entered the lobby, walked towards the elevator bay, and took one to the 5th floor. Upon exiting the elevator, he was greeted by Ms. Sheila, the office manager.

"Good afternoon, Lamar."

"Hi, Ms. Sheila. I'm here for Ms. Armand."

"Certainly. Please take a seat. While you wait, would you like a muffin?"

"Ah no, I'm good, thank you."

"Ok. Please have a seat. Ms. Armand will be just a few more moments."

Lamar sat in the waiting area and turned his attention towards the TV, which was playing the news, and, in the news, Trump was still president and America was still being run by ignorant, inconsiderate racists while black folks were still oppressed and attacking each other.

Lord, I thank you for this opportunity to not only give back but also take my shot at leveling the playing field, Lamar thought to himself while shaking his head as yet another one of America's Leader's tweets were dissected and processed.

It was another 10 minutes before he was called into his attorney's office by Ms. Sheila, who stood to the side of the threshold while waiting for Lamar to enter so she could close the door.

"Hey lady!" Lamar beamed as Ms. Armand was making her way around her desk to hug him.

"How you doing honey?" she inquired as she laid a kiss on his cheek and then gestured for him to have a seat.

"I'm well," Lamar responded as he sat down and made himself comfortable.

Lamar had always been interested in entrepreneurial ventures, and aside from wanting to become the owner of a lounge, he'd always dreamed of getting into Real Estate, and because he'd shared those dreams with Ms. Santi, she'd made sure to introduce him to Ms. Armand. She quickly took him under her wings, mentored him, and ensured that he was exposed to the variety of paths within the Real Estate world to give him a feel. She'd also been the one to formalize the deal in acquiring his lounge. So, over the years, they'd really become close, and he thought of her like an aunt who encouraged you to be yourself as long as it was done with tact and integrity.

Back in the moment, Lamar continued, "I'm super excited about this opportunity and super thankful that it's happening at a time such as this."

"Time such as this?" Ms. Armand inquired as she crossed her fingers together, with her arms resting on her bosom.

"Well, yeah," Lamar began, "For so long, we've sat back and watched each other catch all hell and be denied access to opportunity. I strive to be a bit of light, offering tangible relief in the midst of this chaotic space we're occupying." Lamar finished as he took a sip of his water.

"Well, I'm here for that!" Ms. Armand laughed in appreciation as she leaned forward to pick up a folder in front of her on her desk. "And I know you came for this," she continued as she handed the folder to Lamar.

Lamar received the folder and sat for a few moments, reading over it. He was impressed with the amount of research she'd put into the property. The property was a distressed 65-unit complex that was on the verge of foreclosure. It needed new roofing, new wiring and new plumbing and was just about 2 years behind on its taxes, but Lamar was not taken aback by this because once he brought them up to standard, he'd be able to rent each unit out for an affordable price and his investment would resolve itself. The property was in Carol City at the corner of NW 183rd St and 37th Ave, which was not far from where he'd grown up nor even from where he currently lived. The current owners were desperate to sell the property because they could not afford the needed repairs and could not afford to bring the taxes up to date so they just wanted out.

"This is some good stuff right here," Lamar said as he nodded his head in appreciation. Sure, there was a lot going on, but if he wanted to make a mark, he would have to start by improving lives immediately and drastically. Lamar finished reading through the folder and set it back down on Ms. Armand's desk.

"So, what do I need to do now?" Lamar inquired.

"Well, the 1st thing we need to do is get these documents notarized, which Ms. Sheila can help you with. Then I can get them submitted. I'll then take on the responsibilities of your Registered Agent, which is basically saying that I represent your company and will make sure that your documents are filed when they need to be and make sure that your taxes are taken care of and keep you in the loop so that you're aware of what's going on at all times." Ms. Armand paused as she glanced over the LLC documents to ensure their accuracy. "And then while all of that is sorted out, I'll tie up a few loose ends on my research, and by Tuesday, I'll get back to you concerning the current owner's response, and we'll move forward from there."

"What do you think about the processing of everything? Will it be a smooth transition?" Lamar inquired.

"Yes sir. Once I reach out to the owner, I will let him know how serious you are about the purchase and let him know that we're waiting on the establishment of your LLC and from there, we're going to pay cash for the property," said Ms. Armand.

"So, then you're confident that I will get this complex?" Lamar anxiously asked.

Chuckling, Ms. Armand went on, "Yes sir. I know a few folks in a few places and this property was mentioned to me. I was told that because gentrification had yet to set its sights on the area, the complex is just not considered a good investment at this time, but I believe in you and your vision. I've watched you grow, and I know that if anyone can do anything to turn not only this property around, but the neighborhood itself, it's you." Ms. Armand finished as she began printing out the documents.

Beaming now, Lamar just sat there and soaked it all in. He was becoming a landlord and the thought tickled him so much so that a squeal of joy escaped his lips before he could catch it. At this, he and Ms. Armand slightly bent over from laughing so hard. After composing themselves, Ms. Armand led Lamar out to Ms. Sheila to have her notarize the documents.

"Notarization complete. Next steps, I will reach out no later than Tuesday with a suggested offer price, once I've finished looking into a few more things. Any other questions or concerns?" she asked.

"No. All good."

"Well, all right then sugah," Ms. Armand began as she prepared to walk Lamar to the elevator bay. "Let me walk you out."

Ms. Armand walked Lamar to the elevator where she stopped to hug him again, kiss him on the cheek, and bid him a good day. He then took the elevator back to the lobby, crossed it, and exited the building and headed toward his car. His emotions were on 1000 and his heart would not stop dancing in his chest. He really felt like dancing but opted for laughter instead as a few happy tears slid down his face. He hopped back in his car, and as he cranked his car up and the air started to flow, he thanked God for the journey ahead of him. He was finally living out his dreams, and he was determined to go all in.

Chapter 5

It was around 2pm when Lamar pulled back into his driveway and as he was backing in, his phone rang. He glanced over at his phone in its hands-free holder and smiled, seeing that it was Julia.

"Hey lady," he answered as he got out of his car and began making his way towards the front door. "I'm literally just getting home from my meeting and was about to call you in like 10 minutes."

Laughing, Julia replied, "well I guess this was perfect timing."

"It absolutely was," Lamar answered as he entered the house, locked the door behind him, and headed toward his office.

"So, what did you find out about the building?" Julia asked.

"Well, I found out that the owners are really motivated to sell and are asking for 5 mil. I went ahead and signed my LLC formation papers and had them notarized, so now I'm just waiting on my attorney."

Julia hooted in joy at the great news before continuing. "I am so proud of you for never giving up on your dreams."

"I couldn't. With everything before me, giving up was not an option that I was willing to make. It was either go hard or fade away and that little piece of hope that held fast to me made sure I held fast to it," Lamar replied.

"Amen!" Julia laughed. "Well, hey love, congrats again on all your success. I'm getting off this phone so that I can finish getting ready and I will get together with you in a bit so we can continue our chat."

"Yes mam," Lamar began, "Thanks and I will see you later on."

Chapter 6

Since Lamar had nothing else to do right then, he decided to fix himself a turkey wrap. To complete his meal, he also grabbed some Lay's classic chips and grape juice and made his way into his den. He decided to order Guardians of The Galaxy 2 since he hadn't had time to make it to the movies, and he got comfortable. Before long, Lamar kicked back in his recliner and drifted off to sleep.

It was 4:45pm when Lamar awoke. He got up and stretched and took his dishes into the kitchen where he rinsed them and placed them in the dishwasher. He then headed into his room where he beelined straight for the bathroom. After using the bathroom, he hopped in the shower.

It was around 5:30pm when Lamar got out of the shower. As he stood in the mirror drying off and moved on to grooming himself, his mind began wondering about this cousin of Julia's. He wondered what Devon would look like, and would Devon like him, and would he pick up on the fact that he was gay? He laughed to himself at the fact that he was being anxious for no reason. He then told himself that he was just going to a housewarming party and not out on a date.

Besides, his thoughts continued as he prepared himself, *we don't do that anymore.*

Lamar had been single now for the last 2 years and had made peace with it. His run with guys had been unsuccessful, leading him to conclude that he was going to be single as he held no sexual interest in women.

He thought back on the last relationship he'd had and quickly corrected himself as it wasn't an actual relationship. It was a situationship that had ended once the guy started sleeping with women again, paying Lamar less and less attention until he'd finally had enough and decided to walk away. The arrangement before that had been pleasant enough as far as time spent together, but dude had no drive nor ambition about himself, and Lamar was also tired of visiting him at his brother's house only to watch him watch sports and play video games all day so he walked away from that situation as well.

Now the situation before that had lasted the longest but also did the most damage to Lamar.

Lamar had been 17 when he'd first met Tee and there'd been instant sparks. Tee was about 6'1, 160, and caramel-colored with bowed legs and abs to die for. Lamar took fast to Tee and, in retrospect, realized it was due to his insecurities. During that time, Lamar had been a chubby guy, weighing in at 340 lbs. on a 5'11 frame and he was very self-conscious. In addition to his self-consciousness, there were the aftereffects of being brought up in his household.

In the beginning, his mom had been rough on him and showed him no mercy, having beat him often because the wind was blowing, or berated him on his soft spoken-ness. She even shared how she should have aborted him and how he was gullible and an easy target for the ridicule and torment of others. So, yeah, Lamar was in a fragile place when he met Tee.

Tee was initially very easygoing and attentive, which caused Lamar to crave his attention and he quickly found that he'd submitted himself for the sake of Tee's pleasure. Lamar was so smitten with Tee that even Tee's occasional aggression didn't affect him.

Four years in, things began to change. Tee no longer spent time with Lamar like he used to. The calls had also started to dry up. Again, Lamar didn't really allow the changes to bother him all that much, even though they hurt him.

During this same time, Lamar, tired of going through it with his mom, moved out into his very first place. He'd gotten a 1bdr in Opa-Locka and despite how proud he was of himself, between drama with his momma and Tee, he didn't enjoy the moment.

In his mind, Lamar thought that now that he was in his own place, maybe things would change with Tee, but they remained the same. In fact, the only time Lamar heard from or saw Tee was when Tee's dick was hard. As much as this bothered Lamar, he settled on the fact that at least he had a piece of Tee and told himself that it was enough.

Lamar entertained their arrangement for far longer than he should have until one day, he woke up and realized that he was tired of being mistreated and handled as if he were disposable and decided to walk away. He'd had enough of feeling like he was being granted favors by folks only popping up when they needed him or wanted something from him.

He told himself he wasn't taking mess from anyone anymore and he was starting with Tee. So, the day before Lamar was to turn 22, Tee called, and Lamar didn't answer. Tee continued calling and Lamar continued ignoring him. In fact, Lamar chose to treat himself to a day out on the town. He'd gotten his feet done, caught a movie and had some lunch.

It had been around 8pm when he'd finally made it home. As he was making his way upstairs and to his door, he saw movement out of his left eye. It was Tee who caused Lamar to hurriedly slide his key into the door in a desperate attempt to get in and slam it shut, but Tee was quicker and reached the door before Lamar could even halfway close it, and he shoved Lamar in and onto the floor and then closed and locked it.

"Tha fuck is wrong witchu?" Tee asked angrily as he stood over Lamar.

"Ain't nothing wrong with me," Lamar nervously replied as he slid back to give himself space to get up.

"So, who you fuckin'?" Tee demanded as he stepped in closer to Lamar.

"What?" Lamar asked confused at the question. "Nobody," Lamar added as he quickened his slide.

"Really?" Tee questioned as he stopped moving in on Lamar to allow him a chance to get up. "So why tha fuck you ain't been answering my calls?" Tee finished as he crossed his arms across his chest.

"Because Tee, I'm tired." Lamar sighed as he stood up and faced Tee. "For the past year, you've been everywhere you wanted to be but with me and the only time I ever see you is for sex," Lamar continued as he straightened himself up, "You rarely call and after sex, you clean up and disappear until the next time."

"Ok. So, what chu saying?" Tee asked as he inched in closer to Lamar.

"I'm saying that I don't want to do this anymore," Lamar replied as he began to tense up. "It feels like I'm in this alone, so I'd rather just be alone so please leave." Lamar finished as he unconsciously backed up a bit.

"I ain't goin no muh fucking where." Tee spat as he closed the distance between the two of them. "And neither are you." And with that, Tee quickly reached out and began choking Lamar.

Lamar was caught off guard and, in an instant of self-preservation, immediately began swinging. He caught Tee with a left blow to the jaw, but Tee seemed unfazed and in response, began beating the shit out of Lamar with his right hand.

Lamar wanted to cry out, but that first punch made his mouth swell up, and Tee was now working on his right eye and cheek. Lamar wanted nothing more than to fall out from the pain but felt that if he did, he would never wake up again. At the thought of losing his life this way, he mustered up enough strength to reach out around him to grab the first thing he could lay his hands on, which ended up being a small iron sculpture gifted to him by his bosses. He swung blindly with all his might.

He apparently connected because he was released immediately. He continued swinging and making contact. With the little vision he had left, he saw Tee backing up towards the door in an attempt to unlock it. This enraged Lamar all the more. Tee had just beat the shit out of him and now he wanted to run?

Lamar grabbed the lamp by the door and broke it on the side of Tee's head. Lamar then grabbed the custom made door stopper made of oak and as Tee went to run to the door, Lamar caught him on the side of his neck, which finally drew a response out of Tee as he yelled out in pain. By this time, Lamar's neighbors had come out to see what was going on. Tee finally stumbled out of Lamar's house and attempted to make his way towards the staircase.

Lamar's next-door neighbor, Mike, stepped out just as Lamar took aim and threw the door stopper with as much force as he could, and this time, it caught Tee in between his shoulder blades, which caused him to go down to one knee. Lamar went in to kick the shit out of him, but Mike grabbed him and held him back. Lamar tried his best to get to Tee but Mike would not let him go.

Mike repeatedly assured Lamar that it was ok while Tee remained down on one knee. Mike's brother came outside of the house and tried to help Tee up but upon lifting him, he quickly found that Tee's legs were not working properly so he gently maneuvered him to the top of the stairs and angled him down.

At some point, Lamar took note of the fact that not only were all the neighbors out but the police were also pulling up. They got out and after assessing the situation, led Lamar back into his apartment to ask him what happened. Lamar recounted the story.

"Do you want to press charges?" the police asked after Lamar was done telling them what had happened.

"Yes. And I want a restraining order."

Shortly thereafter, the ambulance pulled up to check on the both of them.

"Lamar, do you want to be taken to the hospital to be checked out?" asked the paramedic.

"Yeah, but I'll ask a friend to take me."

In the end, Lamar was checked out and found out that he'd had a fractured eye socket and a broken jaw. He was checked and then given meds and told to follow up with his doctor to make sure he kept up with his recovery. Tee, on the other hand, once released from the hospital, was immediately taken into custody and off to jail, where he sat for 8 months. Lamar took out that restraining order and moved to another apartment building and he never heard from Tee again.

As Lamar drifted back to the present, he'd had to shake off the anger and the pain that man left on his soul. Tee changed his life, and after reexamining himself, Lamar changed his eating habits, began working out, and got his hair twisted into Locs. He hadn't quite grown out of all his insecurities and issues, but he'd learned enough to know that he deserved more than being someone's disposable.

Returning to the moment, Lamar stared at himself in the mirror and seemed to see himself for the first time. He wasn't quite sure of exactly who he was, but he knew who he was not. He gazed upon himself and for the first time in his life, he was at ease. He had no idea what tomorrow held but he was determined to see it through till the end. Realizing his resolution, Lamar smiled at himself and proceeded to his room and then onto the closet, where he decided on some form-fitting, azure blue jeans with a matching form-fitting cotton tee shirt that had a teal blue smiley face in the middle along. He paired the outfit with black suede, short heeled boots along with a black leather belt fastened together by a silver faced buckle.

He continued getting ready and by 6:30pm, he was ready to go. He did a walkthrough of his house making sure everything was in order and then he grabbed the bottles he had bought from earlier that day and then made his way outside to his car. Once settled in, he headed to Julia's in anticipation of the night ahead.

Chapter 7

Lamar pulled into Julia's driveway right at 6:50pm. He grabbed the bottles and made his way to Julia's door. As he was about to ring the doorbell, the door opened, and Julia drew him into a huge hug and kissed him on the cheek before inviting him in.

Lamar took his shoes off at the door and made his way over to Julia's couch. After sitting, he noted the recent additions to her décor.

"Ok." Lamar smiled in appreciation of the two paintings that caught his eye. "I'm digging these." Lamar stated as he took in the erotic canvases that depicted a man and a woman respectively.

"Thanks, love." Julia smiled as she reappeared from the kitchen with a tray that contained 2 glasses of wine and some cheese cubes, grapes and a few crackers. "I was actually out and about near your lounge a few Saturdays ago and noticed that they were having a small street fair, so I decided to stop through and check it out." Julia paused to take a sip of wine as she moved towards the wall that separated her kitchen from the living room before continuing, "This sculpture is the first thing that caught my attention."

Lamar followed her with his eyes and was momentarily speechless. He got up to take a closer look and was in awe of the beauty before him. The sculpture was about 5 feet tall and was made of some type of stained wood whose foundation was in the form of multiple sets of hands stretched upwards, lifting, a couple who in turn had their arms stretched upwards, lifting a child, who in turn, held onto a stone with the word HOPE carved into it. Lamar was moved but maintained control of his emotions as he appreciated the shades of ebony, which really gave life to the piece.

"Just wow." Was all Lamar could muster.

Squeezing his hand, Julia brought herself closer to Lamar and gazed at her newest treasure. Smiling, she softly spoke, "And don't worry, I made sure to grab the card of the gentleman who created all three of these amazing statements so that you can go visit him yourself."

Now laughing, Lamar turned to Julia and said, "You swear you know me."

"What kind of friend would I be if I didn't?" Julia laughed in return. "So go ahead and get comfortable. I'm about to go ahead and change," Julia stated as she disappeared into the kitchen only to return with the bottle of wine that she'd previously opened. She set it on the tray and told Lamar to help himself and that she would be right back before she then turned to go down the hall to her room.

Looking back at the statue, Lamar allowed a few tears to fall as this spoke to him of the lack he'd experienced in his own life and how he'd had to fight for everything. He appreciated the platform some could launch from, such as his bestie who'd grown up with a single mom. Her mom had also been a RN at Jackson up until her retirement due to her ongoing health issues. Julia's dad, while not in the home, was still active in her life, but the bulk of the responsibility of raising her fell onto her mom, and she'd done an amazing job.

Lamar was so lost in his thoughts that he didn't even notice that Julia had returned to the living room and was sitting in the armchair across from him.

"Earth to Lamar," Julia laughed, snapping Lamar out of his trance. "Where were you?"

Laughing, Lamar replied, "I was actually thinking about your mom. Speaking of which, how is Ms. Precious?"

"Still stuck in front of that damn TV," Julia replied with slight annoyance.

"Is everything ok?" Lamar asked in concern.

"Honestly, I'm not sure what's going on with her anymore these days. I mean I knew that her pressure had gone up and she would get dizzy spells out of nowhere but to be honest, when I stopped by yesterday to check on her, I attempted to talk with her, and it was like she wasn't even there."

Not wanting to think the worst, Lamar grabbed Julia's hand and squeezed it while they both sat in silence for a few moments.

"Anyway, I made a few phone calls to set up some interviews for a caretaker for the times I'm unable to be there. I'm also setting up some doctor appointments to see what's happening with her because while I know what I feel is happening, I want to be sure."

"A few things though. You're talking about a caretaker, but when you gone get a man?" Lamar asked with a straight face. Julia burst out in laughter and slapped him on the leg. After a moment of laughter, Lamar continued, "But seriously though, if there is anything that I can do, please let me know."

Julia gazed at him lovingly and squeezed his leg. "Switching gears for a moment," Julia said, suddenly brightening up. "I have something I want to share with you. I'll be right back."

Lamar smiled as Julia excitedly hurried down the hall. He took the time to refresh his glass and sat back on the couch, wondering what had made Julia so giddy.

He didn't have to wait too long. Just about 3 minutes later, Julia came rushing back down the hall with a notepad, which caused Lamar to sit on the edge of the couch in anticipation.

"So, I've been doodling here and there when I have free time and I created something that I wanted your thoughts on," Julia said as she flipped through the pages in her book. Finally locating what she was looking for, she continued, "Now mind you, this is unfinished and has no title so be gentle" she smiled as she prepared to speak.

You know, my issue was never with your inheritance. Nah, my issue stemmed from the perpetuation of said inheritance as you sit in your gentry a cation.

You sit there and you look, unseeing, at the world before you and because you think yourself above, choose indifference.

Children die, mothers lose their life, fathers are snuffed out and even rest becomes cautionary..

An in all of these things, you sit upon your place of rest because what does any of it mean to me?

What does it mean?

It means justice.

It means peace.

It means healing.

It means restoration.

It means refreshing and that via reckoning.

Oh yes, a full and completely thorough reckoning, the kind of which will hit you as me and mine learn to sit still.

You see there are rules to this thang and they must be honored and in fact, will be because they were set and none can escape them but what I'm presenting you in this hour has the power to reroute..

I present to you an opportunity at recompense: Are you willing to rectify or is indifference your absolute and final desire?

Choose carefully cause come now or come later, recompense... an for yo ass, it shall follow.

Lamar sat back in silence at the weight of her words. This was something different. He looked over at her and just stared in an attempt to understand as questions flew through his mind.

"Mam," he began. "I'm not even sure."

"Well, I will start with this: David slew Goliath with only faith and a few river stones so…" Julia stated as she closed her book and made her way back down the hall to return it to its location before coming back to join Lamar in the living room.

Lamar was still trying to find the words but having settled on the fact that he could not, he decided that this was to be a conversation for another day because there was just not enough time to unpack all of what she'd just presented. He really loved how she stood for black and brown folk. He also knew her heart and understood that there was no hatred, only smoke towards those out there kindling.

He received her love for her community and understood that just as much as he was standing in his space, she'd been standing in hers. They'd both grown tired of the shuckin' and flex of it all. They were over it and it was time for action. She'd clearly drawn her line in the sand and understood that it was time we learned how to band together as one.

So much to be discussed, but as they were possibly about to get into it, a horn sounded outside. Julia jumped out of her seat and flew out of the house before Lamar could get up. By the time Lamar reached the front door, Julia was already making her way back into the house in arms with the finest piece of man Lamar had ever had the pleasure of setting two eyes upon up close and personal. His mouth immediately went dry as he took in this 6'3, 215-230, bow legged, perfect loc havin', obsidian statuesque man before him. And then he smiled. Why this man had pretty teeth an' muh fuckin dimples??

Lamar felt a bit overwhelmed and felt himself slipping. He was having trouble breathing and realized he was out there and didn't even notice that Devon had his hand outstretched while Lamar just stood there staring like one of the slow chulren who only came out on holidays and Sunday mornings. Devon began laughing and that thang did something to Lamar's heart instantly. Lamar finally gathered himself and took Devon's waiting hand and upon looking into Devon's endlessly dark eyes, Lamar knew that he was stuck.

"You must be Lamar," Devon inquired as he pulled Lamar in for a hug. Lamar felt he'd left his body at the strength of the arms that enveloped him in a surprisingly gentle hug. Lamar heard himself letting out a small breath at not only the physical beauty of this man but the scent of him wrapped all up in those arms and that chest and that energy. Lamar caught himself as he found that he was 2 seconds away from laying his head on this man's shoulder.

Finally getting some sense about himself, he responded, "I am." He could have kicked himself in that moment. He'd never behaved like this with any man so why now? Why with him?

"Well, I'm Devon, and Julia's been telling me some really awesome things about you, and I'm looking forward to talking with you." Devon finished as he released Lamar from his embrace.

Lamar felt sucked in again as Devon held his gaze for a moment more. On the verge of drooling, Lamar mentally kicked himself and responded with, "I'm looking forward to you as well." Realizing what he'd said, he quickly cleaned it up with, "...I mean, talking with you. I look forward to talking with you as well."

Devon appeared to be unfazed as he just smiled and finally released Lamar's hand. It was then that Lamar noticed Julia was no longer in the living room and had been gone for a moment or two. Upon realizing that, Lamar moved to grab the bag with the bottles along with his phone and keys. As he turned around to go put on his shoes, he jumped a little. Devon was standing right behind him with an outstretched arm as if grabbing something. Lamar looked down and noticed the bag in his hand and he then realized what was happening but could not understand why Devon was so close to him. Oh, the thoughts that were knocking at the forefront of Lamar's mind. But deciding that he'd made a big enough fool of himself, he fought those thoughts back and handed the bag to Devon. As he handed it over, Devon's fingers lightly brushed across Lamar's, which caused him to gasp. He hoped Devon didn't hear him and quickly moved to go around him to put on his shoes.

As Lamar put on his shoes, he took the moment to do some deep breathing to calm his nerves. He was not at all used to what was going on and honestly, didn't even know what the hell it was, but he had to control himself.

Once his shoes were on, he turned back around to find Devon, of all things, smiling. Devon asked, "You ok?"

Lamar replied that he was and then shared that he had a lot going on in hopes of recovering his image.

"You're fine. You can relax with me," Devon answered back in his deeply rich and smooth, velvety voice.

Lamar heard him, but what caught him was the way Devon responded, which caused Lamar to look up into Devon's eyes.

As the two stared into each other's eyes, they heard Julia coming down the hall and they both moved towards the door. Devon reached it first and held the door open for Lamar and remained there until Julia had passed through the door. He allowed time for Julia to lock up and then all three piled into his black-on-black Tahoe. Once everyone was in and comfortable, they all began their trip to Devon's house.

Chapter 8

The ride over to Devon's house was nice. He proved to be a laid-back guy with a quick wit and warm sense of humor. Between his and Julia's banter and Lamar's occasional comment, Lamar was finally able to relax a bit; although his mind kept circling back to what had happened earlier.

Devon soon pulled into an area known as Miami Lakes. The area consisted of well-to-do middle to upper middle-class families. Devon turned onto a street near 169th and NW 77th Ct and navigated his way through the neighborhood. Lamar had never really had a chance to come out this way, but he nodded his head in appreciation. The neighborhood wasn't far from the town square which had many shops, boutiques, and eateries. He was also close to the 826 and I-75.

As Devon finally began to slow up on the approach, Lamar thought to himself, *Fye!*

They pulled into the driveway of a 2-story gray and black home seductively lit by strategically placed lighting hidden amongst the lush yard.

"Welcome to my humble abode," Devon announced as he placed his SUV in park. Lamar looked towards the rearview mirror.

"Nice place," Lamar complimented Devon on his home.

"Thanks, my parents helped me get it," Devon replied.

They then gathered all their things and fell in line behind Devon as he made his way towards the front door. Devon unlocked and stepped to the side as Julia made her way in first, followed by Lamar, who still felt some type of way at the nearness of Devon as he passed by.

Upon entering the foyer, Lamar was taken aback by the décor. Devon's home was immaculate. The first thing that caught Lamar's attention were the beautifully laid blackish tiles that were as smooth as liquid. The walls were, he noticed as they were guided through the living room towards the kitchen, a unique mix of gray and white with an unidentified color on the crown molding. Lamar also took note of the erotic paintings, sculptures and muted throw pillows carefully arranged on Devon's super plush, black leather sofas. As they passed through the formal dining room, Devon took the lead and directed them towards the kitchen.

As they were passing by, Lamar also noted the beautiful dining table that looked to sit 6. It was beautifully stained with a very unusual base. He also appreciated the dark gray-colored glass top. He made a mental note of the centerpiece.

As they rounded the corner into the kitchen, he thought to himself, *I wonder what that bedroom looks like?* He quietly chuckled at how giddy he felt.

Upon entering the kitchen, Devon set all the bags on the counter by the fridge and offered them something to drink. Both Julia and Lamar took a bottle of water while Devon went about grabbing pans from the fridge. "I have the ribs and chicken going already so they should be ready in another 30 minutes," Devon stated as he arranged the pans on the counter in an order that suggested he was locked and loaded for action.

"You need any help?" Julia asked as the scents of whatever in those pans wafted up.

"Matter fact," Devon began, as he nodded towards the pantry area. "If you would, grab about 7 pans and warmers and bring them outside,"

Devon said as he moved towards the fridge and grabbed various sauces. "You will see the tables outside to your right," Devon continued as he uncovered the first pan and proceeded to pour sauce over it. "Lamar, can you grab those coolers over by the sink?" Devon asked as he moved towards the patio door with the uncovered pan of what looked to be full of snapper, salmon and mussels. "Be careful cause they're full of wine coolers, beer, and water. Let me know if you need help." He finished as he exited the kitchen.

Julia and Lamar went about setting up the pans with the warmers and coolers and moved on to setting up the chairs that had been on the left side of the patio. It was when Devon popped back out of the house with candles and floaters that Lamar recognized Devon was a different type of dude. He was something special and Lamar took a quick moment to appreciate this beautiful man.

Who is he and where the hell did he come from? Lamar thought to himself as they set about situating the candles and sending them on their way across the pool.

As Devon was busy turning the meats and placing the fish on the grill, he called for Julia and Lamar and asked them to go to the garage and grab the 4 bags of ice that he'd placed in his deep freezer earlier. When they returned, they went about filling the coolers with ice. Upon finishing, Lamar took a moment to look around the yard and was pleased with the privacy and liveliness of the scenery. As he gazed around the yard, he noticed a table that he hadn't seen earlier that was against the wall behind the grill. It was covered with various liquors and juices for chasing.

The more I learn about this guy the more I think I like him, Lamar smiled to himself.

It was around 9:15pm when everything was in place. All the food was done and sitting in the warming pans. The drinks in the coolers were chilling and the ambiance was perfect. Devon, being the studious host that he was, was busy running a last audit of everything to make sure things were as he wanted them. As he seemed to mentally check off his to do list, he asked Lamar if he would go unlock the side gate that the guests would use to enter. As Lamar made his way back towards all the action, he looked at Devon in the midst of final touches. Taking note of the contentment in Devon's eyes, he realized he'd never wanted anyone so much. Devon seemed perfect in every way, and it was driving Lamar mad just being near him, smelling him, and hearing him.

He composed himself and rejoined Devon who, by now, was chatting with Julia about the expected crowd and overall goal of bringing awareness about the Community Center that was to open in Overtown off NW 20th St between 1st Ave and 1st Ct. Devon let them know that the building was 95% completed and that within the next 2 weeks, they were going to be doing a Community Event. He then shared that quite a few of the folks coming were hopeful sponsors to make sure that the Center could meet the needs of the surrounding communities.

The more Devon spoke, the more Lamar felt himself falling.

A man after my own heart? Say it ain't so, Lamar smiled as he watched Devon with admiration. *He don't know it yet but he gone get this eagle tonight,* he thought. Lamar laughed which caused Devon to pause momentarily as he and Julia looked at him quizzically.

"I'm sorry, my mind was wondering again." Lamar laughed lightly, "I tend to do that from time to time."

Smiling now, Devon picked his conversation back up. This time Lamar joined in and shared his gratitude for what Devon was doing and let him know that if he could help in any way, to please make sure he reached out. As they continued their prep talk, they were interrupted by a "Hey Hey," coming from the direction of the gate. They all looked over at the first of many guests who'd begun arriving, and with that, the party was officially underway.

Chapter 9

The night wore on like a perfectly fitted pair of jeans. The music was ambient, the drinks strong and the food superb!

At a certain point, Lamar made his way to the patio and stood there, taking it all in. He understood that if nothing else, he was in the right place at the right time. Devon had proven himself to truly be a jack of all trades. The way he floated through the crowd of joyful people warmed Lamar's heart specially at the way Devon waited on them and made sure that they were all right and didn't need anything.

Lamar apparently got lost in his thoughts again because, one moment, he was reflecting on Devon's hospitality and the next, he was hearing his name. When he returned to the party, Devon was standing inches away from him asking if he was ok.

Laughing, Lamar replied, "You must think I'm a nut at how I just float off like that."

Laughing as well, Devon responded, "Not at all. I find it intriguing how you're able to disappear within yourself at the drop of a dime."

Lamar's laughter came to a smile as the word *intrigued* occupied his thoughts.

"I tend to get in my head probably more than I should," Lamar began as he shifted his feet. "But I'm really enjoying myself and love how you're handling the crowd."

"I'm glad to hear it," Devon paused as he took a sip of his cup. "As that's why I made my way over here. I have a few folks that I'd like you to meet." He finished as he nodded towards a group of four people that were standing near the pool in deep conversation.

As Devon turned to move towards the group, Lamar fell in line behind him. Upon reaching the group, everyone stopped talking and looked towards them.

"Lamar, this is Deena, Joseline, Carlos and Richard. Everybody this is my cousin's friend Lamar. I figured you all would have quite a few things in common," Devon began as Lamar smiled at each of them while shaking their hands.

Devon informed Lamar a bit about them. "These four, in addition to partnering with me on the community center, are the owners of a forth coming condo tower that we broke ground on a while back. We're about 3 weeks out from taking applications and we couldn't be more proud of where we're heading and what this means for not only the city but the region as well."

Lamar found himself beaming with pride at this information. "That's what I'm talking about!" Lamar replied in pure joy. "Where's it located and when can I get a tour?"

Deena responded that it was on the corner of NW 79th St and 22nd Ave. She went on to say that they could set something up for him.

Devon then went on to share a few things about Lamar that he'd learned from Julia as he really hadn't had a chance to really speak with Lamar, but he was planning on fixing that later in the evening.

As the quintet engaged each other in conversation, Devon backed off in pleasure at his handy work.

"Congratulations again to you guys. It's truly an honor to meet individuals whose actions speak to my heart. How did you guys even get started on this work?" Lamar began.

"Joseline here," Deena began, "is an Immigration Attorney, Carlos is a Pediatrician, Richard is a Real Estate Mogul, and I am a licensed Psychologist." Denna paused for a second as she took a sip of her drink then continued, "So, let's see, probably about 2 years ago, Devon and the gang here met up at a Clean Up The City Day being hosted by the Miami Rescue Mission down in Overtown. It was an amazing event, and it drew a healthy crowd of volunteers. When all was said and done, we ended up having a late dinner where we were still reflecting on the success of the day and, while it felt good, the common consensus was that we believed there was more that could be done in the community. I mean sure, there was food being given out and even some rent vouchers for single mothers and a few single fathers that were bold enough to seek help, but we couldn't help but wonder about what these families would do next month and the month after that." Deena finished as Carlos picked up the conversation.

"So, we decided to all meet up again that following Saturday with a variety of ideas to find out what we could do to make a permanent mark in the community." Carlos finished as Joseline spoke up next.

"So, we met up the Saturday after that and concluded that a lot of the issues plaguing the community had to do with a lack of access to affordable housing, jobs that offered livable wages, access to adequate daycare and organizations that were willing to offer people a second chance at life. So, after prioritizing what should come first, we ended up honing on something to do with affordable housing." Joseline ended as Richard stepped in.

"With my access, I began searching and seeking through properties in the general area to gauge where we would be jumping in and discovered a gem. If you're familiar with the area, there was a large plot of land off 79th between 22nd and 23rd," Richard paused as he looked upon Lamar.

"Yea. It's been empty since forever," Lamar confirmed.

"Well, I found out that it had been for sale for over 15 years but because it was in Liberty City, nobody was interested in it so I dug into it and found that it could be acquired for a steal, so I reached out to the gang and presented the price, and they all asked how soon I needed the money. I told them to give me an opportunity to put together the paperwork and that I would reach out to them within the next 48 hours. So, I had everything processed and we picked up the property that following Wednesday," Richard finished as Deena picked the conversation back up.

"So, once we were the owners of the property, we still needed to figure out what to do with it. So, we met up that following Saturday to sit down and strategize," Deena finished as Carlos then took the reins.

"We agreed that while, single family homes would have been great for a few folks, we wanted to maximize the space for the most possible people. With that in mind, Devon was the one to suggest the condo tower and, in that moment, we knew where we were heading." Carlos finished as Richard again took over.

"So, I reached out to some of my contacts with the city and presented the idea. They let me know that they would get back to me. About 3 months later, they reached out and said that they loved the idea and let me know that not only would we have to meet up with the zoning board to present but suggested that we also do an additional presentation to the community since most folks were not able to make it to city meetings. So, we met with the board and a few members of the community and won them all over. 2 months later, we were able to organize a community meeting that became a whole thing. We laid everything out on the table, letting them know about the mental health services, medical services, social services, job services and daycare services that would be on the first 3 floors of the building in addition to the 4th floor of the building being dedicated as multi-purpose uses for the surrounding areas." Richard finished as Joseline jumped back in.

"And they loved the idea immediately. Of course, they were wondering how it was going to be funded but we let them know that we, along with a few partners, were going to be footing the bill and from there it was a matter of getting everything zoned, and permits issued and getting with a developer, and we took off from there." Joseline ended as she took a sip from her cup.

Lamar could not believe what he was hearing. This amazing group of individuals not only came and saw but they conquered and all in the name of humanity. He could not believe his good fortune to have been introduced to such stand-up folks.

"So how did you guys get the funding together so quickly?" Lamar inquired.

"Well, we've known each other since college, and ol Richard here was a finance major. Through his guidance, along with instruction from our parents, we all invested in quite a few things early on, and those investments panned out very nicely, so we had a nice collective piece of change." Carlos laughed.

"And what we didn't have, Richard was able to get from a few of his business partners," Joseline added as she lightly tipped her cup towards him.

"So how did you guys meet Devon?" Lamar asked.

"We actually all went to UF, and we met on the first day of freshman orientation. Me and Deena knew each other from growing up around the way." Richard began, "And during our orientation, Carlos, Joseline and Devon were sitting all the way in the back next to each other and it so happens that their section was the only section that had seats available. So during those long and uninteresting speeches, we all exchanged small talk amongst each other and by the time we all ended up leaving the auditorium that day, we were inseparable." Richard smiled as he fondly recounted those memories.

Lamar smiled at the bond they shared amongst themselves. He loved how they supported each other, learnt from each other and helped each other as much as they could. He also loved how they maintained their bond well after graduating from school.

"So, tell me Lamar, what is it you do?" Deena asked.

Smiling, Lamar began. "Well, I'm the owner of a lounge in Opa-Locka called Ed's. I initially started out working there when I was 16. During that time, my mentor connected me with a few folks, and through them, I learned financial literacy, budgeting, and saving. By the time I was 22 or so, I'd taken some Business Management courses at Miami Dade and by the time I was 24, the former owners were ready to retire, and they offered to sell the business to me for a fair price as they were just ready to live out their days in peace and relaxation. Thankfully, I'd been disciplined enough to build my credit and set some money aside, so when I purchased, I was given favorable terms and was able to cover my down payment. About 3 years in, I refinanced the building and made some renovations and it's been booming ever since."

Lamar paused as he took a sip of his drink before continuing. "As far as my other ventures, because I was a product of low income housing and a mother who battled drug addiction, I learned early on what it meant for a child to have a healthy environment. This led to my interest in Real Estate. As I studied and questioned and began to understand, I realized that I could make a difference in people's lives simply by allowing them to lay in peace and calm while the world fell apart around them, which is how my vision for affordable housing came into play. So, with that being said, I believe that come Monday, I'll have some amazing news to share with you guys!" Lamar smiled as everyone around smiled in celebration at the direction of Lamar's life. He felt welcomed here in this space and, oddly, as if he'd found his tribe. Of course, Julia was always and forever more, but to have more than one witness really spoke to him of his future.

"I believe that if we truly want change, we need to first be it and everything else will fall into place." Lamar closed as everyone raised their cups.

"To change!" They all decreed in unison before breaking out in laughter in more small talk. Lamar made sure to invite them to the lounge, where he assured them everything would be on him, and the group exchanged their contact information. Deena again reminded him that they would be getting together with him to give him a tour of the building. Lamar shook hands and gave hugs and then excused himself to go in search of the restroom.

As he made his way towards the kitchen, he smiled when he saw Julia coming out.

"Hey best friend!" Julia exclaimed as if this was the 1st time seeing him today which caused Lamar to burst out in laughter. He loved this lady.

"Yo crazy ass," Lamar laughed as he stopped for a second to look over her. "You ok?"

"I am. I'm having a really nice time and am glad to have gotten out of the house for a change. How are you?" Julia asked as she squeezed his hand.

"I'm exactly where I'm supposed to be." Lamar smiled matter of factly. "Hey, where's the bathroom?"

Julia gave him directions and Lamar hurriedly followed to relieve himself.

Lamar let out a sigh of relief as his bladder emptied. He stood there for a moment; a bit tipsy but mostly grateful at the alignment of it all. He then flushed, got himself situated and then washed his hands. As he was drying them, he took a moment to take himself in. He observed the angle of his jawline and the unique shape of his eyes, in addition to their amber-colored lenses. He also took note of his well-proportioned nose and he smiled and blew a kiss at himself. He cut the light off and as he exited the bathroom, and made a right, he headed back towards the kitchen. But he ran into a wall. He knew it wasn't a wall because hands reached out to steady him almost immediately.

"Ooh," Lamar softly cried out as he looked up and right into Devon's mischievous eyes. He didn't realize it, but he'd involuntarily latched onto those building biceps and felt himself going dark at the thought of this stolen moment. The moment was further enhanced as Devon's hands slid to the small of Lamar's back and pulled him forward. Lamar's heart raced in nervousness at their closeness. As Lamar continued staring into Devon's eyes, his mouth went dry.

The two stood like that for what seemed like forever, until Devon softly smiled before sharing, "You don't have to be so nervous around me. I'm interested." And with that, Devon gently released him and went around him into the bathroom.

"Did he just?" Lamar found himself unable to move for a moment. He could not have possibly heard what he thought he just heard. In fact, he was sure he had not just heard what he thought he just heard so he shook his head attempting to clear his thoughts and headed back towards the party.

Chapter 10

The rest of the evening was blissful. Lamar met a few more folks but he found that even though he engaged in the brief conversations, his mind was stuck on his previous exchange with Devon. In fact, as he moved around the yard chatting and occasionally replenishing his drink, he found that Devon's eyes followed him and he seemed amused at how giddy Lamar was. What Devon didn't know was that Lamar was no longer giddy, he was struggling to not beeline towards him and kiss and grope him. It was such a difficult thing to do, and Lamar even thought to himself, *I think he knows what he's doing.*

It was around 3am when the first wave of folks made their rounds with hugs and good nights. 3:45am rolled around and the only ones left were Devon, Julia, Lamar and the 4 amazing individuals that Lamar had been introduced to earlier that evening. They, too, shared their hugs and goodbyes, along with promises to keep in touch.

After securing the house, the 3 of them immediately set about cleaning. They started with the food by making sure everything was in a pan before taking it into the kitchen and placing it on the counters. Devon then went into his pantry and grabbed multiple Ziplock bags which he then placed on the island counter. After sorting out all the food, Devon took everything that could be frozen to the garage while Julia and Lamar placed the rest in the fridge. They then made it back outside, where Devon set about emptying the coolers of all the melted ice, and then he took them into the garage as well. Meanwhile, Julia and Lamar made sure there were no loose pieces of garbage around the yard before wiping down the tables and then breaking them down to set them on the side of the house. By the time they were folding up the chairs, Devon was back with them. Once the yard had been cleared, Julia asked where she was sleeping, and then, after placing kisses on both Lamar's and Devon's cheeks, she made her way to her quarters for the evening.

"Lamar, do you want a drink?" Devon asked.

"Sure, why not," Lamar replied.

Devon headed into the house to fix them both a drink. When he re-turned, he asked Lamar to hold his drink. After handing his drink to Lamar, Devon went about setting up two of the now stacked chaise lounges next to the pool. When he was finished, he turned around and invited Lamar over to sit across from him.

"So did you enjoy yourself?" Devon began and he adjusted himself to be more comfortable.

"I really did, and I thank you for not only having me but for your hospitality, culinary skills, and your awesome friends!" Lamar answered as a smile had taken over his face. "How did everything turn out for you?

"It was truly my pleasure." Devon smiled back as he raised his plastic cup. "And honestly, it went better than I could have imagined. I've got several meetings coming up over the next few weeks but enough about that for now, since we never actually had a chance to talk, tell me about yourself." Devon finished as he leaned back a bit.

The way Devon gazed at him made Lamar's heart flutter and his lower parts thumped in response. This brought on an unanticipated wave of pleasure that caught him off guard, making him tremble a bit. He hoped Devon didn't notice. Taking a sip from his cup, Lamar began.

"Well, I'm the oldest of three who grew up with a single mom. When I was 10, we moved to Miami from Bristol, PA. I met Julia that same year." Lamar paused as he took another sip to calm his nerves at the way Devon's eyes seemed to sweep over his entire being. "We came down to live with a cousin because my mom's drug addiction was pretty bad, and she figured that she'd do better by starting over. So, she reached out to her cousin Carolyn who invited us down."

"As far as where I am today, I've been through a lot and I just never wanted to go backwards so I made sure that at every opportunity, I took advantage of my resources. I learned, asked questions and worked hard." Lamar paused as he stared off into space with a half-smile before continuing. " And I can say that I am pleased with my life so far, even though I have no personal life but it's all good. Sacrifice is necessary to travel the road less traveled." Lamar concluded.

"So, tell me, what moves your heart? I mean I get that you come from humble beginnings, but even more than that, what is the thing that pushes you when you feel tired or unmotivated?" Devon asked.

Oh, he wanna know know, Lamar thought as he chuckled to himself. "Well," he paused as he thought of how he wanted to respond, "I've really been through it, and I made it out. The thing that keeps me going, no matter what, is this innate sense that, regardless of what I do, where I go and how I get there, refuses to let go of me. I'm not honestly sure what it is, but it is only satiated when I help and when I give back, and when I plot and plan on changing the most lives." Lamar stopped to ponder as a smile broke across his face. "That is what pushes me and motivates me and gives me reason when everything else around is shit."

"Ok Mr. Lamar. I see you." Devon smiled as he laughed a bit. "So, are you seeing anyone?"

Laughing, Lamar replied, "I'm not and haven't in the last few years."

"Why not?" Devon inquired.

"Where do I begin?" Lamar laughed sarcastically. "Let's see, the first guy was a fling, the second guy was basically a bum and the last guy beat the shit out of me. So, after that track record, I just became uninterested." Lamar paused as he sipped from his cup, "What about you? Who are you and what's your relationship status?"

Laughing, Devon began, "Well, I'm 31 and from Gainesville. I'm an only kid so I'm used to getting my way." Devon said as he leaned up and towards Lamar a bit. "I've got my major in Social Work with a specialty in Mental Health." Devon paused as he took a sip before continuing. "I love helping others, traveling and speak Spanish, French and Mandarin." Devon paused as he gently placed his hand on Lamar's inner thigh and began softly caressing, "And I go after what I want."

Lamar was in ecstasy at Devon's touch. He could not believe what was happening. He finally managed to gather his thoughts before speaking, "But are you single?"

"I am for now, but I am hoping that can change," Devon responded as he leaned in even closer to Lamar and was now only inches from Lamar's face. By this time, Devon's direction had changed, and his hand had moved up under Lamar's shirt and was slowly sliding back and forth across his stomach.

Attempting to swallow and get some moisture, Lamar asked, "Are you bi?" Lamar knew that this was probably not the time but the way he figured, it might as well be. He'd been down that road before and it was not a game he wanted to play again.

Laughing softly while still caressing Lamar's stomach, Devon replied, "I don't believe in labels."

This caused Lamar to stiffen up in disappointment, and he tried to move back, but Devon's other arm reached around and held him steady, which caused Lamar to gaze upon him.

"Listen, I understand what I just shared with you and want you to know that you don't have to worry about any issues from me. I'm not here to hurt you. I also only believe in being with only one person at a time." Devon shared while making sure Lamar could go nowhere. "So can we get to know each other better?" Devon asked as his hand had finally found its way to Lamar's right nipple where it began to gently encircle it.

Again moaning, Lamar struggled to find the words. "Umm umm," Lamar stuttered as Devon's big, hard, warm hands closed in on his nipple, causing him to gasp.

"Oh, you like that?" Devon chuckled as he moved in and began kissing and licking on Lamar's neck while intermittently applying pressure to Lamar's hardened nipple.

"Ooooh," was all Lamar could get out as Devon then brought his face around to Lamar's and began gently and deeply kissing him, which inadvertently caused Lamar to open his legs, inviting Devon to which he obliged as he simultaneously let the lawn chair fall back as he moved his body over Lamar's.

Lamar was losing it at how fast all of this was happening. Not even 8 hours ago, they'd just met, and now Lamar was already giving him permission to enter his space.

Realizing this, Lamar pressed his hands against Devon's chest while biting his lip from the pleasure Devon was still giving his nipple.

"What?" Devon asked as he returned to Lamar's neck with the licking and kissing and occasional nibble while all the while pulling up Lamar's shirt with his left hand.

"You..." lick "want..." kiss "me..." nibble "to..." lick "stop..." kiss "now?" And this time, Devon's mouth took ahold of Lamar's left nipple while gently squeezing and tugging on the right with a passion so intense that Lamar cried out loud as he felt he was about to explode.

Devon quickly covered his mouth and continued his quiet torture and Lamar felt himself beginning to slowly leak and throb and leak some more as Devon focused his attention now on the right nipple with his mouth as his left hand squeezed and tugged on the left. Realizing that Lamar's right nipple was his spot, he paid special attention to it, which caused Lamar's body to surrender to Devon's desire.

Devon eventually came up for air and began kissing Lamar while fondly caressing his face. "You ok?"

Lamar lay there trembling in pleasure at the touch and thought of this man. He had no words. He honestly wanted to live in this moment forever but then reality set in and he finally pulled back and answered, "We should stop."

Devon paused to look at Lamar and obliged him. As he moved to get up off Lamar, he was surprised when Lamar grabbed him and pulled him back down but this time, Devon was next to him.

Realizing what Lamar wanted, Devon easily slid into position so that Lamar's head rested in his armpit and Lamar's leg rested across Devon's big, muscular arm that held him close. They lay there quietly, lost in their thoughts as they stared off into the sky when Lamar finally broke the silence. "Why me?"

Devon pondered the question for a few moments as he took in the instant chemistry they'd had from earlier that day. "Honestly, it was the battle I saw in your eyes when I stepped into Julia's." Devon paused as he pulled Lamar even closer to him. "I saw the desire, the pain, the joy, the restraint and the tenderness and I just wanted to be there to protect you and make it better."

Completely thrown off by Devon's response, he couldn't stop the few tears that slowly rolled down his face. All his life, he'd felt alone and misunderstood, and even though he had the love of his mom, his siblings, Julia, Ms. Santi and Angela, it somehow felt different with Devon. In those shared words, Lamar felt exactly what was said and it touched him in a way that he never would have thought possible.

Devon must have felt the tears on his arm because he leaned over and kissed Lamar on the neck and moved to wipe his eyes. Afterwards, they then lay there quietly, just enjoying each other's presence for at least another hour before Devon suggested that they go get some rest. He led Lamar back into the house and upstairs to the room that he'd prepared for Lamar. He kissed Lamar again and held him close, allowing Lamar to feel, for the first time, the pressure that hung low in those shorts. He gasped and instinctively looked down at the bulge and back up at the now smiling Devon. He leaned back in and kissed Devon deeply as his hands explored the thick curvature that was Devon's love below and he moaned in pleasure. This time, Devon was the one who stopped the intimacy.

"Look man. You got about 5 more good minutes before I give you what we both looking for and I don't think Julia would like to be woken up by what I wanna do to you. Cause I'mma start off gentle but when I get up in there, is over."

Lamar looked up at Devon and was turned on. A bit afraid of the hunger in Devon's eyes, he realized that he'd better heed the warning. He then gave Devon a light kiss and thanked him again for the night.

Devon hugged Lamar one last time and after assuring himself that Lamar was ok, he left the room. He closed the door softly on the way out, leaving Lamar there with a burning fire and utter satisfaction.

Lamar got comfortable and cut off the lamp next to the bed and he lay there in awe, appreciation, desire and admiration of the man that had just left his room. Something about that man, in that moment, caused him to submit himself to him. He decided that he wanted to be whatever Devon needed him to be and do whatever Devon needed him to do. Mostly, he wanted to make Devon happy.

Lamar had no idea what position he'd placed himself in at that moment, but life, being as sure as the day, had a way of making sure you knew. Lamar finally drifted off to sleep, oblivious at the journey ahead. Because had he known, he would have prepared but rarely do you see a storm coming.

Chapter 11

It was around 11am when Lamar's eyes fluttered open. As he took in his surroundings, he was a bit confused about where he was until he recalled the gathering last night and more specifically, Devon. The thought of Devon caused Lamar to smile. He was immediately transported to bliss at the conversation and Devon's touch. For a moment, he wondered if last night was even real.

I mean, he thought to himself, *we were drinking.*

Shaking those thoughts away, he finally pulled himself out of his happy place, swung his legs over the edge of the bed and sat up as his mind still swirled with thoughts of his potential future with the man of his dreams. He sat for a few moments soaking in the moment before getting out of bed and stretching and then moving towards the adjoining bathroom. After relieving himself, he washed his hands and face, and brushed his teeth with the toothbrush and toothpaste Devon had so thoughtfully placed there at some point last night. After brushing and wiping off the excess, he stood at the mirror, reflecting upon himself. He'd fought so hard to learn to appreciate himself and, in this moment, he was really pleased with his work.

As he was about to move towards the room to get dressed, he noticed something out of the corner of his eye. Stuck to the wall between the light switch and the shower was a sky blue sticky note. Lamar moved towards it and smiled as warmth flowed through his chest upon taking it off the wall.

The note simply said, *"I meant what I said. I want you and I'm here to protect you if you'll allow me to."*

Devon's thoughtfulness brought tears to Lamar's eyes. The thought of someone showing as much consideration and intent as Devon when Lamar had given up on love moved him in ways he just did not think possible for him and yet here it was, right in his face.

Lamar took a moment to take it all in before heading back into the room to get dressed. He stripped the bed down and neatly placed the sheets and blanket at the foot of the bed. He then made his way downstairs to see what was going on with everyone.

As Lamar made his way towards the kitchen, the scent of something beautiful met him, making him move faster. As he entered the kitchen, he observed Devon and Julia moving around the kitchen, cooking, laughing, and setting up plates on the island.

Upon sensing Lamar entering the room, Devon looked up and over towards Lamar and smiled. "Morning sleepy head," Devon started. "How'd you sleep?"

"Very well, thank you." Lamar smiled.

"Well, I'm glad you finally joined us. Julia was just about to go fetch you." Devon laughed.

"So, what's all this?" Lamar gestured at the spread.

"Just a lil something to officially welcome my cousin to the city." Julia smiled in reply. "Now sit down so we can say grace and get our grub on."

Once all the plates were fixed, Julia led them in a small prayer and they all dug into their servings of home fries, turkey sausage, over easy eggs and guava pastries. The food was so delicious that they were all silent until everything was gone and washed down with a nice cup of café con leche.

Since Julia and Devon had been responsible for breakfast, Lamar took it upon himself to clear the counter and wipe everything down. Once everything was loaded into the dishwasher, they held small talk about the party last night and their plans for the day. Julia said that she would be working on setting up those interviews for a caretaker and then she would relax. Devon replied that he was free for the evening after organizing and cleaning up. Lamar felt a tingle shoot up his spine at the possibilities. Lamar quickly gathered himself and said that he was going to be meeting with his lounge manager to go over the numbers from last night, prepare for that evening and do a little online shopping for his house.

"Matter fact," Lamar continued, "In the continuance of your welcoming Sir, I'd love to have you guys come through and hang out with me if you're able."

Devon replied that he'd definitely be there and Julia concurred. Julia and Lamar then gathered their things and piled into Devon's truck.

Chapter 12

The ride back to Julia's was light and cheery, especially now that Devon and Lamar had become so familiar with each other. The three bantered back and forth and laughed the whole way to Julia's driveway.

They pulled into Julia's driveway where they sat for a few moments as Devon shared with them how thankful he was they came out and how he hoped for more gatherings. Julia seconded that emotion and leaned over to give him a hug and a kiss on the cheek. She then turned around as Lamar leaned forward to also receive his hug and kiss and then she got out.

Lamar again thanked Devon for everything and made sure to give him his number. As Lamar went to get out, he turned back to give Devon a handshake, to which Devon cocked his head back and laughed.

"Come here," Devon demanded. Lamar scooted his way towards the middle of the bench and was about to say yes when Devon, having undid his seatbelt, leaned into the back towards Lamar and grabbed Lamar's neck and brought him towards his. He began kissing Lamar gently which caused Lamar to moan in response. Devon laughed and pulled back to gaze upon him.

"I'm thinking that we've got more exploring to do, so after we leave the lounge, I'm taking you on a date, so be ready," Devon said as he lightly gripped Lamar's chin before repositioning himself back in his seat. "Have a good day and make sure you think about me." Devon ended with a wink.

Laughing, Lamar got out of the truck and waved Devon off before making it to Julia's door, where she'd left the front door open. Lamar pulled open the screen door and kicked his shoes off to have a quick chat with Julia before heading home.

"I'm in here," Julia called from the kitchen. Lamar closed and locked the main door behind him and made his way towards the kitchen.

"So, what did you think of my cousin?" Julia asked as she pulled 2 bottles of water out of the fridge and handed one to Lamar.

"I honestly think he's amazing and I find it hard to believe that someone of his caliber and sentiment is real," Lamar answered honestly.

Laughing, Julia replied, "I see, just as clearly as I saw how you practically fell at his feet," Julia answered as she began laughing even harder. Finally composing herself a bit, she continued, "Chile, I thought I was gonna have to get my shovel." She continued as one hand held her hip and the other wiped away the tears that had fallen from her laughter.

Not really amused but tickled at the truth of it all, Lamar responded, "Anyway. He aiight."

"Ok aiight," Julia replied as she sat down at the kitchen counter. "No, but seriously, I kind of figured that my cousin was into both men and women just from his interactions with folks over the years. Of course, he's never came out and said it, and me, being one to mind my business, never asked, but there are certain things that you pick up on when you know someone."

"Oh, so you set me up?" Lamar asked as he laid his hand over his chest in feigned insult.

"Boy, bye," Julia laughed as she dismissed Lamar's sarcasm. "You know you like that boy."

"That is besides the point mam," Lamar answered back as he giggled at the realization that he was apparently now dating.

Still laughing, Julia got up from the counter and moved towards the front door. "I've got to get on these interviews."

Following suit, Lamar made his way towards the front door where he put on his shoes.

"Will I see you tonight for sure?" Lamar asked as he leaned in to give Julia another hug.

"I will definitely be there," Julia replied as she watched Lamar walk out and make it to his car.

Lamar unlocked his car, got in and cranked it up. The air was already on blast so he opened his windows to let the trapped heat escape. He sat there for a few moments taking in the surrealness of how quickly his life was changing. He'd been introduced to some incredible people and couldn't help but wonder if he'd finally found someone who not only physically drew him but was able to simulate him mentally and emotionally. He found it hard to believe and yet here it was. As he returned to the moment, he put on his seatbelt and, after backing out of Julia's driveway, went on autopilot as he headed home.

As he cruised the short distance to his house, he was again lost in the world of Devon. He was surprised at how easily he'd begun falling for this guy. He briefly considered that maybe he was moving way too fast but brushed it off with yet another fantasy involving lifelong commitment and hell, a puppy.

Lamar had to laugh at that last one but thinking on the seriousness of it, he realized that he meant it. He realized that as much as he attempted to fight off the feeling that he should avoid this space, he was running out of good reasons to keep his guard up.

As Lamar pulled into his neighborhood, he decided he was going to simply take it day by day. With this new resolve, Lamar pulled up into his driveway, got out of his car and made his way into the house in order to begin preparing for later that evening.

Chapter 13

It was around 5pm when Lamar woke up from his nap. He woke up smiling and refreshed and thankful. He basked in the feelings of being wanted and appreciated and his heart was warm. Despite his previous situations, he didn't feel like he needed to hold back at the thought of his future with Devon.

Devon was a dream come true, from the tone and texture of his voice, to his eyes which held intelligence, desire and a mischievousness that drove Lamar wild, onto his perfectly sculpted frame that felt so damn good next to him.

And to top it all off, Lamar found himself mesmerized by the pressure that hung low and to the left between thighs that he couldn't wait to lick. Devon was truly something to behold.

The more he laid there and thought about the perfection that was Devon, the more he became aroused to the point where he found himself salivating at the thought of all the things he wanted to do to him. Laughing at himself for behaving like a horny teenager, he finally got up and began moving around.

Coming back to the moment, he heard his phone ringing as he relieved himself. He finished, washed his hands and then went back into his room to see who'd reached out to him. He saw that the missed calls were from Ms. Armand. He immediately called her back.

"Hey there, Lamar. Have I caught you at a bad time?" Ms. Armand said.

"Not at all. Everything all right?"

"Oh yeah... Just wanted to let you know that my team has handled the purchase with urgency and that everything is ready to go. I'll have everything officially submitted on Monday and I'll follow up with you should anything come up," she informed him.

"Thank you for the update. Have a great weekend then!" Lamar said before ending the call and returning to the bathroom to wash his face and brush his teeth. He then headed back into his room to throw on something decent and he grabbed his phone as he then moved towards the kitchen. Upon entering the kitchen, he heard his phone chime, alerting him that he'd just received a text message, so he stopped what he was doing and looked down at the message. Smiling when he noticed it was Devon, he opened the message. It simply said:

DEVON: *What up lil daddy? Last night was nice and I just wanted to reassure you that I'm really trying to spend time getting to know you. We can go as fast or as slow as you want but I'm here. I look forward to our date tonight so be ready.*

Lamar couldn't help the grin that spread across his face. He'd never been courted before, and it felt strange to be handled in such an intimate and tender way. He was thrilled about later and could hardly wait until the two of them linked up.

Still smiling from the text, he sent a quick smiley face emoji and proceeded to fix himself a cup of green tea with honey along with a tuna spread over a quickly toasted pita slice with provolone cheese. He enjoyed his meal, and once he was done, he headed into his office to power up his PC.

Once his PC was on, he went into his emails and reviewed the numbers from last night along with the set-up for tonight's open mic that Angela had sent him earlier that day and he smiled at the continued growth of the lounge. He really appreciated the support that he was receiving from the community and emailed Angela back, informing her that he wanted to sit down with her to go over something that they could do for the folks who continued to support them.

In a separate email, Angela also let him know that she would be at the lounge an hour before opening just to make sure everything was in place and looked forward to hearing from him about the housewarming. Lamar responded that he would update her and thanked her again for being awesome.

Lamar then energized, began scrolling around various websites to look for things for his house. He settled on some candles and accessories for his bathrooms. Content with what he'd purchased, he powered off his PC and then made his way to his den where he turned on Netflix and selected Girlfriends.

As he settled into the series for the 1000th time, he remembered Julia telling him that she grabbed a card for the artist she'd made her purchases from. He picked up his phone and texted her a reminder to get him that card so that he could check out his work.

Lamar then settled into the episode where Joan was being Joan in preparing everyone to go out Christmas Caroling. He kicked his chair back and enjoyed their world for a few hours.

Eventually, he picked up his phone and saw that it was 7:15, so he decided to go ahead and get ready for the night ahead. He turned the TV off, went into his room, turned his Bluetooth speaker on, selected Monica radio, and set about getting ready for the night.

Chapter 14

Lamar took his time getting ready. He took a nice, long, hot shower and then got out and dried off. He followed this with applying lavender oil to his hair and body and then moved on into his room. After throwing his towel across the top of his closet to dry, he entered and, after looking around for a few moments, settled on a black, form-fitting cotton tee shirt along with some form-fitting black jeans. For his shoes, he chose a pair of red ankle boots with a nice heel on them and a black leather belt that had a matte black finish buckle in the shape of some unknown figure. Pleased with his selections, he laid everything out and set about getting himself together.

It was 8:15pm before he was done dressing and heading out the door. The ride over was short and pleasant enough. When he reached the lounge, he circled by the front as was his custom, and hung a left and then another quick left into the alley behind the business. He pulled up to the security gate, swiped his badge, and waited while the gate opened. After entering the parking lot, he pulled up next to Angela's car. He made sure that he had everything he needed before he made his way into Ed's.

As he passed through the kitchen, he spoke to everyone and inquired about their day. He made sure to let them know that if they needed anything or just wanted to talk to be sure to reach out to him. He then exited the kitchen and made a left and then a quick right down a short hallway where Angela's office was located on one side and his on the other.

"Knock knock," Lamar said as he lightly rapped on Angela's door frame. She was, as usual, hard at work.

As he entered, Angela took a moment to take her eyes off her computer screen. When she saw it was Lamar, she got up with a smile and made her way around her desk to give him a hug.

"Hey my love!" Angela began as she gestured towards the two chairs in front of her desk and made her way back around to her seat.

"Hey there lady!" Lamar answered back as he took a seat and got comfortable. "How are you?"

"All is well. Just wrapping up a few things," Angela replied as she turned back towards her PC. "And you've got perfect timing but before I get into all that, tell me about last night."

Lamar took a moment to allow last night to replay in his mind before he responded. "It was perfect." Lamar began. "The guests were super nice and very inspirational, and I even made some contacts who're more or less moving in the same direction as myself." Lamar paused as he considered telling her about Devon. Not that he was ashamed or anything, it was just new and he wanted to give it some time before introducing him to people.

"Uh uh," Angela said, interrupting Lamar's thoughts. "What was that?" she laughed.

"What was what?" Lamar asked, feigning innocence.

"Really? That's what we're doing now?" Angela asked as she crossed her arms over her chest.

Laughing, Lamar decided to go ahead and share. "Well, I did meet this guy. His name is Devon and he's perfect." Lamar began as he felt his heartbeat pick up. "He's super smart, well versed, connected, is kind, compassionate, has great taste and is even a bit of a renaissance man."

"And what else?" Angela probed with laughter in her eyes.

"You and Julia get on my nerves thinking ya'll know me." Lamar laughed as he realized that he'd fallen for Devon more than he knew. "Ok, so he is phyne!! And baaabay!! He got it... Do you hear me?"

They both burst out in laughter at the implied business.

"So, this guy has really captured your attention huh?" Angela seriously quizzed Lamar.

"He really has. He is unlike anyone I've ever met before. I mean, he literally gives me butterflies," Lamar answered as he chuckled at the realization.

"Well, I can definitely tell that you're into him because I've never seen you this giddy about anyone. Hell, I've watched plenty of handsome men approach you over the years only to be met with polite disinterest." Angela smiled as she continued, "What was different about him?"

Lamar took a moment to think before answering, "Honestly, I believe he sees me."

"I get that. Trust me I do." Angela paused as she gazed at him. "To be seen and heard is everything." Angela paused as she switched up the mood. "I look forward to meeting this guy." Angela crossed her hands over her chest. "He must be something special to have caught your attention."

"Well, he and Julia are supposed to be here this evening so you will definitely get your chance." Lamar smiled.

"All right now." Angela laughed. Getting back to the business at hand, Angela transitioned, "So about tonight, everything is lined up for our speakers and I got your email about setting up something for our patrons. I'm working on a few ideas that I'll share with you when I feel better about them. Also, those vendors I mentioned to you earlier this week finally reached back out and after a bit of negotiations, we've come to an agreement on the partnerships moving forward. Once I have all the paperwork, I'll reach out to you to go over everything. As far as everything else, there are no issues, and I will see to it that there's a table for 3 set up." Angela stopped as she shuffled through some paperwork on her desk. "I think that's about it for now."

"I love and appreciate you lady." Lamar smiled.

"You know I got you." She smiled as she again returned her attention to him. "Was there anything else that you wanted to cover while we're here?"

"I think that's about it. If you can direct me to my table, I'll just hang out there until the doors open," Lamar responded.

"Yes sir boss." Angela laughed as she got up and rounded the corner with Lamar in tow. She directed him to the bar for a few moments while she got with the head server for the floor. After a few moments, she looked over at him and nodded for him to follow.

It was in that moment that Lamar knew what he was going to do for Angela. He was sending her and her kids to Caribbean for a week and he was not taking no for an answer. Smiling to himself, he took a moment to appreciate how strong Angela was to have completely started over with herself and her babies and it made him proud to see that despite how difficult it must have been, she never gave up and never let her kids see her sweat.

He reflected on the night she told him that she left her husband. She'd been married for 7 years and was the assistant manager at Esther's and had two small children aged 2 and 4 at the time. She said that she'd come home from work, and it was storming out. She'd dropped her kids off at her mom's earlier that day to spend the week with her, so she was looking forward to spending some alone time with her man. She said she came into the house and found it odd at how quiet it was, especially since it was fairly early, and her husband's car was in the driveway. Not thinking too much more about it, she kicked off her shoes and headed towards the bedroom where she stripped out of her pants. Upon opening the door, she tossed her pants towards the hamper while expecting to see her husband in the bed asleep or at the very least, dozing in and out, but he was not there. She said she knew something was weird when she saw the bathroom light on with the door closed. She said as she neared the door, she heard soft talking. She opened the door, and her husband was startled but that was not what broke her heart. She said that he was in the bathroom naked, hard, while face-timing some chick. She immediately turned around and ran back into the room to throw on the pants that she'd kicked off. She said that as she was leaving the room, he grabbed her by her hair, yoked her around, and slapped her as he asked where she was going.

Stunned, because he'd never hit her before, she just stood there looking at him. This apparently pissed him off even more because he slapped her again. This time, she swung back and rushed out of the room and towards the door but before she could get it open, he grabbed her by her shirt and spun her around into his fist. She said he'd hit her three more times and would've hit her a fourth had she not kicked him in his balls.

When he went down, she ran out of the house barefoot, jumped in her car, and never looked back. She said that she filed for divorce the very next day. She'd told Lamar that her husband called her phone back-to-back, leaving her messages apologizing and saying he would never do it again, but she remembered the abuse she witnessed her mom go through and was adamant that she was never going back to him to be disrespected and possibly beat again. She said this was around the time when she ended up getting into the program that he met her through.

As Lamar followed Angela, his heart swelled with even more pride. This woman was so resilient, and she never allowed her past to poison her future. He was beyond pleased with this woman and hoped that the trip he was planning for her showed her a fraction of how grateful he was to her.

Upon reaching the front end of the lounge, Lamar was taken aback by the view. He never tired of looking at his biggest accomplishment to date. The care Angela took to make sure that it was clean, fresh, and full of ambiance made his heart even warmer. He also appreciated Angela's suggestion to have an interior decorator come in and reimagine the space. He was a bit hesitant at first because he was a creature of habit, but he had to say that Angela's vision was exactly what was needed. The lighting throughout the public areas of the lounge had been recessed and dimmed a bit, along with diffusers that were strategically placed throughout the building, creating yet another layer of comfort. The thing, however, that really did it for him, was the way the booths were sectioned off.

The interior decorator had gone above and beyond with various fabrics that were in natural tones and hues. These fabrics were inconspicuously hung from the ceiling and encircled the booths giving the sensation of privacy. They also allowed for whoever occupied the booths to adjust them so that they were completely enveloped in intimacy.

He continued to his table where he thanked her with a hug and a kiss to the cheek upon sitting down. Once comfortable, he checked the time and saw it was 8:47pm. He decided to go ahead and send out text messages to both Julia and Devon to let them know that he was at the lounge, and they were free to drop by whenever.

As he sat there, lost in his thoughts about his future, his phone sounded off, alerting him that he'd just received new messages from Julia and Devon.

JULIA: ☺ *Wrapping up to head out soon.*
But the second text from Devon set Lamar on fire.
DEVON: *I'm enroute. Looking forward to our date later in the evening. And oh, I'm not gonna hold myself back, so if you don't wanna be rocked to sleep, you better behave yourself.*
Smiling at the thought of Devon's everything, Lamar replied:
LAMAR: *you should be the one concerned.*
Seeing that it was now 8:56pm, Lamar decided to go ahead and make his way towards the front of the building to be there with Angela to welcome his guests. While enroute, he slid his phone into his back pocket and made it just as Angela was unlocking the doors and with that, the night began.

Chapter 15

Lamar was humbled by the inflow of patrons. The place was filling up fast. At some point, Angela pulled out her walkie and called for the hostess to come and man her position. When the hostess got to the front of the building, Angela asked Lamar for a more accurate description of Devon and then sent him back to his table.

Smiling to himself, Lamar made his way back. As he was sliding into the booth, one of the servers came up to the table with a pitcher of some type of tangerine-colored liquid and 3 glasses. Lamar thanked and tipped the server, poured himself a glass, and was immediately taken to a place of pleasure at the drink's subtle sweetness and thick consistency. He pulled the glass away from his lips long enough to look at it and then took another sip.

As Lamar began to feel the warmth from the liquid filling him, he leaned his head back in contentment. Amazingly, he did not allow his thoughts to run away from him. As he sat there in silence, he was startled at the depth of the voice that spoke to him. "Is this seat taken?"

Lamar's eyes shot open as his head tilted back into position in order to look around to see who that was. Upon laying eyes, he smiled, and the warmth spread into his nether regions. It was Devon, accompanied by

Angela who stood just off to Devon's right, smiling. Lamar attempted to stand to give him a hug, but Devon placed his hand on his chest and gently pushed him back down as he slid into the booth next to him.

"So, this is Mr. Devon? I'm Angela, Lamar's 2nd in command around these parts." Angela smiled as she moved forward with an outstretched hand that Devon received and gently shook. "Welcome to Ed's and I really hope you enjoy your evening."

"Really quick before you go, what is this drink?" Lamar asked as he held up his glass.

Laughing gently, Angela replied, "That's a Tequila provided by one of the vendors whose paperwork I've yet to send over to you but since you're here, what do you think of it?"

"It's incredible. It's smooth and flavorful without being overly sweet," Lamar paused as he took another sip, "We've got to get this on the menu asap."

"Consider it done," Angela replied, satisfied, before excusing herself. "Nice meeting you again Devon and if you need anything, please don't hesitate to let your server know."

"Thank you and it was a pleasure meeting you," Devon replied.

"Likewise." Angela smiled as she left the two of them to engage with themselves.

"This is nice," Devon began as he looked around, taking it all in. "It's definitely grown and sexy, but I also get a feeling of comfort here. Like people are completely at ease. It's almost as if they've come to the cookout." Devon finished as he scooted a little closer to Lamar.

As Lamar moved to adjust himself at the nearness of Devon, he felt Devon's hands on his chin and his face turned to meet Devon's. Devon glanced at him for a few moments before leaning in and kissing him. Lamar moaned as Devon's left hand caught Lamar at the small of his back in order to pull him closer. As Lamar was being brought closer to Devon, Lamar put his arms between the two of them by placing them on Devon's chest, which caused Devon to pull back with a smile.

Lamar looked into Devon's eyes and could have stripped naked right there at the desire that swirled through Devon's eyes. "Sir, we are in public." Lamar playfully laughed.

"You see the same thang I see, and you know ain't nobody thinking about the booth in the back, nor can they really even see in here." Devon smiled back as he reserved the right to rub Lamar's back.

"You sir, are nasty." Lamar laughed as he turned back to face the going's on of the lounge.

"You have no idea," Devon whispered as he quickly nibbled Lamar's ear lobe.

The two of them sat back and watched the activities of the lounge while chit chatting here and there.

This moment is so right, Lamar thought to himself as he felt Devon's left-hand interlocking with his right. With his left hand, Lamar fixed Devon a drink and passed it over to him and leaned his head on Devon's left shoulder.

As the two of them sat in silence, the lights dimmed even more, and a single light shone onto the stage that was fairly centered to their line of sight. As the crowd quieted, Angela appeared out of the darkness before the mic to claps and cheers from the crowd.

"Good evening, ladies and gentlemen." Angela began in her husky, vibrato voice. "Thank you for coming out to share your time, space and energy." Angela paused in order to allow the crowd time to respond.

"Tonight, we have 4 individuals who want to bless us with their art." Angela paused as the crowd responded with their approval.

"All right now. Coming to the stage first is a brother who goes by the name I, Harpo." She finished as the crowd clapped in anticipation.

"Evening folks. As previously stated, I am I, Harpo and I thank you for having me. This piece is titled Home."

Home?

I was asked did I feel at home.

I paused because I've never understood the concept.

You see, betwixt many moons and trees that sway gently in breezes which soothe, the sun often found me in varying spaces.

I didn't initiate this phaze, and I knew not how to correct it.

Home...

The place of one's ancestry, being able to link lineage to thought.

A Smile.

An action.

A skill but, where is that place for me?

Its' deeper than a mortgage or an inheritance passed down by the faithful.

It's wider than the multitude of property lines spread far and wide, being the sum of what wasn't taken.

It's more obvious than hues of skin kissed by the son and kept by the same.

Home...

What does it mean to an alien? A being here, not of this place as they navigate their way through this space of deeply tinted mirrors finally making their exit.

But to where?

These are the questions I ponder as I come into the recognition of fact that I am but a vapor.

My hope is that when I've covered this last bit of somethingness that I return ta origins that breathed me into this thing called time to finally taking rest in knowing..

Home

"Thank you." I, Harpo ended and walked off as the crowd whistled and snapped their gratitude.

"Oh, so it's gone be one of those type of nights.." Angela exclaimed as she returned to the mic. "My brother said Betwist many moons and trees that sway gently.." She smiled as she allowed time for the crowd to settle back down.

"Well all right. Now it's time for our next presenter. Coming to the stage is a brother by the name of Mark." Angela finished as the next artist approached the mic.

"Evening folks. I'm Mark and this piece is called The Hills."

The Hills

As I sat there at the corner of destiny and favor, I smiled.

I smiled because for the 1ˢᵗ time I was able to receive that we would make it.

I was so inspired that I got up and dared at a journey down this Ave.

I saw the pain.

The pressure.

The rejection.

I took note of rulings governed by ignorant eyes and hearts full of shadows.

I looked out and heard the silent cries and I was comforted.

I was comforted because as I looked out, I saw off in the distance, dawn, slowly making her way towards this Ave of ebony junctions.

I continued down this lively street and saw nothingness being gathered up as fruit before beauty's eye and for the first time, in a long time, I laughed and I'm talking gut-wrenching, heart-filled, tear-flowing laughter and I was taken back to the day when I'd, in desperation, consumed the holiest of holies in a fit to drive away the void that lurked just beyond my vision.

In that moment, I was reminded of the sweetest instruction and was at once transported back to the corner and destiny and favor and I somehow knew that dawn was on our side.

"Thank you." Mark ended as he, too, exited the stage to more whistles and claps.

As Angela made her way back towards the mic, Devon leaned over and kissed Lamar gently on the forehead, causing Lamar to snuggle up against Devon even more. Smiling, Devon removed his hand from Lamar's, wrapped it around Lamar and pulled him as near as he could possibly get. Once settled, they both turned their attention back towards Angela.

"I know it often looks bad but we must remember that joy comes in the morning!" Angela said to shouts of joy and laughter as she continued. "We must continue supporting one another and looking out for one another and standing as a unit." Angela paused as the crowd clapped their approval.

"Before getting into this next presenter," Angela began as she looked out and around the crowd, "I just wanted to say thank you to each and every one of you for standing with us and believing in us."

"Now for our next presenter, we have someone who has not graced this stage in many moons." Angela stepped back for dramatic effect before returning to the mic to continue, "Please welcome to the stage, my girl and yours, Julia!!" Angela finished as the crowd cheered and whooped as Julia made her way to the mic.

Lamar and Devon looked at each other and smiled in anticipation of what Julia had to say. Lamar laid his head back on Devon's shoulder as Julia finally approached the mic.

Laughing, Julia began, "Thank you all for having me. It's definitely been a while, but I wanted to drop off some thoughts and also surprise my bestie with something new and fresh since he likes to concern himself with when I'm gonna get a man." Julia paused as the crowd laughed. "So, this piece," she began again, "is titled A Cocktail."

A Cocktail

You ask why I am alone, and I reply, choice and circumstance.
You see, I have loved, and I have dated but the 2 were never exclusive.
So why am I alone?
It's because exclusivity seemed to dance upon the fringes of my reach; taunting me with promises of together and forever only to leave me with the facts of never and he thought he was clever.

For me to cleave requires the mind of one whose heart desires me and the woman that I am.

For me to submit requires the vision and sight of a king who sees.

Understand that the endless tricks of young men caused me to bridle my girdle tight and not for lack of want.

See, she, through whom juices flow, is ever ready but that heifer not logical and we've grown past the state of ignorance.

This ride requires depth and a man who comprehends the rock pon which I cling to.

Home to me?

And this is why I am alone.

Check please...

As Julia finished, the crowd erupted in laughter and applause. Lamar was personally tickled at her reference to her lady parts being an illogical heifer. They continued cheering, laughing, and whistling as she made her way over to where Devon and Lamar were on their feet, welcoming her with hugs. She gave them both kisses and told them to sit back down and to get back to being comfortable. She took her seat and fixed herself a drink, and Angela made it back to the mic.

Laughing still, Angela spoke into the mic. "I can't stand that heifer right there." She paused as she slightly bent over forward in laughter.

Finally gathering herself, she continued, "Ok, you guys, I'm sorry. Coming to the stage next is our last presenter for the evening. I bring to you, Son of Us." Angela finished to snaps as the next presenter made his way to the mic.

"Good evening, everybody. I'm glad to have followed on the heels of laughter." He paused as the crowd prepared themselves for whatever he was going to present.

"Again folks, my name is Son of Us and I bring to you Observation."

Observation

I talk about it because I am about it.

My community.

I see how we've been divided and played against each other, and I stand to unite.

I see how we were denied access to equality while being reprimanded to the sidelines, watching other nations stand upon the backs of our ancestors and I stand to renovate.

I see how we were stripped of our dignity and pride as others amassed and placed foot to neck with assured threat of death, now or later, and I speak to heal and convict.

I see how we were robbed of our resources and lands while delegations rationed scraps, and I stand to reclaim, re-vitalize, and restore.

I see how, concerning my community, mercy was a nonstarter as our lives were viewed as inconsequential, and I declare worth.

I see how my people were stripped, starved, and humiliated, then provided with guns, drugs and sentences as our government sat back, watching us kill ourselves before waging war against a war they underwrote, and I stand to cleanse our streets.

You see, I sat back, and I watched how a legacy of fear and servitude slowly morphed into a legacy of death.

At first, vengeance was to be mine until I realized that every up exists because of down and I took note of time.

It was then that I relaxed, and patience became as precious as my next breath.

See, as I sat back and watched and waited, I saw your end.

The blood and horror of it flowed just as easy as the poison you drank that led you there.

An note, it was not by our hand that your end befell you.

So now I no longer sit by and observe, no, now I take action, for the window is small and the opportunity great.

My people, my hand is extended.

Let us rise together that we be carried above the flood that is to come.

Let us take our place as we then sit back, watching and waiting, for recompense to have its fill.

"Thank you," Son of Us finished as he stepped away from the mic.

At first, you could've heard a pin drop at the thick silence. Then suddenly, someone began softly crying, and someone else began snapping, and someone else began clapping, and before you knew it, everyone was on their feet in unified appreciation. Lamar looked around and saw many wet faces and even more people hugging each other at the emotion of it all. Lamar even found that a few stray tears slid from his eyes, which Devon also noticed and, in response, drew him into a hug just to let him know that he was there for him, which caused more tears to fall.

He couldn't explain why he'd been triggered but it felt good to just let the tears flow and even better to be held by this man who continued to amaze him. They stayed this way for what felt like forever until Lamar felt an additional hand rubbing his back. He and Devon pulled apart and he smiled when he found out that it was Julia.

"I'm heading home. I've got 3 more interviews tomorrow for the caretaker for my mom," she said. They all hugged, and Devon and Lamar kissed her cheek and then Julia was out.

The two of them sat in silence as they sipped their drinks and enjoyed the ambiance flowing through the building by the now soothing house music coming out of the speakers.

Devon looked at his phone before asking, "Are you ready?"

"Yeah, I'm just gonna let Angela know," Lamar responded.

The 2 of them made their way towards Angela's office where she'd disappeared a few moments before.

"Hey love, we're leaving. We just wanted you to know we had an amazing time and appreciate you for everything," Lamar said.

"Ok babes. I'll reach out to you tomorrow," Angela said as she looked up from her monitor. "And Devon, it was really nice meeting you."

"It was nice meeting you as well," Devon replied as the two of them turned around and headed out to the front parking lot towards Devon's truck.

In a shocking twist of events, Devon not only held open the passenger door for Lamar but also helped him up into the seat. Lamar was tickled at the thought of him being treated with such care and he couldn't contain the giggle that came up.

"You are the silliest person I know." Devon smiled as he secured the door and rounded the vehicle to get into the driver's seat. "Where's your car?" Devon asked as he cranked up his vehicle.

"Oh, it's in the employee parking lot behind the building," Lamar replied. "I can get it later."

"Copy," Devon responded as they both put on their seatbelts.

"All right lil daddy. You ready for this evening?" Devon smiled as he put out his right hand for Lamar to grab with his left.

"I am." Lamar laughed as he realized that lil daddy was his official nickname.

As they set off into the night, Lamar was in pure bliss as he held the hand of the man he was falling in love with. He was ready to face the world with Devon and couldn't wait to show him how much. He squeezed Devon's hand and took in the scenery as Devon navigated them through the sultry South Florida streets.

Chapter 16

As Devon navigated his way through Opa-Locka towards, Lamar assumed, was SR 9, they talked about the evening up to this point.

"I'm really impressed with Ed's. How about a personal tour sometime?" Devon asked.

"I'll set it up asap," Lamar said while personally thinking to himself, *and you can get a personal tour of me tonight.*

Smiling, Lamar continued, "Thank you for your kind words about Ed's. It's been a labor of love. How are you adjusting to officially being a resident of Miami?"

"I'm adjusting just fine. I'm actually looking forward to getting started next week and continuing to impact lives."

As Devon dug into the specifics he hoped to accomplish such as alleviating mental anguish and assisting with not only personal achievements but people's professional goals as well, he made a left onto SR 9, which connected Miami Gardens, N. Miami Beach, N. Miami, Norwood and 95 North and South.

As Devon continued with his dreams of reaching as many people as possible, Lamar's heart melted completely, and it scared him. Here he was with this guy he'd only met almost 2 days ago prior, and he was already wide open and caught up. Realizing this fact, he was suddenly assailed by an intense sensation that he'd not experienced since childhood. It hit him hard and fast, causing his heart to race.

Sensing change, Devon squeezed Lamar's hand while asking, "You ok?"

It took Lamar a moment to respond because in all honesty, he was scared shitless. This feeling was familiar, yet foreign, and he'd done everything he could to fight it off for years. It seemed to have stilled and left him over the years but tonight was an apparent reminder that it was never far away.

"Yea, I am now," Lamar replied weakly as he leaned as close to Devon as he possibly could considering the design of the truck. In the aftermath, he was in a strange space but was brought back to the moment as Devon squeezed his hand and assured him that he was right there and that he wasn't going anywhere.

For a few moments, they rode in silence as Devon had since navigated his way onto 95 South towards the city. As the city passed by in somewhat of a blur of lights to Lamar, he looked out of the left corner of his eye only to find Devon watching him out of the corner of his right eye.

"You sure you're ok?" Devon asked, still a bit concerned about Lamar spacing out. He wasn't sure what was going on with him but in this moment, he just wanted to comfort him and let him know that he was not alone. He also hoped where he was heading would bring that beautiful smile back to his face.

"Yes, my long and strong piece of chocolate," Lamar responded, hoping to shake up the awkwardness of the moment.

It definitely had the effect Lamar desired because Devon immediately burst out in laughter before saying, "Now that will get you in some real trouble."

Laughing as well, Lamar replied, "Well that's the plan."

Getting back to a sense of normalcy, the two of them continued their talk with Lamar now also sharing more of his dreams and visions for the future as he continued observing the scenery passing by in an attempt to guess where he was heading. They talked about dark days that they both had seen, how they'd gotten through them, the lessons they'd learned, and the ones they still held onto to this day. Lamar was loving their back-and-forth banter. It felt so natural and Devon never let his hand go all the while.

As they continued their back and forth, Lamar also took a moment to take in the city scape. Miami was an incredibly beautiful city with so much to offer and even more obstacles to overcome but Lamar was confident that between Devon, himself and the fabulous 4, things were bound to change.

At some point, both of them fell back into silence as they took in the scenery. By this time, they were crossing NW 62nd St exit and downtown was coming in hot. For the next 15-20 minutes, they took in all of the glory of Miami and the many changes that had occurred.

They eventually exited on Brickell Ave and Lamar perked up. The only times that he really ever came down this way was to ride through on those nights when he wasn't quite sleepy and had nothing else going on. He'd slow stroll to witness the wealth and growth of the area before heading back to his neck of the woods, so he wondered what Devon was up to.

Sensing Lamar's excitement, Devon said, "When I date, I want you to be comfortable in knowing that I've got you. I just want you to enjoy us." Smiling, Devon continued onto SW 4th Ave and then made a left onto SW 8th St. He then took the next left and pulled up to the very first building on the left. He stopped in front of the doors, hit the emergency flashers and got out to speak with the valet. After a moment or two, he made his way back towards the truck but instead of going to the driver's side, he made his way around to Lamar's side of the truck. Lamar undid his seat belt and grabbed Devon's phone and turned to open the door, but Devon had already pulled it open and grabbed Lamar's hand to help him step down from the truck.

Yea, you gone get all of this tonight, Lamar thought to himself as he smiled.

Devon led him into the building and navigated towards the bank of elevators. All the while, he never let go of Lamar's hand which caused Lamar to pull his hand up and gently kiss it. As they stopped in front of the elevators, Devon stood behind Lamar and reached around him with his left arm to press the call button. While they waited, Devon's left arm rested around Lamar's waist while Lamar had took the moment to lean into Devon and slightly lay his head on Devon's shoulder.

As they waited on the elevator, people passed by. Some of them smiled, at which Lamar smiled back, while others shot looks of disgust to which Lamar leaned in all the more into the comfort that was Devon.

The elevator finally came and they stepped in. Devon pressed the button for the 40th floor and Lamar's excitement went up another notch. Was this to be a romantic rooftop experience? He was so excited that he almost squealed but maintained his composure as Devon gently kissed him behind his right ear and held him even more tightly.

The elevator finally stopped, and Lamar's heart rate increased in anticipation. The doors opened to an exquisitely styled foyer. They made their way through the double doors and ahead, Lamar finally saw that he was to be wined and dined at Sugars. He made a mental note to bring Julia here.

They were greeted by 1 of 2 hosts to whom Devon mentioned his reservation. The host confirmed their reservation in her ledger and then led them into the establishment. They walked through the main area of the lounge and then were guided outside onto the patio area which caused Lamar to involuntarily gasp at not only the décor but the view. In addition to downtown, he was able to see clear up to midtown and across towards the beaches. Still walking in front of Devon, Lamar let out a little giggle as Devon leaned forward to nibble on the back of his neck. In return, Lamar tooted up into all that manliness to let him know that he was very appreciated, to which Devon softly chuckled.

They were finally led to their table where Devon even held out Lamar's chair before sitting down. As Devon spoke with the waiter, Lamar was in pleasure overload. He'd never seen something so beautiful before in his life. From the alcove-like setting to the walls made of the natural bush onto the lights speckled throughout the bush to the antique look of the table and chairs. And again, that view. Lamar had never had the pleasure of Miami from this angle, and it literally took his breath away.

As he looked around to take it all in, he finally came back around to this Adonis before him, and he leaned over and kissed him tenderly and with lots of tongue. As he was kissing on Devon, his hand slowly made its way up Devon's thigh where he made contact with the tip of Devon's aroused member and he slowly squeezed and caressed it, which caused Devon to moan.

Smiling, Lamar pulled back and after giving him one last kiss, just looked at him and then said, "Thank you."

Grabbing both of Lamar's hands, Devon pulled them onto the table and kissed both of them before saying, "For you, I believe it's worth it."

As they sat there in silence, looking into each other's eyes, their waiter returned with water and some lemons. She set them on the table and asked if they were ready to order.

Devon looked at Lamar who nodded and Devon responded with, "Let me get 2 orders of bang bang shrimp, a sugar roll and keep the chilli parador's flowing until I say when."

This brought laughter from all 3 of them, and their server, whose name Lamar learned was Jess, made her way to get their orders submitted.

Lamar leaned back over when she was gone and kissed Devon as deeply as he could while desperately squeezing his hand. When he finally came up for air, Devon was smiling, and Lamar felt tears rolling down his face. Before he could wipe them, Devon reached across the table with both hands and wiped them away for him.

"I'm here, lil daddy. I'm here and I promise I'm not going anywhere." Devon started as he reached for a napkin to dry the new onset of fresh tears. "This is real. You can trust this, and you can trust me." Devon paused as he wiped away the remaining tears. "I just want to see your smile and help you accomplish your dreams." Devon stopped as he got up to walk around to Lamar and squat down in front of him. "Bae, you don't have to cry because you will never be alone again as long as I'm alive. Do you believe that?" Devon stopped as he waited for Lamar to respond.

Sniffling, Lamar looked upon Devon before him. He hated that things were moving so fast but he thought about the instant chemistry and how Devon's energy matched his words. He thought about how hurt he'd been in his past and that this guy was totally different. He was spending time with him. Keeping his word and he wasn't some secret, so he went with his heart and answered, "Yes. I do."

With that, Devon gently kissed him while wiping off the newest set of tears. Then he pulled Lamar up into a hug, holding him tightly for what seemed like forever before making sure he was secured back in his seat before returning to his.

They soon had their drinks, which they both agreed were amazing, and their food arrived shortly thereafter. As the night wore on, they realized there was no need to talk much. They were enjoying each other's company and the libations were definitely up-to par.

It was around 2:30am before either of them decided to call it a night. They thanked Jess and left her a healthy tip. They then exited the lounge, hand in hand, and made their way back to the elevator. The ride down was very comfortable seeing as how they'd bonded even more.

They made it to the 1st floor and back outside to the valet. When the truck was brought around, Devon again walked Lamar around to his side and helped him back up into the truck before getting back in his driver's seat and they again held hands as they made their way into the city.

Chapter 17

Lamar was in heaven. He'd just had the perfect date with the man of his fantasies, and he was wide awake, living through it all. The warmth that spread through his chest caused him to lovingly gaze over towards Devon, who pulled Lamar's hand up to his mouth, where he planted a gentle kiss in response. Lamar laughed quietly to himself wondering if life could possibly get any better.

Seeing that they were back on Brickell and heading further South towards Coconut Grove made Lamar curious as to what was next. Sensing the inquiry, Devon simply relayed that he wanted to spend some quiet time together and he'd brought along a few accessories. This set Lamar's curiosity on fire as to what could possibly be next for the two of them.

At some point during their drive, Lamar realized that they were not going towards Coconut Grove at all because Devon ended up making a left towards Virginia Key. Lamar was really puzzled now because, as far as he knew, besides the multiple strips of sand along the water, there was only Virginia Key Beach and what looked to be a hole-in-the-wall bar as soon as you crossed over the first bridge. Everything else was residential. Settling on patience, Lamar sat there in quiet anticipation, waiting to see what was next.

He didn't have to wait long because as soon as Devon crossed over the 2nd bridge, he shortly pulled into the parking lot to their right. He then made a quick left and proceeded to drive towards the end of the parking lot that was furthest from view of the road.

It didn't take them long to reach the end of the parking lot and there was only 1 other vehicle there and that vehicle was parked towards the front of the parking lot. Having settled on a particular location, Devon angled his truck, backed the Tahoe up, and stopped. Before getting out, he opened the back of the truck and then, after telling Lamar to give him a few minutes, hopped out and made his way around to the back of the truck to move around whatever he had planned for the two of them.

Lamar's excitement was on 10 again and he could not stop the smile that slowly spread across his face at their location and what was about to happen.

Calm yo fast ass down boy, Lamar laughed to himself. *What if he just wants to talk or sit here in silence?* Lamar continued in his thoughts. *Relax.*

The suspense was killing Lamar at this point and just as he was about to undo his seatbelt and get out of the truck, Devon was there, opening the door for him. He again helped Lamar out of the truck, and as they rounded the back of it, Lamar's breath caught in his throat. Laid out on a thin piece of sand between the back of the truck and the water that was not too far away was a quilt set up with a bottle of Tequila, two cups, two candles, and a pillow.

Lamar was at a loss for words at the thoughtfulness and simplicity of it all. He quickly turned around to face Devon, who was standing there smiling. Lamar leaned up into Devon and slowly kissed him as tears slid down his face. He'd never felt so treasured nor cared for in his life and the beauty of it all turned Lamar into an emotional wreck for a moment. He really couldn't believe it. He recalled the days he was beat because the wind was blowing too hard, or the clouds were too gray. He thought how his grandfather would call him faggot and sissy and hit him whenever he could.

He thought about how he was touched as a child but quickly moved past all those things to return to this moment with this man and he was, for the first time, unashamed at the tears that flowed down his face. All the while, Devon just held on while slowly rocking him.

When the last tear fell, Lamar picked his head up to look into Devon's eyes, and he asked, "Where did you come from?"

Laughing, Devon responded, "From a galaxy far, far away."

As the two of them laughed together, Devon led him to the quilt, had him take off his shoes and helped him sit down. Before sitting himself, Devon went back into the truck, realizing he'd forgotten something, and he returned with Guava Nectar for the drinks along with a shaker. He went ahead and fixed them both drinks and sat behind Lamar, who in turn, leaned back into Devon's strength and slowly sipped on his drink while gazing out upon the water.

The night was gorgeous. The temp felt to be in the low 80's and the breeze was really breezing. The moon was full in the sky and there was not a single cloud to obstruct the view. Lamar's favorite part was the path of light that trailed its way across the water and seemed to stop right where the sand below their feet ended. It was quiet, save the gentle waves that rolled up against the shore.

The two of them sat in silence, lost in their thoughts as they slowly sipped. Devon wondered who'd hurt Lamar so bad while Lamar thought if he would ever get over the pain of yesterday.

Devon finally broke the silence by asking, "I know you may not want to get into it but who hurt you?" Though Lamar had shared a bit about his tragic past at the party at Devon's house, Devon wanted to dig a little deeper and understand the trauma behind Lamar's hurt.

Lamar, taking a few moments to think about how he wanted to answer the question, responded, "There were many people and things that hurt me."

"Have you ever thought about facing those issues because it sounds like you just tossed them into the back of your mind and tried to forget," Devon inquired.

Lamar was again floored by this man's ability to see him. He took another sip of his drink before responding. "I've honestly never given it much thought. I mean, life being what it is, who has the time or opportunity to just sit back and deal with it? I mean, you've got to live."

"Agreed, but bro, you can't just not deal with it. You know what I'm saying? You stifle yourself doing that and you are an amazing person with so many wonderful traits and characteristics about yourself. I think that for you to fully work out your destiny and give your best self to those you want to affect, you're going to have to yoke those muh fuckin issues up and let them know that they no longer have you. You must let them know that you are in control," Devon countered.

Lamar had no response to that because Devon wasn't lying, but Lamar's thing was, how? Even if only in the world you've created for yourself. Lamar didn't know but what he did know was that he was not about to ruin the moment with his baggage, so to change the course of the conversation, Lamar simply replied, "you're right but can we not dig into that tonight. I want to enjoy you and all of your efforts."

Devon looked upon Lamar and determined that he would let it go tonight but he was going to see to it that Lamar dealt with his shit. He was too amazing and gifted not to. "Deal."

And with that, the two of them snuggled up even closer while continuing to sip on their drinks and look out over the water.

Chapter 18

They had been sitting there for a little over an hour in their comfortable silence when Lamar leaned up slightly so that he could set his now empty cup to the side, and he turned around and kissed Devon. Devon then put his cup to the side and engaged Lamar's desire.

The kissing intensified and the next thing they knew, they were kissing while struggling to get out of their clothes. Once they were fully naked, Lamar finally had the chance to see Devon's love below. His mouth immediately began to water. He'd heard about them, but he'd never seen a pretty piece of meat rack before. It was deliciously thick with pronounced veins running the length of what appeared to be a 9.5-inch course that met at a perfectly shaped helmet. And that wasn't the best part. The best part was the way this fine specimen curved to the left. Before Lamar realized what was happening, he was beelining for that deliciousness but he was stopped just as he was about to put hands around it or mouth on it.

Lamar actually pouted causing Devon to lean back and laugh. Lamar didn't see what was funny at all. Finally composing himself, Devon said, "I'm sorry but 2 things. I brought you out tonight to please you and 2nd, I need to get my condoms." And with that Devon leaned over and went into his pants, grabbed his wallet and surprisingly some lube.

Understanding and appreciating but still pissed, Lamar wasn't sure what to do with himself, so he leaned back on his arms and crossed his legs while watching Devon.

As Devon began to return to him, Lamar then asked, "When were you last tested?"

"Just last week. I test every 6 months just to be safe, even though I always have safe sex," Devon responded.

"Do you have proof?"

"Yeah, of course." Devon reached into his wallet and pulled out a small piece of paper, almost the size of an index card and handed it over to Lamar.

After reading over it, Lamar was contented, and he then moved to reach for his pants while telling Devon, "I was tested last month and have not had sexual contact with anyone other than myself for several years now." Lamar found his phone and went into his gallery. He found what he was looking for and showed it to Devon.

"You keep a picture of your status?" Devon laughed.

"Yes sir. Just to remind myself of why I need to keep it to myself." Lamar laughed in returned.

"Oh. " Devon said, his voice dropping an octave as he moved towards Lamar.

As Devon hungrily crept towards Lamar, he tossed the condom near where their drinks were. As he neared Lamar, he gripped him and pulled him under his body and then began kissing Lamar passionately while his hands explored Lamar's willing body.

The heat between the two of them shot up a notch as Devon lowered his head to Lamar's right nipple, which caused Lamar to softly cry out. As much as he couldn't stand it, he absolutely loved the way Devon teased and tortured him with his tongue and fingers. Lamar wrapped his legs around Devon's waist, which caused Devon to laugh in between the teasing and torturing of his new bae.

Devon took his complete time learning Lamar's body and, in the process, teaching Lamar about it. Lamar never knew how erogenous he was until Devon's touch. This exploration left Lamar trembling in desperate need as he longed for Devon to be inside him.

Having learned how to set him off, Devon returned to Lamar's right nipple, which he gently bit down on, but this time, he simultaneously began stroking Lamar's leaking member as it stood at full mast. Devon smiled mischievously as he alternated between gently biting down and sucking on Lamar's nipple while slowly stroking him. He gazed at Lamar in hunger as Lamar's eyes rolled into the back of his head while releasing incoherent sounds of pleasure.

Wanting to feel what was to be filled, Devon's hand left Lamar's member to find the spot he was eager to pleasure most. He was thrilled at how warm and soft it was. He licked his finger, and he began gently massaging Lamar's darkness until he'd entered the foyer, which brought a gasp out of Lamar, along with his hands pushing against his chest. Devon looked down at Lamar and Lamar removed his hands. Devon then slowly descended Lamar's pleasure with his long and thick finger, which soon thereafter, landed on Lamar's g-spot. He realized this because Lamar instantly gripped him, and he felt a bit of moisture. He gently massaged Lamar's center and just as he noticed that Lamar was on the verge of release, he immediately pulled out which caused Lamar to sigh in frustration, which caused Devon to laugh.

Devon came up and began kissing Lamar again while slowly grinding up against his wetness with his now throbbing member that had begun to slowly leak as well. At this point, Devon was ready to dive in. In the heat of the moment, and with their status shared, the condoms lay forgotten to the side. Right before he pushed to enter, he locked Lamar's legs in place, and began sucking on Lamar's neck. As he sucked and nibbled and licked, he slowly pressed against Lamar's softness. He felt Lamar tensing up, so he began pleasuring Lamar's left nipple while continuing to suck on Lamar's neck. He slowly pressed again and again and again until he felt himself slipping inside.

Lamar tried to run, but realizing that he didn't have anywhere to go, he placed his hands on Devon's shoulder's as he cried out in a little pain and a lot of pleasure. Devon took his time, careful not to give Lamar more than the tip of his pleasure until Lamar finally relaxed and that's when he began to dive.

Devon's initial stroke was slow and steady. He'd come out to the tip and then slowly slide back in until he was fully resting inside the enchantment that was Lamar. The pleasure of Lamar's tight, warm, wetness drove him crazy and he began picking up speed which caused Lamar to cry out a little louder each time. At a certain point, Devon realized that he was touching Lamar's bottom, which he found led to another door. In tapping on that door, Lamar's occasional trembling turned into Lamar trying to flee the scene. Lamar pleaded with him, but Devon covered him with kisses so as to not draw any attention and he continued giving Lamar what they both wanted.

After a few agonizing moments of deep diving, Devon decided that at that moment, he was going to honor his word, so he pulled out while adjusting Lamar's legs, and then he angled himself and reentered Lamar, only this time his goal was to create as much friction as possible on Lamar's g-spot. As he slowly began applying that pressure, Lamar called out his name and began trembling heavily while begging Devon to stop. Devon refused to listen even when Lamar's hands came back up to his chest trying to push him off. Instead of stopping, Devon switched up the rhythm and angle of the stroke, which caused Lamar to start leaking from his member, creaming from his wetness and stuttering from his lips.

Devon smiled as he watched Lamar's eyes roll, yet again, to the back of his head.

"Please…" Lamar begged, pleasure in his plea.

Lamar struggled, which caused Devon to re-angle and hit it at a different angle just before leaning down and whispering in Lamar's ear, "I told you what was gone happen." As he continued stroking Lamar. "You said this was what you wanted, didn't you?" Lamar mumbled something unintelligible to which Devon asked, "You said I was gone be the one in trouble, right?" Lamar cried out in response. "So, now that you got it, take it." And it was at that moment that Lamar's cries of pleasure intensified, and Devon felt his wetness starting to contract. Devon could sense that Lamar was about to blow. And blow he did.

Lamar had never, ever in life, had an orgasm so intense. It caused him to open his eyes and push sound out of his throat as wave after wave of pleasure overcame him. Tears flowed down Lamar's face as his body continued to convulse at the pleasure of Devon. Devon, however, showed no mercy. He re-angled and dove past his now contracting g-spot and he began to beat Lamar down, which caused Lamar's already intense orgasm to go up even more.

Having had enough of torturing Lamar, Devon began long stroking Lamar, careful not to enter that 2nd door. He released the lock on Lamar's legs and then pushed them down towards Lamar's chest while leaning up to watch himself slide in and out of Lamar while simultaneously watching Lamar. Lamar's facial expression almost caused him to burst out in laughter, but he wasn't laughing anymore after looking back down at his stroke and all the cream it produced.

Devon felt himself about to let go, and after one last dip into Lamar's depth, wave after wave of pleasure overtook him, so much so that he caught a cramp in his left leg.

When what seemed like the longest bust was over, Devon released Lamar's legs altogether, which fell almost limply to either side and he weakly lowered himself onto Lamar's chest where he lay listening to Lamar's heart.

Lamar finally managed to prop his right leg up and let it fall lazily at Devon's side. He'd never known sex could be this amazing nor intense. He was giddy at how much pleasure this man brought him. There was no denying his skill and as Lamar lay there with this man laid on top of him and still partially erect in him, he realized that he was in love.

Chapter 19

Devon was the first to wake. He noted that it was still dark. He then looked upon Lamar, who was sound asleep. He kissed Lamar on the forehead, pulled himself off of Lamar, and began cleaning up and putting things back into the Tahoe. Upon clearing out everything that he could, he made his way back over to Lamar and picked up his phone, which was still, amazingly, on the comforter up near Lamar's head, and saw that it was 5:17am. He knelt and gently tapped Lamar on his chest, softly calling his name.

Lamar was in the midst of a dream. He couldn't quite recall what was going on, but someone kept calling his name. He stirred and at first, he was disoriented because all he saw was darkness. It took him a moment to realize that he was still on the beach and the voice he'd heard was Devon. At the recognition, he smiled as he moved to get up.

As Lamar moved to get up, Devon reached down to pull him up. Upon realizing that they were both still naked, Lamar laughed and kissed Devon, who, after kissing Lamar, led him back to the truck.

"We're not getting dressed?" Lamar asked as he took Devon's help getting up and into the passenger seat.

"I thought about it but with all the sand that got in our clothes, I just didn't see the point," Devon replied as he then shut the passenger door and made it around to the driver's side.

The two of them sat in comfortable silence as Devon made his way back into the city. As Devon made his way onto the airport expressway, Lamar wondered where they were headed. He did not have to wait long for an answer.

"I hope you don't mind, but I figured that we would go ahead and head to my house. We can get cleaned up there, order some breakfast, and kick back today," Devon said after merging into northbound traffic on the Palmetto.

"I'm game." Lamar smiled.

The two soon pulled into Devon's driveway, where he opened the garage, pulled inside and parked as the door came back down. They got out of the truck and Lamar helped Devon grab everything out of the truck. After setting the things where Devon instructed him too, he followed Devon upstairs to Devon's room. Lamar fell in love with Devon's room instantly. It was done in shades of gray and black and had a huge king-sized canopy bed with solid wooden posts. Sheer gray and black curtains that were tied to the posts hung from the canopy at the top frame. All of this was backed up upon a plush-looking leather headboard that adorned the wall like a piece of art. The floor shone like liquid except where there were purposely placed throw rugs. As he looked around the room, he also noticed the big ass TV hanging from the wall across from the foot of the bed. He continued his inspection of the room and really appreciated how Devon didn't over-do it with his décor but rather had only the pieces that he needed. As he stood there, appreciating the space and the placement of Devon's things, he didn't initially hear Devon calling to him. He wasn't aware until Devon came up behind him, grabbed him and gently kissed him on his neck, which startled him.

Laughing, Devon grabbed him by the hand and the two headed towards the bathroom. They showered together and made more love while in there before washing and drying off and getting into Devon's super comfortable bed. Lamar snuggled up against Devon's chest and Devon turned on the TV and pulled up a live image of a fireplace and they lay there in silence, gazing at the burning logs.

At some point, they both drifted off to sleep and slept until around 12pm when Devon quietly got up so as to not disturb Lamar and he grabbed his phone. He ordered them some brunch and got back into bed and back into position with Lamar laying on his chest. Once the food was 5 minutes out, Devon kissed Lamar on the forehead and told him it was time to get up so he could eat, and then he threw on some basketball shorts and a tee shirt and made his way downstairs to get their food.

When he came back up, Lamar was coming out of the bathroom. After stripping back down, Devon sat the food on the bed and he and Lamar said grace and ate their meal. Once done, Devon found a movie on Netflix, and they got comfortable and that was their entire Saturday.

Chapter 20

Sunday morning found Lamar, yet again, wrapped up in Devon's arms. Between the chemistry, sex, ordered food and the cuddling, Lamar didn't think a more perfect experience existed.

He looked up at Devon, who was snoring lightly and he smiled. He leaned up and kissed him on the cheek and then carefully pulled himself out of bed. He grabbed one of Devon's oversized tee shirts and made his way downstairs into the kitchen where he began rummaging through the fridge to figure out what he was going to cook for breakfast. After a few minutes of searching, he settled on oatmeal, fruit and turkey bacon.

After everything was done cooking and sliced, he fixed some green tea with honey, grabbed a serving tray out of the pantry and slowly made his way back upstairs. As he entered the room, he heard the water running in the bathroom. He headed towards the bed, careful not to spill anything, and set the tray down. As he was turning around, he was greeted by the beautiful sight of a naked Devon. He smiled and felt himself throb a bit at the semi swollen thickness that swung heavily back and forth as if calling out to him. Devon drew closer, pulled him in and began kissing him while squeezing his rear.

"Good morning, bae," Devon said as he led Lamar back towards the bed.

"Good morning sir sexiness," Lamar replied to which Devon laughed.

The two of them ate their breakfast in silence and once the tray was removed from the bed, Devon turned on some soft and slow music that played from speakers Lamar hadn't noticed until now. As the music serenaded them, Devon pulled the shirt off of Lamar and took his time appreciating Lamar's body.

Devon really took his time letting Lamar know how beautiful he was, and Lamar loved every moment of it. After an intense session of foreplay, Devon finally entered Lamar where he made slow and passionate love to him. Upon finishing, the two showered and got back in bed and watched movies until they again drifted off.

The rest of the day was spent talking about the week ahead and planning their next get together. At some point, Devon ordered dinner and they feasted on Salmon, wild rice and asparagus paired with a nice white wine that Devon pulled out of his bar. Once dinner was over, the two of them talked well into the night before realizing that it was coming up on 11:30pm. They both decided that it was definitely time to head out so that Lamar could pick up his vehicle and Devon could get ready for Monday morning when he and his partners would be opening the community center in Overtown.

Devon gave Lamar back the shirt he'd had on earlier and a pair of basketball shorts and they both made their way downstairs and towards the door leading into the garage. Before they stepped out, Devon handed Lamar a bag in the laundry room that was off to their right. Lamar looked in, saw it was his clothes from Friday evening, and made a mental note to drop them off at the cleaners the next day.

Once in the garage, Devon remote-started his truck and opened the garage door. As he was making his way to open the passenger door for Lamar, Lamar stopped him.

"While it's much appreciated, you don't have to keep going out of your way doing all this."

Devon laughed. "It's nothing."

Lamar responded by kissing Devon and proceeded to open the door for himself and climb in while Devon stood there shaking his head and smiling. Once Lamar was in, Devon came back around to the driver's side and climbed into his seat, and when his truck was ready, he backed out, closed the garage, and pulled off towards Ed's.

The ride to Ed's was uneventful. They rode in silence while holding hands, and about 25 minutes later, they pulled into the alley behind Ed's. As Devon neared the gate to let them into the parking lot, Lamar clicked his remote to open the gate, and Devon slowly pulled into the employee parking lot.

Lamar undid his seatbelt and grabbed his bag. He leaned over to kiss Devon who'd already undid his seatbelt. Devon kissed him back then placed his hand behind Lamar's head and deepened the kiss.

"You gone make me take it right here in this front seat," Devon said huskily between kisses.

Smiling, Lamar replied, "Anytime you want it."

"Get cho ass out my truck." Devon laughed.

Laughing in return, Lamar got out and made his way towards his car. Unlocking the doors before he was close, he made it to his rear driver door and opened it and placed his bag on the back seat. As he closed the door and turned back to wave at Devon, he saw that Devon was still sitting in the same spot, only now he had his door open.

"C'mere real quick," Devon said hungrily.

Lamar was instantly aroused. He made his way quickly over to Devon, where he found that as he neared him, Devon was slowly stroking his throbbing beefcake. Lamar began kissing Devon, grabbed his meat and began slowly stroking it for him, which brought out a few moans from Devon as they kissed. Having had enough of not tasting Devon, Lamar decided to go for it and he was not stopped this time.

He slowly took Devon's curved dick into his mouth, sucking on the head until there was enough moisture before taking in more. Lamar then began teasing Devon with licks and kisses and sucks coming at random, driving Devon wild.

Lamar then began honing back in on the head, which he began slowly bobbing on while simultaneously stroking his now drenched shaft. Striving to please him, Lamar began descending on Devon's deliciousness inch by juicy inch until the head was at the back of his throat. By this time, he'd removed his hand and gave him slow, steady neck action. He allowed the head of Devon's dick to knock on the door of his throat, and at one point, opened the door for Devon to come in. That initial grip of his throat caused an already reclined Devon's mouth to fall open as his eyes rolled back. The further Lamar allowed Devon to enter, the more Devon began to tremble. When Lamar found his safe space, he began slowly deep diving where he'd go down to his comfort and then slowly come off while applying the jaws of life.

As liquid flowed down Devon's beautifully, melanated shaft, Lamar brought his hand back to it and while finding his groove, implemented timed strokes. This brought guttural sounds from Devon's throat as his hand moved to grab the back of Lamar's head, which Lamar gently pushed away. He drove Devon wild with the way he was up and down and in and out with Devon's dick.

At one point, he felt Devon tense and he knew that it was about to go down, so he applied even more pressure with his mouth on Devon's head and dove even deeper into his throat. Lamar felt Devon begin to shake and tremble and just as he was diving one last time, he felt Devon release into his mouth. Lamar had never been a swallower, but in that moment, for him, he received Devon's juices until Devon was spent, and then Lamar continued his groove, which caused Devon to begin trembling heavily. Lamar continued working Devon until Devon could take no more and he yoked Lamar up by his shirt halfway between a moan and a laugh.

Disappointed that he was forced to stop, Lamar sucked his teeth and looked up at Devon, who was looking down at him with a mix of desire and aggression.

Devon then just shook his head and cupped Lamar's face. He leaned forward and kissed Lamar on the forehead and said, "Listen, lil daddy, you got it, and you got me, but I got something for you. Not gone have me out here folded up, taking advantage of me," then placed himself back in his shorts. "Go on to your car and call me once you get home."

Lamar reluctantly replied, "ok," and then floated back to his vehicle.

He got into his car, turned it on, and allowed the AC to kick in. As he sat there, lost in the moment, he watched Devon out of his rearview mirror whip his truck around and then out of the parking lot. He was in bliss. He officially had a man who not only wanted him as much as he wanted him, but he was smart, sexy, direct, and had the best sex ever! He could not believe what he was experiencing. As his AC finally kicked in, he too whipped around and exited the parking lot, enroute to his house. He was literally on cloud 9 and had no thoughts of coming down and he was happy about it. At that moment, there was a tinge of something foreign, but even the odd sensation could not stop him from feeling his feelings. What he didn't understand was that the sensation ran much deeper than he had ever processed.

He finally made it to the house around about 15 or so minutes later. Then he texted Devon:

LAMAR: *Made it home. Looking forward to hearing from you soon. I'm about to get ready to shower and prep for tomorrow. Thanks for everything.*

Lamar then went about his nightly routine of preparing for bed. Once he'd finished his routine, he grabbed his pillow, his blanket, and his phone and made it into his den, where he turned on Hulu and began watching Golden Girls while checking for messages. He saw that Devon had responded:

DEVON: *just walked in the house a few moments ago. About to shower and get ready for bed. The pleasure is all mine and you don't need to thank me for anything. I'll reach out tomorrow at some point after everything dies down at the center. Hope you have a great rest.*

DEVON: *good night, and oh, I still have something for you. ;)*

Lamar's heart was warm and full. He set his alarm and he watched Golden Girls until they were watching him.

Chapter 21

Monday found Lamar tied up in his sheets as his body writhed from some apparent nightmare. In this dream, he was out on a date with Devon when all of a sudden, he found himself in the middle of this huge space where there was no light. He called out for help several times only to be met with silence.

As he stood there, he could feel the presence of something else there in the darkness with him and it was then that he began running. He had no idea where he was, and he still couldn't see but he knew that he must put distance between himself and whatever that thing was.

As he continued his sprint, he noticed a faint light up ahead off to his right, so he aimed towards it and pressed himself harder than he'd ever pressed himself before. As he drew closer to the light, he again felt the presence of the unknown thing that he'd been running from, and it seemed to be closing in, so he continued pushing himself to avoid contact with it.

Sweat was now running down his face and his eyes stung from the streams pouring down his face, but he pushed through the discomfort and the threat of exhaustion at the ever-growing source of light. Feeling that he was almost there sent a surge of hope through him, and it caused him to drive his legs even harder. As he continued his dash towards what he hoped was an escape from the darkness and the thing within, he began to make out a room of sorts sitting just ahead in the glow.

As he neared the threshold of this unknown room, Lamar's fear began to subside a bit at the thought of safety. Just as he was within reach enough to grab ahold of the door frame, he was hit from the left with such force that, for a moment, he was weightless just before crashing to the floor on his right-hand side. Dazed from the crash, Lamar's fight or flight instincts kicked in and he was immediately on his feet and ready to fight but surprisingly, nothing came.

Finding this odd, Lamar made a mad dash towards the room again, only to be tackled from the front. Whatever it was fell with him this time, landing on his chest, knocking the air from his lungs. Struggling to breathe, Lamar began swinging for all he was worth and even managed to land a few blows on this unknown assailant. As he continued swinging, he realized that there was no longer anything there.

What the hell? Lamar thought as he quickly jumped to his feet. Lamar then recognized that the thing that kept attacking him simply did not want him to leave the darkness of the space and apparently nothing more. This ignited a fire in Lamar to get across that threshold, so with more determination than ever before, he tore off again towards the room. This time, he was met with a heavy blow to the stomach just as his foot stepped through the frame. Not wanting to succumb to the pain and believing his life depended on it, Lamar began throwing blows for all he was worth.

Lamar had never fought so hard in all his life, and what was more, he seemed to land blows less and less. It was like this thing knew Lamar's next move and was quick to counter. With the doorway being so close, hope once again flared through Lamar's heart and caused him to wail like he never had. At one point, Lamar made to strike but switched it up at the last moment and reached out with his left hand, grabbed whatever this thing was by what Lamar could only describe as hair and he began landing blow after blow into what he assumed was the face of his attacker. In return, his attacker began throwing body blows that threatened to double Lamar over, but Lamar refused to bend and thought to himself, *I have to get in there.*

Realizing that no number of blows would get this thing off of him, Lamar knew then what he had to do. He recognized that this thing wanted to keep him out of the light, so Lamar made sure his grip was sure, and he pivoted to where his back was facing the doorway. In one last effort, Lamar allowed himself to fall backward onto the floor of the room with his assailant in tow.

About to swing again, Lamar realized that his attacker had stopped fighting him immediately. With that in mind, Lamar quickly pulled himself up while maintaining his grip on this intruder, and upon his eyes adjusting to the light, his mouth fell open. In front of him was a mirror, but that wasn't the issue. It was who he was holding onto that caused him to pause. The assailant that had been fighting him so vehemently, Lamar's mind finally processed, was himself.

At that recognition, Lamar woke up while simultaneously sitting up. His heart was racing, and he was sweating profusely. He looked around and realized that he was still on his couch and Hulu had long ago paused.

Realizing that it was all a dream, Lamar took a few deep breaths and turned to the side so that he could place his feet on the floor. He held his head in his hands as he absently looked towards his feet. He was not sure what any of that was about and it disturbed him that it felt so real.

As he sat there pondering over what the hell it could have been, his phone rang. Leaning to his right to grab his phone off the arm of the couch, he saw it was his mom.

Still trying to clear his head from sleep and that dream, he answered, "Hello?"

"Hey, baby boy. How are you?" his mom, Linda, asked.

Her voice immediately soothed and comforted him. He was so thankful that he and his mom had reached this place of peace. Just a few short years ago, things weren't so nice.

"Much better now." Lamar smiled. "How are you?"

"I'm good," his mom replied. "What's wrong?"

Lamar's heart warmed at his mom's concern. "I just had a really weird dream is all."

"What was it about?"

Lamar explained the dream, referring to Devon as a friend instead of a boyfriend, as he wasn't ready to introduce him to his family. His mom sat silent for a few moments before responding.

"Well, son, it sounds like you need to pray about it."

Lamar wouldn't say that he was religious at all and hadn't grown up in the church, but he did recall his first encounter with faith. Prior to moving to Miami with his family, Lamar had regularly attended Sunday services at Faith Baptist Church in Fairless Hills, PA and the experience had been awesome. The church had been full of wonderfully kind folks of every race and ethnicity, and he honestly felt the love.

Outside of that, he'd attended a service here and there, and prayer was more of an afterthought than anything to be taken seriously. He'd come to believe that if you wanted it done, you had to do it yourself, and that's the life he'd built for himself.

"Ok. I'll think about it," he replied.

Laughing, his mom replied, "All right, son, but remember, the only thing holding back your relationship with God is you. He is waiting on you but don't take too long. None of us know how much time we have left."

"I get it, and I will do better," Lamar responded as he got up and stretched. "So, what you got going on today?"

"Oh nothing. Just a few doctor visits and then a little shopping for the girls," she answered.

Lamar's sister, Sharena, had 2 girls, and his brother, Peirre, had 2 girls and a son, and his mom spoiled them all rotten. As far as the doctor visits, Lamar was stunned when his mom first told him that she had breast cancer, but she quickly calmed him and let him know that everything was under control.

"Ok. How you feeling? You need anything?" Lamar asked. Between he and his siblings, they'd retired their mom and she lived comfortably.

"I'm ok. I haven't been feeling my best, but I'll get by," his mom responded.

Lamar thought of his mom often these days and just wanted her to be comfortable. Her life coming up in Bristol had not been easy, but she'd always been a soldier and always seemed to come out with Lemonade. He was proud of the woman she became and the life that she now led. He thought about his siblings and how they'd also taken a page from her book of The Perfect Lemonade. His brother was a general contractor and had his own business and was doing well. While they didn't have the best relationship, his sister owned a boutique clothing store and a salon, and she was doing well.

As Lamar continued pondering his mom's life, he thought to himself, *Yea, lady, you did well.* She'd really gone hard and fought even harder for her children and her sanity. He'd never known anyone so strong and solid.

"Well, I will be seeing you soon, so you be safe out there. I love you," Lamar said as he made his way towards the bathroom in his room.

"All right then buddy. I look forward to seeing you. Love you," his mom said before she hung up.

Lamar brushed his teeth and splashed water on his face before using the bathroom. After using the bathroom, he turned on the shower and his YouTube music app and selected Jill Scott radio before getting into the shower.

He took a nice, long, hot shower as he reflected on Devon and their budding love before his mind drifted off to that weird dream again. He really couldn't make sense of it and shook it off as Jill serenaded him. His thoughts gradually drifted back towards Devon.

He finally finished his shower, got out, dried off, and then made his way into the kitchen. Observing the time on the fridge, he was surprised that it was only 7:30am. He prepared himself a breakfast smoothie, grabbed a bottle of water, and made his way into his office.

While waiting for his PC to start up, Lamar shot Devon a quick good morning text. He also wished him success and greatness and told him to call him later. Lamar smiled as he hit the send button. He then set his phone down and pulled up his emails while sipping on his smoothie.

After going through his emails, Lamar sat back in his chair, his gears grinding. With the prospect of property management in his very near future, Lamar had been playing with the idea of digging deeper into Real Estate. He thought over the lack of ownership in the black and brown communities, and he wanted to change that narrative and show that it could be done if you only believed and worked towards it. Curious now to see what was out there, Lamar began searching for available land in Miami Gardens. He didn't notice anything significant, so he decided to shut down his PC.

Lamar decided to put on some underwear and went back into his den. He pulled his blanket and pillow from his couch and transferred them to his recliner. He then turned on Netflix and tuned into Girlfriends while still sipping on his smoothie.

As he was watching his show, his phone sounded off that he'd received a text message. He smiled when he saw it was from Devon.

DEVON: *thanks bae. Call you later.*

Lamar giggled as he sent the kissy face emoji in response.

Before Lamar could set his phone down, his phone went off letting him know he'd received more text messages. Re-opening his phone, he saw the first text was from Julia:

JULIA: *I want to do brunch. Available? If so, be ready around 1pm.*

LAMAR: *I'll be ready.*

The 2nd text was from his attorney:

MS. ARMAND: *just checking in with you and hope your weekend was well. I have some great news and look forward to our meeting tomorrow.*

Since Lamar still had his phone in hand, he decided to reach out to Ms. Santi:

LAMAR: *Hey lady. Are you free for a late lunch tomorrow?*

Ms. Santi had been such a blessing to his life. She had been instrumental in the healing between him and his mom and turned out to be the aunt he never knew he needed. He'd met her through his mom who'd met her at a job fair for the housing authority. Over time, she and his mom had become close, and his mom introduced her to her kids and out of all of them, Lamar was the only one who stayed in touch and their relationship continued to blossom.

After finishing the text to Ms. Santi, he placed his phone on do not disturb. He then set an alarm for 11am and he tuned back into Girlfriends. By the 3rd episode, his smoothie was gone, and he felt sleep nipping at his vision. Before he knew it, Lamar was out.

Chapter 22

Lamar woke up from his nap right at 10:59am. As he pulled himself from the comforting grip of his recliner and sleep, his alarm sounded. After shutting it off, he made his way to the bathroom, where he relieved himself, splashed water on his face, and then brushed his teeth. After brushing, he made his way into his closet to gather something to wear.

He settled on a pair of melon-colored cotton shorts and a graphic tee. As he transitioned his clothes from the closet to the bed, he noticed his bag from the weekend. He went ahead and grabbed it and moved towards the kitchen where he went out onto the patio and opened the bag and began shaking out any extra sand that may have lingered. He then placed the clothes back in the bag and dropped them at the edge of his living room on his way back to getting dressed. He washed his hands before touching his clothes, threw on his shorts, and moved to grab some colorful socks out of his drawer. He then chose a pair of pastel-colored slides and then grabbed his tee shirt and made his way back into his den where he resumed watching Girlfriends.

As he sat there watching Girlfriends, his phone alerted him that he'd received a message. He looked down and saw that it was from Ms. Santi.

MS. SANTI: *A late lunch would work perfectly for me. Can't wait to get together with you.*

Lamar then set his phone down and resumed watching Girlfriends.

After 40 or so minutes in, Lamar's phone rang. He looked down at his phone and saw that it was Julia.

"Hey love. How are you?" Lamar smiled.

"Hey there, best friend. I am well," Julia replied.

"So what's up?" Lamar inquired.

"I'm running a little earlier than I thought I would be so I wanted you to know that I am heading your way now and will be there in 20 or so minutes. Will you be ready?" Julia asked.

"I've been ready. Just let me know when you're pulling up," Lamar responded.

"Will do and see you soon," Julia answered just before she disconnected the line.

Lamar got up, folded up his comforter and set it on his couch where he also placed his pillow on top of the comforter. He then put on his shirt and placed his slides by the front door along with the bag of clothes to be dropped off at the cleaners, and he grabbed 2 bottles of water, one for himself and another for Julia, just in case she wanted one. He then went back into his den and sat back in his recliner and waited on Julia.

He didn't have to wait long because about 15 minutes later, his phone rang. He answered and said that he was coming out. He grabbed his keys and wallet, headed out of the kitchen, slid into his slides, and picked up the bag of clothes. He headed outside, locked up the house, and made his way to Julia's passenger-side door. After getting in and putting on his seatbelt, they headed off into the city.

Chapter 23

After piling into Julia's car, he leaned over and kissed her on the cheek.

"Hey boo," Julia began as she backed out of Lamar's driveway and began her way towards their destination. "How are ya?"

"I'm pretty good," Lamar replied as he settled in for the ride. "Where we headed?"

"Today, I thought we'd hit up Sundays."

Sundays was a restaurant in Miami Gardens near Joe Robbie Stadium aka Hardrock Stadium. It was owned by Trick Daddy and was known for its famous Southern Cuisine. Lamar had been there once and remembered how amazing the food was. As they were making their way through Miami Gardens in route to Sunday's, Lamar quickly settled on fried ribs with greens and mac and cheese.

"So what you been up to?" Lamar asked.

"So you know I had a few more interviews yesterday with potential caregivers for my mom, and I decided on a young lady by the name of Belinda," Julia responded as she made a right onto 183rd St off of NW 47th Ave.

"Really? What stood out about her?"

"Well, one of the reasons was that she came highly recommended by one of my co-workers who was going through the same thing as myself," Julia answered as she made her way towards NW 27th Ave. "And she was really sweet and had such a gentle disposition about herself."

"That's what's up!" Lamar exclaimed, knowing how hard it was for Julia to trust her mom to someone else's care. "So how is this going to work out?"

Julia took a moment to respond as she looked around to make sure it was safe to go before turning left onto NW 27th Ave. "I actually took this week off just to work with her side by side and get her acclimated to my mom, her house and my expectations," Julia began as she shifted over into the far right hand lane headed North. "And I also made it known that I was looking for someone who would be willing to live with my mom Monday through Friday as I would take over on the weekends."

"I'm super happy to hear that. I know you're super relieved," Lamar stated as he gazed at his friend. He hated that she even had to experience this but understood better than most that life often presented you with challenges and rarely were any of them desired. "Does she have kids?"

"She does but she also has a husband who she says fully supports her career. She also shared that her kids were aged 19 and 14 so she was comfortable leaving them for extended periods of time."

"She sounds like she's got all of her ducks in a row." Lamar smiled.

"It definitely seems that way and we're actually going for dinner tonight so that I can meet her husband and kids just to make sure everyone is on board because I know how important family is. I want everyone to be ok with her decision."

Lamar sat there admiring how amazing his friend was. Here she was, dealing with the steady decline of her mother's health and yet she still found time to accommodate other people. As Lamar sat there, lost in thought about what his friend was going through, he didn't initially hear Julia until she nudged him.

"Come back to earth sir," she said smiling. "I was asking you how'd Friday go?

Lamar's face broke out in the biggest smile before he could even form the words which caused Julia to laugh. Composing himself, Lamar responded, "It was absolutely perfect! Devon was such a gentleman and he really took time to consider me and hear me. He had the whole night planned, and his thoughtfulness literally blew my mind. After our late dinner, we then ended up heading towards Virginia Key where we spent time getting to know one another and we actually fell asleep there. The next day, we just lounged around at his place watching movies and eating and on Sunday, we did more of the same up until it was time for me to head home because of course he had to get some rest for the grand opening of their Community Center today and I had a few things that I needed to take care of. All in all, though, to be quite honest, I do believe I'm in love with your cousin."

Julia squeezed Lamar's left hand with her right before responding, "I'm really happy for you friend. My cousin is a really decent guy and I definitely knew that should ya'll hit off that he would be good to you."

"I appreciate that and am really happy that you introduced us. I can really see us building together," Lamar answered as he squeezed Julia's hand back.

"Absolutely," Julia replied as she made a right onto NW 207th St and then a quick left into the parking lot.

Observing the mostly empty parking lot, Lamar said, "Oh wow. I guess Mondays, around this time, is the best time to come here."

Normally Sunday's had lines out of the door, down the sidewalk, through the parking lot and down the street. Because this was not the case at this moment, Lamar became excited that he would be bussin down his plate in no time.

"Hell yea, especially when they opened not all that long ago." Julia laughed.

After parking in front of the restaurant, the two of them got out of the car and made their way inside. They saw once they got inside that there were only 2 people ahead of them so they took a moment to take in the décor while their mouths watered a little at all of the delicious aromas wafting from the kitchen.

Once they got to the counter, Lamar placed his order along with a Blue Raspberry Lemonade. Julia then ordered the fried Snapper with yellow rice and yams and a half and half. Once their orders were placed, Lamar attempted to pay but quickly replaced his wallet upon seeing Julia's neck slide back. Laughing, he backed away from the register and let his friend cover their meals.

While waiting on their food, they went ahead and grabbed a seat by the windows and made themselves comfortable. They didn't have long to wait as their order was being called out 15 or so minutes later. Once they received their food, Julia led them in a quick prayer and they both dug in.

After finishing their food, they thanked the cashiers and made their way back to Julia's car.

After getting in, Julia asked, "What do you have planned for the rest of the day?"

"A little online shopping and then go check on my mom. And afterward, I'm gonna be hooking up with Devon," Lamar responded.

Upon hearing this, Julia smiled and said, "that's what's up."

Having piled back into the car, Julia made her way back towards Lamar's house, while chatting along the way. Once they reached Lamar's house, they sat in the driveway for a few moments with Julia sharing that she wanted to cook Sunday dinner to which Lamar replied that it would be cool.

Having confirmed everything that was to come Sunday, Julia removed her seatbelt and leaned over to hug Lamar. As they both concluded their hug, they then wished each other well and Lamar got out of Julia's car. As Lamar put his keys into the door, he heard Julia backing down the driveway. As he next unlocked the door, he turned to wave Julia off but she'd already angled out of the driveway and was headed West towards home.

Lamar made his way into his den, where he kicked off his shoes, socks and clothes until he was back in just his boxers. He then tuned into Golden Girls.

As he was watching, Lamar thought of the 4 people that Devon had introduced to and decided to shoot them a group text inviting them to come out the following Saturday at 11am to have brunch and discuss a few things.

After sending out the group text, he then set his phone onto the arm of his recliner and got into yet another episode of Golden Girls like he'd never seen it before. As Lamar went on watching the show, he felt himself becoming sleepy and before long, he was outta there.

Chapter 24

It was around 4:30pm when Lamar finally stirred from his food induced nap. He smiled as he got up and stretched. He smiled because he was in a great space. He had an amazing support system, a thriving business, more opportunities on the way and a man with whom he could finally entertain sharing it all with.

After stretching, Lamar grabbed his phone off the arm of the recliner. As he turned it to face him, he saw that he had 5 new messages. He opened his phone to read through the messages and saw that he'd received replies from the group chat that he'd sent out earlier to the folks he'd met at Devon's house warming. In the chat, they said that they'd love to meet on Saturday for brunch and were looking forward to checking out the lounge and all that it offered. Lamar replied:

LAMAR: *looking forward to our conversation. Guarantee you will be more than satisfied with the food and drink selections.*

Lamar then moved onto the last message that he'd received. Seeing it was from Devon, warmth shot through his body which caused him to smile and feel excitement in anticipation of Devon's response to his earlier text. Upon opening the message, Lamar instantly became aroused. Devon had simply replied:

DEVON: *Thinking about you and can't wait until later on.*

Lamar felt his member throb as memories from the weekend flashed through his mind. Smiling mischievously, Lamar replied with an eggplant, peach, and smiley face emoji followed by a few hearts and a kissy face before setting his phone back down.

Lamar made his way into his bathroom, where he relieved himself, washed his hands, and splashed water on his face. He stood there for a moment looking at himself in the mirror before gargling some mouthwash. Once done, he cleaned up his mess and went back into the den to grab his phone and call his mom.

"Hey lady," Lamar began once his mom answered on the 3rd ring. "How are you?"

"Hey son," Linda began. "I'm just a little tired but come on over. I told your brother and sister that you were stopping by so they will be here soon."

Lamar smiled. Even though he and his sister didn't always see eye to eye, he was always happy when they all came together. He felt that it made his mom smile, and after the life they'd all experienced growing up, anything that brought joy to his mom's life, he was always down for.

Besides, he didn't get a chance to get together with his siblings often, since they all had their careers and personal lives.

As he walked back into his room and made his way towards his closet in order to grab some cotton shorts and a tee shirt, he asked his mom what she wanted to eat. She said it didn't matter so he told her that he would grab some food and then be on the way. They said their I love you's and disconnected their call.

Lamar took no time getting dressed, so he went into the den to grab his keys and then made his way outside towards his car. As he sat there, letting his car warm up so that it could cool down, he ran through places with a large enough menu where he could grab a few dishes to suit everyone's tastes. As his AC kicked in, he decided on Pollo Tropical. With the food

selection in mind and his AC blowing, he began making his way towards
N Miami Beach.

Chapter 25

The ride to and from Pollo Tropical was uneventful so it didn't take him long to make it to his mom's house which was located in an area known as Biscayne Gardens. She lived in a cozy 2bdr duplex along with her cat. The neighborhood was attractive and well kept. It consisted of a variety of ethnicities and everyone, for the most part, was really friendly.

His mom had lived here in this neighborhood for the last 10 years and Lamar had met quite a few of her neighbors and it pleased him that most of them were so pleasant. It also pleased him to know that should she ever feel the need for people, she did not have to go no further than her porch.

As Lamar pulled up to his mom's house, he saw that Peirre and Sharena were already there.

Life must be good, Lamar thought to himself as he looked over their vehicles. Sharena was pushing a new and shiny Lexus SUV while Peirre was pushing the newest Dodge Ram. As Lamar got out of his 2017 Nissan Altima, he smiled. His siblings had always possessed a desire for the finer things.

He parked at the curb in front of his mom's house and upon gathering everything, got out and made his way around towards the front door. He smiled as he reflected on how well his mom had done with her children.

As he drew near the door, he heard the laughter of his family coming from around the side of the house so he re-routed. Upon reaching the side gate, he saw that it was partially cracked so he pulled it open and made his way inside, being sure to secure it on his way in.

"No, no, I got it." Lamar smiled sarcastically as he made his way around the side of the house to join in on the ruckus.

"Well, that's good then. I'm glad to know you're capable of not dropping the food," his brother Peirre replied, to which everyone burst out laughing.

Lamar set down the food on his mom's patio table, which had been adorned with a pastel-colored tablecloth, and then moved towards his mom, where he gave her a big hug and a kiss on the cheek. He then made it to Peirre and the two embraced and patted each other on the back. When he got to Sharena, the two of them shook hands and nodded. Things had never been great between the two of them, but they'd since decided they would always put their differences to the side in order to keep the peace when it came to their mom. Lamar knew his mom did not like the fact that the two were so distant, but she respected the fact that they respected her enough to be cordial in her presence.

After all the pleasantries, Sharena made her way inside to gather the paper plates and cups and napkins while Lamar took his seat across from his mom. He took a moment to gaze upon her and he felt that something wasn't right. She didn't look sick or anything, but he sensed that something was off. He brushed it off thinking maybe she just needed rest and he then made the mental decision to enjoy himself.

Rejoining everyone at the table with the food ware, Sharena took her seat next to their mom, and they all began fixing and passing the food around. Once everyone had what they wanted, Lamar's mom led them in a prayer of thankfulness. Once she was finished blessing the food, everyone began digging in.

"So how has everyone been?" Lamar began. It had been a minute since he and his siblings all sat down like this, and he understood that it was sometimes hard to catch up with everyone's schedule.

"Well between my shops and my girls, I've been all over the place. But other than that, everything has been fine. How about yourself?" Sharena responded.

"Tell my girls I said what up," Lamar began. His nieces were 9 and 10, and he didn't get to see them often, mostly because he and his sister did not mesh well, and he never wanted any conflict to come up between them, so he checked on them whenever the opportunity presented itself. "But as far as me," he continued, "I've been great. Business is going well. I'm looking into expanding my portfolio and will have some work for you soon bro, but everything is good. I cannot complain. How about yourself brah?" Lamar asked as the floor was given to Peirre.

"I've been doing fine man. Me and Nicky are hanging on in there and the kids are sprouting on up and eating up everything in the house so in between working, feeding them and paying bills, I try to sleep as much as I can." Peirre was in an amazing relationship with Nicky, whom Lamar affectionately referred to as sis-in-law, and they had 3 kids aged 12, 6, and 1. Lamar often got a chance to hang out with them because he and Nicky were super close. He was super happy for his brother because he'd seen his share of disturbed women. He never gave up hope and learned to work on himself in the process, and he'd finally found his happiness. They'd been together since forever, it seemed, and there couldn't be a better couple.

"How bout you old lady?" Lamar smiled.

Taking a moment to smile and lean her head back in thought, his mom began, "I've had better days, but I've also had worse, so I will not complain. I'm just thankful to be able to have my babies here with me, even if you and your sister don't see eye to eye. I just hope it's not always that way. But God got me, and as long as I hold on, I am ok." His mom finished.

Something about the way she said that bothered Lamar, but he decided not to make a big fuss about it because he knew that when his mom wanted to talk, she would make it known. So, for the remainder of the impromptu lunch, the four of them enjoyed the rest of their meal, their mom, and each other. They all agreed to meet back at their mom's house with the rest of the family in tow in the next two weeks for a BBQ, which made his mom smile.

After another hour or so of hanging out, they all decided it was time to go. The three of them joined in to clean up so that their mom did not have to and made sure that she got back into the house ok. Peirre and Sharena left first after kissing their mom on the cheek, while Lamar lingered behind.

He'd told himself that he would wait until she was ready to talk but his concern would not let him wait that long.

"Mommy, what's wrong?" he asked.

"Nothing God can't fix," she replied.

"Would you like for me to set you up with someone to help you out around here?"

"Aww. That's nice but I assure you that I'm fine. Just going through the motions of being old and tired." His mom laughed and sat down in the living room where she turned on her TV and began to relax.

"Well, all right, but if you need anything, you call me," Lamar said as he kissed her on the forehead and made his way outside, being sure to lock the door behind himself.

As he was making his way towards his car, his phone rang. Looking down, he saw it was Devon. "Hey bae. How you doing?" Lamar asked as he cranked his car, closed the car door and let down the windows.

"I'm great," Devon began, "I'm off and am about to head your way. Did you want anything to eat?"

"Not really," Lamar began, "Julia took me out to brunch and then I had an early dinner with my mom and siblings so I'm actually full."

"Ok, well, I'll grab you a salad just in case," Devon replied.

"Cool beans. So how was your day?" Lamar asked.

"We'll talk about all of that when I get there," Devon replied.

"Well ok, daddy. I look forward to seeing you then." Lamar laughed.

"Oh yes. You definitely gone see me..." Devon grinned.

By the time he hung up with Devon, his AC was kicking so he rolled his windows up and made his way home in order to get ready for Devon.

Chapter 26

I t was around 7:15pm when Lamar pulled into his driveway. He cut the engine to his car and sat there, lost in thought. He reflected on his mom and couldn't help but be concerned even though she said not to be. He knew there was more to his mom's fatigue than she was letting on but she was his mom and he could not push her to do anything she was not willing to do. Reluctantly accepting this reality, Lamar finally decided to receive his mom's claims and made a mental note to try not to worry about her so much. After a few more moments of sitting there in silence, Lamar begrudgingly got out of his vehicle and made his way towards his front door.

After letting himself in, he quickly went through his house, turning on lamps and lighting candles. Finally, after being satisfied with the ambiance, he opened his YouTube music app and settled on Anita Baker after scrolling through his favorite playlists. He then powered up his surround sound system and was immediately comforted by the sultry tones of Ms. Baker as he then made his way into the den, where he sat his phone on the couch and proceeded to make sure everything was in order. Content with everything now being in its place, he grabbed his phone off the couch and made his way into his bedroom where he set his phone on the nightstand to the left of his bed and eagerly set about making his bed up. Now satisfied that everything was as he desired to be, Lamar then stripped and made his way towards his bathroom, where he took a quick shower just to wash away the concerns of the day and be fresh for his lover.

Lamar was still in the bathroom when his phone rang. As he was in the process of oiling himself down, he set the bottle of oil down and carefully stepped towards the nightstand to grab his phone up. It was Devon on the line. Answering, Devon let Lamar know that he'd just pulled into his driveway. Lamar responded that he needed just a few more moments to finish gathering himself and then he'd be at the door.

After patting himself dry, Lamar went into his dresser, grabbed a wife beater and some basketball shorts, threw them on, slipped into some house shoes, and made his way towards the front door. As he rounded the corner to the living room, his heart sped up at the sight of all that sensual chocolate standing in front of his door with several bags. As Lamar reached for the door handle to open the front door, he broke into a smile as some unidentified fragrance, blended with Devon's natural scent, wafted in. Upon opening the screen door, Lamar instinctively leaned on his tip toes and gave Devon a light kiss before offering to grab some bags out of his hands. Devon, of course, declined and followed Lamar back inside. Lamar pointed Devon towards the kitchen, closed and locked the screen door, and proceeded to do the same with the front door, and then he, too, made his way towards the kitchen.

Lamar walked in just as Devon was setting the last bag on the counter. As soon as Devon's hands were free, he pulled Lamar towards him and cupped Lamar's bottom, kissed him tenderly, and then held him for a few moments before letting him go. Lamar was floating at the thought of how gentle and intimate Devon was with him.

"This is nice," Devon began. "Very warm and inviting. And what's that smell?" Devon inquired as he began inhaling deeply.

"Those are some candles I made." Lamar smiled.

"Seriously?" Devon asked in a bit of disbelief.

"Yes sir. There is this BYOB Candle Making shop up in Pembroke Pines that me and Julia went to maybe 2 or 3 months back on a little outing and after several cups and some laughs, these candles are the result." Lamar stated as he pointed out a few of the candles that were visible in their line of sight.

"Nice. What's in it?" Devon inquired.

"If I told you, I'd have to kill you," Lamar replied, to which they both laughed. "So tell me about your day," Lamar asked as he took a seat at the island that spanned a good portion of his kitchen.

"So you really not gone share what's in them?" Devon asked as he moved in close on Lamar and placed his hands on the small of Lamar's back, which caused Lamar to gasp, which was perfect for Devon as he leaned down to plant another of those tender kisses on Lamar's lips.

Caught somewhere between moaning and laughing, Lamar managed to get out that he had some additional candles in the back and that he would send a few home with him. This seemed to satisfy Devon, and he broke away from the moment, but not before lightly nibbling on his neck and set about unloading the bags of food.

Turned on and slightly irritated that Devon had broken the moment, Lamar stuck his bottom lip out and even pouted a bit, to which Devon laughed out loud and followed it up with an "aww". This caused Lamar to laugh at himself as he watched Devon set everything on the countertop. Lamar pointed out where the plates, silverware, and cups were. As the food took over Lamar's senses, he made a point to look at the name on the bags. He smiled when he saw that it was Carrabba's. He'd definitely had them a time or two and really enjoyed their cuisine.

As Devon set about fixing them both a plate, Lamar smiled in pride at this beautiful man who seemed to constantly consider him even though he didn't have to. While Devon was situating the plates and wine he'd also grabbed, he began sharing his day.

"Babe, it was everything I thought it would be and then some," Devon started. "We started off with a few speeches from myself, the folks I introduced you to at the party. We then had a few performances from, get this, The Betty Wright, Angie Stone, Trick Daddy and Trina herself!" Devon paused as he let that sink in.

Devon's excitement was contagious, and Lamar found himself filled with expectancy at what was next.

"After the performances and a few words given by Trina, we then introduced our featured guests which included several medical professionals in various fields along with 15 hiring managers and all of the case managers we have on staff to get the ball rolling for those in need." Devon paused as he finally sat down across from Lamar in front of his plate.

"Once that portion was finished, we then had a ribbon cutting ceremony to commemorate the opening of our Condo tower, which you have to come see. And then we had several giveaways and finally we fed the people and thanked everyone for coming out. It was truly an amazing affair and I'm so thankful to have been a part of it, man." Devon paused as he became lost in the activities of the day.

Lamar, sitting there beaming with pride, lifted his glass in tribute. "To an amazing man with an amazing network of partners. May their lives only go up from here as they work to counter all that has gone wrong in this world."

They both dipped their glasses towards each other and then they took a sip. Devon then blessed the food and while Lamar wasn't really hungry, he managed a few bites of his meal, having resolved that what remained would be his lunch for the following day.

They both sat in their thoughts. Devon's mind was on the next thing to do to further benefit the people of the neighborhood they were serving. Lamar's mind was on how much he loved this man before him and how he wanted to crawl over to him and slowly swallow him in appreciation.

Laughing at himself, Lamar broke the silence between the two of them.

"What happened?" Devon asked as he took another bite of food.

"Just me being silly," Lamar responded. "But in keeping with the theme, I love how you guys have taken ownership to the next level. Why was that so important to you guys?" Lamar asked.

After taking a moment to process and finish chewing his food, Devon answered, "Well, when you look around in this country and in this world, it's impossible to miss how black and brown folks are such huge consumers but represent a minuscule percentage of actual product and/or services. That was a problem for me and my partners, so this was our line in the sand to reverse that tide."

"I'm with you when you're right," Lamar began, "I've often shared that sentiment with others myself and have felt that sometimes I'm fighting a losing battle against a wall of complacency."

"You're not alone," Devon began, "White folks are sometimes uncomfortable having conversations about it, but slavery, Jim Crow, and the government really did a number on our people. It left many of us more broken than we will ever know, and that trauma was passed down through generations, producing fruit such as anger, resentment, and mental health issues." Devon paused as he stared off into his thoughts while absently sipping from his wine glass.

Lamar sat there in awe of this man before him. His passion. His drive. His mind. It was all there for the picking. Composing himself, Lamar looked at this man with a newfound admiration, respect and desire to give him everything and then some.

Taking his time with the vision of beauty before him, Lamar finally spoke, "Babe, what you guys did here today in our city is legendary and will inspire generations to come, and I want you to know that if you guys do nothing more, it is enough."

Finally returning from his thoughts, Devon looked upon Lamar with a particular intensity on his face and gazed for a few moments before speaking, "Is it really though?"

Lamar took a moment to let that question sink in. He understood that Devon's vision seemed larger than his capability allowed for, and he recognized the frustration in his question. It caused him to get up and make his way around the island in order to stand behind Devon and embrace him while softly laying his head against Devon's back. For what seemed like forever, the two of them remained this way as Devon's question still lingered in the air. Finally, Lamar spoke, while still resting upon Devon's back, "It is. It is because you are enough." And with that, Lamar laid a tender kiss on the back of Devon's neck and made his way back towards his seat.

As Lamar situated himself once again, he looked up at Devon and was shaken. He was shaken because Devon still sat there in silence but was looking upon him with a hunger that he'd not seen before and as much as it aroused him, it also made him a little nervous because he did not know what to do with it.

Devon didn't even realize how much he craved to be inside Lamar at that moment until he noticed how Lamar seemingly backed away. This caused Devon to smile within himself. In keeping with their conversation though, he finally composed himself and Devon began, "Sounds like between the few of us, the world better watch out." Devon laughed.

"You damn right," Lamar began. "Hey, I also forgot to mention to you that I sent out a group chat to Joseline and nem asking them to come out to Ed's this Saturday to go over a few things I'd like to run past everyone. I'm also inviting Julia and my attorney and I'd love for you to be there if you're free."

"I'm there," Devon responded as he pushed his plate away from him and leaned back.

For the remainder of the evening, the two of them enjoyed their wine, their music and each other. They sat in silence, mostly just appreciating each other, and often found themselves gazing into each other's eyes at the fact that this thing between them was happening and how much they shared in common.

At some point during the evening, the two of them cleared the countertop and put everything in its place. Devon said he would grab a shower, so Lamar led him into his room, where he grabbed a rag and towel out of the closet and a toothbrush. As Devon got himself situated to shower, Lamar made his way back into the kitchen and grabbed the one bag that remained. In it, Lamar found Devon's clothing for the next day. He headed back to his room, where he neatly laid out Devon's outfit across the bed, carefully so as not to wrinkle them. He placed Devon's underwear, socks and undershirt near the polo and placed Devon's socks on the legs of the polo. Satisfied, Lamar made his way back towards the den, careful to grab another blanket and pillow out of his closet. Having made it back into the den, he turned on the TV and selected Netflix. After scrolling, he settled on Memoires of an International Spy, then covered the couch with one blanket and spread the other out and then got comfortable.

Moments later, Devon entered the den, naked, where he grabbed the extra pillow that Lamar had set on his recliner, and he neared Lamar and stopped in front of him. Anticipating pleasuring Devon, Lamar instantly sat up which caused Devon to laugh. Devon then pulled Lamar up and situated himself in the space behind Lamar. In the time it took Devon to situate himself, Lamar came up out of his clothes, and as his shorts hit the ground, Devon reached for him to lie back down. Lamar obliged, and the two got comfortable on Lamar's oversized couch. They quickly drifted off to sleep with Devon's arms wrapped around a deeply snuggled Lamar.

Chapter 27

Lamar stirred in his sleep as he dreamed. In his dream, he was lying in bed with Devon and Devon was grinding up on him and playfully nipping at the back of his neck, which drove him wild with pleasure. As Devon continued nibbling on his neck and grinding up against him, he suddenly gasped with a mix of pain and then intense pleasure as Devon entered him. He woke up from the sensation, disoriented, because he realized that it wasn't all a dream. He finally recognized that Devon had woken him with his hunger.

Lamar cried out in pleasure as Devon slowly and achingly dug deeper and deeper into him with his slow and steady stroke. Lamar reached back with his left hand to grip Devon's neck as Devon's stroke began to intensify.

As Devon finally slid all the way into Lamar, Lamar cried out and tried to jump off, but Devon held him firmly by the waist and began to again assault that hidden space. Devon then lifted Lamar's left leg and as he moved on top of Lamar, he pulled Lamar over towards the right side of the couch and then he lifted Lamar's right leg and locked both in place and began drilling Lamar, causing him to scream out his name. This time,

Devon did not hesitate to give Lamar the dick he'd been holding back. He'd since learned that Lamar could take it; it just took some coaxing.

Remembering Lamar's spot, Devon switched up the intensity of the stroke and came out enough to where he could now focus on applying pressure directly to Lamar's pleasure box. Slowly thrusting himself against Lamar's darkness caused Lamar's juices to flow and Lamar's cries and screams of pleasure to fall silent. Devon felt Lamar's body tense as he seemed to briefly struggle with receiving Devon's strokes.

Devon took his time working that spot before slowly increasing his speed. As he did, he felt Lamar reopening. It was in that very moment that Devon sank to the bottom of Lamar while simultaneously releasing an intense amount of pleasure just as Lamar began clinching and trembling as he too climaxed.

Devon collapsed on Lamar's chest, spent and breathing heavy. The two of them lay there listening to each other's heartbeats.

Finally breaking the silence, Devon asked, "You ok?"

Still trembling at the pleasure of Devon's semi hard thickness still very much so inside of him, Lamar managed a yes.

Realizing that Lamar was still riding the high of Devon's manhood caused Devon's thickness to stiffen, at which time Lamar tried pushing Devon off, but it was too late. Devon grabbed both Lamar's hands and slowly stroked him as he gently nipped at Lamar's nipples.

Feeling the moisture once again flowing, Devon slowly increased the intensity of his dive as he felt Lamar's darkness welcome him once again. Once again finding Lamar's bottom, Devon was serenaded by the mixture of moans, screams eend cries, and he began losing it. He began beating Lamar as if Lamar had wronged him in life, which increased the volume of Lamar's pleasure. In turn, this amplified Devon's speed to the point where he'd lost all control and grabbed Lamar by the throat and showed him who he was.

As Devon crashed into Lamar, the thought of how juicy and tight and hot Lamar was caused Devon to stiffen even more to the point where he desired nothing more than to become one with Lamar. He pushed inside him as hard and as fast as he could in hopes of unison until he felt the edges of his world disappear as his body became locked into a trance so intense that all he could do was go with it until the last drop of him was spent. Only then did he collapse upon Lamar's chest, gasping for air.

When he finally came, he noticed that Lamar's heart was racing, and his body trembled like crazy. Devon groggily caressed him and gently kissed his face, and, after a few moments, he felt Lamar's body relax and his heart rate slow down.

"Bae, you good?" Devon asked, his head still resting on Lamar's chest.

Lamar needed a moment before responding. He'd never experienced such an overload of pleasure like he'd just experienced and it scared the shit out of him. Don't get it twisted, it was amazing, but the animalistic hunger that overcame Devon shook him a little.

Struggling to find his voice, Lamar tried to speak "I...umm..." he said weakly as he was still distracted by Devon's semi hard thickness inside him.

Recognizing that his beefcake was interfering with Lamar's thought process, Devon laughed as he slowly pulled out. He almost didn't make it out as Lamar's body clenched and seemingly held on, refusing to let go. He would have given it to him again, but he realized that Lamar, in spite of what his body wanted, was done for the day.

Still struggling to gather his thoughts, Lamar weakly asked, "What time is it?"

Softly laughing, Devon reached towards his phone which was on the end table before stating that it was 5:45am.

"Oh," Lamar weakly began again, "I, umm, I'm ok." Lamar finally got out.

"You sure?" Devon asked as he got up and used his screen saver to get to the light switch for the den. Devon examined himself and looked over to examine Lamar who was still on his back but with his arms across his eyes. He made his way over to Lamar and he lifted his right leg to see if Lamar was in fact really ok. Not seeing any blood on him or under him, he received Lamar's declaration. He was a little concerned because he'd never let go like he had this morning. He realized that when it came to Lamar, it was hard to control himself; plus, Lamar felt so damn good that he had to open up at least once.

Recognizing that he still had a few hours before he had to be at the Center, Devon went into Lamar's bathroom, turned on the shower, and set the temperature. When he was satisfied with everything, he returned to the den, gathered Lamar up into his arms, made Lamar throw his right arm around his neck, and carried him into the bathroom.

"Can you stand?" Devon asked.

Weakly laughing, Lamar tried to stand but found that his legs were a bit wobbly, making him reach out to Devon for support. Steadying him, Devon made him stand and even walk in a circle before they both got into the shower.

Devon washed Lamar thoroughly before washing himself and then he rinsed them both off and turned off the shower and then led them out and dried them both off. He then led Lamar to the bed and sat him down while he went into Lamar's closet and grabbed another blanket to replace the one, they'd just used up. After replacing the blanket, he took the discarded one and tossed it in the washing machine, which was just off the kitchen, along with 3 tide pods and a little bleach, and then he went back for Lamar.

After again gathering Lamar up, he carried him back to the den and gently laid him back on the couch. He then cut the light out and carefully got back behind him. He set his alarm for 8am and set it back on the end table. He wrapped Lamar up in his arms, kissed him on the back of his neck, and heard Lamar's soft breathing before he closed his eyes.

Smiling, Devon pulled Lamar in even closer, snuggled in, and drifted back off to sleep.

Chapter 28

It was around 8:15am before either Devon or Lamar stirred. Lamar actually opened his eyes first but was content to lay there for a moment. Devon was also half awake, he just hadn't opened his eyes yet.

The two of them lay there super comfortable, and neither wanted to break away, but Lamar finally decided that he wanted to go ahead and get up and get a start on his day, and that included fixing Devon's breakfast before sending him off into the world.

Lamar made to get up but found that he was firmly gripped in Devon's embrace. This caused him to smile tenderly but because he needed to get up, he lightly rubbed Devon's hands while softly calling his name. At first, Devon didn't respond, but he finally managed to grumble what Lamar assumed to have been "huh," which made Lamar laugh lightly.

Lamar made to get up again, feeling that Devon's grip had loosened a little. As he was about halfway up and off the couch, Devon suddenly pulled him back. Laughing a bit louder now, Lamar slapped Devon's arm and told him he was trying to fix breakfast for him, to which Devon groggily replied, "Kiss."

Still laughing, Lamar leaned down and gave Devon a tender kiss, and as he was pulling away, Devon deepened the kiss and began caressing Lamar's thigh, to which Lamar pulled himself away laughing while responding, "No! You not finna have me stretched out all day when I've got stuff to do and you gotta be in your office soon."

Devon reluctantly released him but not before grabbing him and biting his right butt cheek.

"Animal!" Lamar laughed as he made his way towards his bathroom to relieve himself and perform his morning ritual.

Once his morning duties were finished, he made his way, still naked, back into the kitchen and he began rummaging through his fridge to find what he could whip up really quick. He settled on two multi-grain bagels and some chicken sausage with a berry whip he'd made.

After taking everything out, he began sauteing the sausage and he popped the bagels in the toaster. While those things were going, he took out two espresso cups to place into his Keurig machine, and then he grabbed two coffee mugs and set them under and began that process.

Once everything was completed, he went about fixing two small plates and setting them up. As he finished placing Devon's plate, he turned around, intent on going to wake Devon, and was startled.

As soon as he turned around, Devon was there. Apparently, he'd jumped up not long after Lamar started cooking because he was fully dressed except for his shoes and work polo.

Devon pulled in closer and began caressing Lamar's left thigh while leaning in for a kiss. As the kiss deepened, Devon pushed his food to the side, lifted Lamar onto the island, and moved even closer between Lamar's legs as his mouth found Lamar's hardened nipples and he gently tortured Lamar.

"Bae, stop," Lamar mumbled.

"Keep going?" Devon laughed as he began biting Lamar's neck while lifting his legs to his shoulders.

"No, please stop. I don't wanna go back to sleep. I have stuff to do." Lamar pleaded as he tried to squirm away.

"I won't be long," Devon replied as he lowered his head to Lamar's chamber and began to have Lamar for breakfast.

Lamar's eyes rolled into the back of his head as Devon's tongue slowly stroked him. He cried out in pleasure as Devon's fingers soon followed suit, quickly finding his spot.

Taking pride in the fact that he had Lamar trembling, Devon pulled his now throbbing member out of his pants and quickly entered Lamar and began rocking steady.

With his legs now thrown across Devon's shoulders, Lamar could only cry out and shed tears as his man stroked him with a point to prove.

The lovemaking was intense and it was deep and just as Devon had promised, it was short. Within 5 minutes, Lamar felt Devon tense up and he then released.

Shaking uncontrollably, Lamar began clinching upon a still-stiff Devon, who'd at this point chosen to focus on Lamar's spot. As Devon continuously pressed in upon Lamar's responsiveness, Lamar's head was thrown back in ecstasy as the pressure mounted. Devon felt Lamar's body preparing to let go, and he began applying even more pressure. And as he dug in, he leaned forward to bite Lamar's right nipple. By the time he'd made it over to Lamar's left nipple, Lamar was convulsing and talking incoherently.

Devon lightly stroked Lamar to make sure that he'd gotten it all out of his system, and then he picked him up, still inside him, and walked them to Lamar's bathroom. Once inside, he carefully pulled himself out so as not to flop onto his pants, and then he cleaned himself up at the sink with the rag that Lamar handed him. Satisfied, Devon made his way back into the kitchen while Lamar released Devon's pleasure and hopped in the shower for a quick wash.

After a quick moisturizing and drying, Lamar made his way, naked, back into the kitchen where he saw that Devon had straightened up the kitchen and was digging into his meal. Lamar walked up to Devon and, inserted himself in between Devon's legs and leaned on the left one with his hands across his chest.

"Can I help you?" Devon laughed as he finished up his bagel and began working on the remaining sausage.

"You gone make me cut you," Lamar said through his smile.

"And you gone make me beat you down again and be late if you keep up with all that ass hanging out," Devon replied as he grabbed a handful of Lamar's cheeks and gave them a squeeze.

Laughing, Lamar responded with, "whatever."

"You better be glad I gotta go." Devon countered. "But hey, how about you come over to my place tonight and I'll cook for you and try to keep my hands to myself," Devon said as he pulled Lamar even closer and laid his head on Lamar's chest.

Lamar could have stood like this forever and was sure to let Devon know with the way he embraced him and placed a tender kiss on his forehead.

"I'll think about it," Lamar responded coyly.

"Aiight. Don't show up and watch what I do," Devon answered.

"What chu gone do?" Lamar laughed.

"Don't show up and find out," Devon answered as he winked and got up from the island. "But seriously, thanks for breakfast, bae, and as much as I hate to leave, I gotta go."

"Awww," Lamar began, his lips poking out. "I don't want you to go."

"I know but we got dreams to realize, remember?" Devon said as he pulled Lamar in to give him a hug and kiss on the forehead.

"I know, and goals to accomplish," Lamar replied as he sucked his teeth at the fact that Devon had to go.

"Well, I'll see you later tonight and I'll check in with you later on today," Devon said as he lifted Lamar's face to his. They stood this way for a moment, staring into each other's eyes. Devon finally broke the trance by leaning down and gently kissing Lamar and then hugging him before heading out to his truck.

Lamar stood there for a few moments smiling before finally heading into his office and powering up his PC. While his PC was powering up, he went into the den to grab his phone. Upon checking his messages, he saw that he'd received a text from Ms. Armand:

MS. ARMAND: *Hey Lamar. Are you free to meet up at 1pm this afternoon? I have some news for you.*

Lamar's heart immediately began racing with excitement. He texted back:

LAMAR: *1pm is perfect. Looking forward to the news.*

Moments later Ms. Armand responded back with a black fist.

Making his way back into his office, Lamar sat back down and began going through his emails. Of course, he'd received a notification from Angela, and after going over the numbers, he was very pleased with what had gone down over the weekend and made sure to respond.

He next sat there thinking about the brunch that he'd invited everyone to this Saturday, what that would look like, and what exactly he would be speaking about. As he sat there pondering over the needs of his community, he had an itch to hop onto Zillow and look for available land in Dade County. He took note of several commercial properties, but nothing quite caught his eye until he came across a piece of land that was stated to be 10 acres, and the best part was that it was right there in Miami Gardens. He quickly shared it with Ms. Armand and then himself. After searching through some more pages, he decided that it was time to wrap it up, so he shut down his PC and got up and decided that since he wasn't getting with Ms. Armand until 1, he might as well take a nap. He then made his way back into his den, where he turned on Netflix and selected Girlfriends, and then he nodded off for a quick nap.

It was around 10:45am when Lamar woke up. As soon as he opened his eyes, the first thought that came to mind was that he was leveling up. It was all surreal to him because he remembered that not all that long ago, all of what he'd hoped to accomplish was no more than a dream and here he was not only getting ready to take over ownership of an apartment building but he was hopefully going to be acquiring 10 acres of undeveloped land. He lay there as his mind ran with all of the possibilities that lay ahead of him and, for the first time in a long time, he smiled from his heart.

Lamar finally decided to put his visions on hold and get up to begin preparing for his meeting. He made it to his bathroom, relieved himself and then freshened up. He then headed into his closet and stood for a moment, looking around before deciding on some dark tan khaki shorts, a dark peach-colored polo and some brown loafers. He also grabbed a brown leather belt that had a dark brown buckle on it, and then he headed back towards the den, where he laid everything across his recliner. He was bubbling with joy in this moment and decided not to wear socks because he was feeling all fancy.

Satisfied with his choices, he picked up his phone and noted that it was only 11:25am so he decided to check out the website of the artist whose card Julia had given him. Pulling the card out of his wallet and sitting himself down on the couch, he took his time scrolling through the various pieces. He'd purchased 3 paintings and 2 sculptures when it was all said and done. He'd also grabbed something that he thought his mom would like. He set up the shipping for the items and then he checked the time again. It was 12:00pm and he found himself getting a bit restless so decided to have a cup of tea. He quickly brewed a cup of lavender tea to calm himself.

After finishing his cup, he went back into the den and proceeded to get dressed. After he was dressed, he realized he'd left his deodorant in his room along with the body oil. He rushed over to his room, put on some deodorant, carefully oiled himself up, and then cleaned his hands. He checked himself out on the mirror and, after smiling at himself, went back into the den, grabbed his keys, phone and wallet and headed out to make his way over to his attorney's office.

Chapter 29

Lamar pulled into the parking lot at Ms. Armand's office at 12:35pm. Realizing that he still had some time, he just sat there, comforted by the thought of the news he was about to receive. He couldn't contain his smile and even did a little jig in his seat to which he immediately began laughing at himself. As he sat there in his happy place, his phone rang. Looking over at his phone, he saw that it was Joseline.

"Hey lady. How you?" Lamar smiled.

"I'm well, honey. How you doing today?" Joseline smiled back.

"I'm excited! I'm about to meet up with my attorney in the next 20 or so minutes about the apartment building I was telling you about."

"Yassss baby!!" Joseline exclaimed.

"Right," Lamar laughed. "So what's up? Everything ok?" Lamar continued.

"Absolutely," Joseline began. "I was reaching out to thank you for the invite Saturday and wanted to ask if it was ok for us to bring a plus 1?"

"Most definitely," Lamar began. "The more folks we can get involved with this movement, the better off it will be."

"Amen, baby. There is absolute strength in numbers." Joseline laughed before continuing, "I wasn't sure of what we were going to be discussing but in the event that coins were required, I definitely wanted to make sure that we had folks in place."

Lamar couldn't contain his appreciation and shared his thanks in between the tears that Joseline couldn't see falling. He could not believe what he was experiencing. It was like everything was happening at once and not just in his dreams but in real time.

"Listen baby, you don't have to thank me. We are all in this together and when we decide to move as a unit, things get done so I am grateful to you for being willing to even share your vision. I'm here for all of it!" Joseline responded.

"I'm truly thankful for that," Lamar responded as he wiped his tears away.

"You got it baby!" Joseline replied. "And you said it was going to be at 11 right?"

"Yes mam, and all I ask is that you bring yourselves and your ideas. Everything else is on me," Lamar responded.

"10-4," Joseline began, "Well I'mma let you go and we will all be seeing you Saturday. Enjoy your day, Congrats on the building and make the rest of the week great!"

"Thanks, love, and you do the same!" Lamar smiled.

After hanging up, Lamar checked the time and saw that it was 12:45pm. He decided to go ahead and make his way up to Ms. Armand's office.

He turned his car off, put his phone on vibrate, grabbed his keys and then got out of the car. After locking his doors, he pocketed his keys and phone and entered Ms. Armand's office building.

He didn't wait long for an elevator and upon getting off on his attorney's floor, was once again greeted by Ms. Sheila who let him know that Ms. Armand would be ready for him in another 5 minutes or so. He thanked her and took a seat facing outside and allowed his mind to flow.

He'd apparently allowed his mind to flow a little too deep because he didn't hear his name being called.

"Lamar, honey, Ms. Armand is ready for you," Ms. Sheila said softly as she lightly tapped him on the shoulder.

Laughing lightly, Lamar got up and again thanked her as he followed her to Ms. Armand's door.

"Good afternoon, Mr. Hicks," Ms. Armand began as she stood, extending her hand, "Thanks for joining me today."

"It's my pleasure," Lamar replied as he embraced her hand before taking their seats.

"So besides busy, how have you been?" Ms. Armand inquired.

"I've been well. Just in my thoughts as usual, trying to figure how to best position myself that I may be able to position others," Lamar answered.

"I hear that and after you hear this news, I believe you will be 1 step closer," Ms. Armand answered with a smile.

"Are you serious?" Lamar beamed with excitement.

"I am." Ms. Armand smiled back in adoration of this young man before her. Although she did not get involved much in his personal life, she knew about a few of the struggles he'd experienced in his younger years, and for him to have pushed through all of them, swelled her heart with pride and respect for him. She admired him for never giving up and for not allowing his circumstances to determine the trajectory of his future. She knew that he fought long and hard to get here and it was with the utmost satisfaction that she not only represented him but covered and protected him.

Getting back to the moment, Ms. Armand continued, "Your offer was accepted and due to some necessary repairs, I was even able to negotiate a few dollars off of the asking price."

Lamar sat back in his seat in order to process the fact that he'd just leveled up. Here again he stood in this place of manifestation and even though it was happening right in front of his eyes, he found it hard to believe.

"So what happened?" Lamar inquired, still in shock at the realization of it all.

"Well, the property was a pre-foreclosure, in need of some work. It was originally listed for 5 million, but with the owner just wanting out and the estimated cost of repairs needed, I was able to submit an offer of 4 million, which was countered with 4.1 million, and I took it," Ms. Armand said as she crossed her hands on her desk to allow Lamar another moment to take it all in.

Lamar sat there in silence as he thought about the lives he was about to change. He knew that affordable housing was the foundation for any stable family and this was only just the beginning. He sat there and thought about all of the hard work, sacrifice, and effort he'd put into being in this position. He welcomed the tears as they fell. They were tears of joy. They were tears of persistence. They were tears of strength. They were tears of relief and he sat in it and enjoyed the reality that he was officially a landlord.

Ms. Armand grabbed some tissues and got up to make her way around to him. She hugged him tight and dabbed at his eyes. "I'm so proud of you, Lamar. When I first met you, you were 18, but the look in your eyes said that you'd lived and you were determined to make it out and I knew right then that you were going to be not only a generation changer, but a world changer. Understand that you will face many more trials and tribulations, but you are covered, and there is favor on your life. You may not understand it right now but it's only up from here and that's not to say that you will be without issues but when you go through those dark places, you'll look back and recall the victories that you've bore witness to, and you'll hold fast to your hope. Now in this moment and this season, take the time to celebrate and enjoy. The road ahead is going to be there so get your balance now but know that you've got this and I'm always here." Ms. Armand then released Lamar and made her way back to her chair.

Lamar, finally gathering himself, began, "I'm so grateful. I really appreciate you being in my life and for helping me along this journey.

"It's my honor and pleasure," Ms. Armand began, "I saw that your vision was cut from the same cloth as those whose backs we stood on to get here and I would be remiss not to do my part in feeding and nurturing that vision," Ms. Armand paused as emotion overtook her as well. She took a moment to gather herself before continuing, "I know that it appears this is your starting point, but truth is, you've been pressing your whole life, even when you didn't know it, which is why I know that you will not stop until you've moved through this earth spreading your love, kindness and inspiration to live."

Stunned at the depth of faith Ms. Armand had in him, Lamar was momentarily without words.

How do you even begin to respond to that? He thought to himself.

"And you don't have to say anything. Your actions speak enough," Ms. Armand countered, seemingly reading his thoughts.

"Now enough with all this mushy crap. Let's get back to business," Ms. Armand stated abruptly with an attempt at a stern face. It held for a moment but then they both burst out into laughter.

"So, the next thing I wanted to discuss was the paperwork. Because I'm still waiting on your LLC to be made official, I wanted to talk with you about an earnest deposit." Ms. Armand stated as she maneuvered through her PC.

"Earnest deposit?" Lamar asked, having never heard this term before.

"So, an earnest deposit is a percentage of the total sales price that's placed as a down payment on the desired property to reflect your seriousness about purchasing the property in question. I would recommend 5% and advise submitting that within the next 48-72 hours. That money is then placed into an Escrow account and will be held until closing, when it will be returned," Ms. Armand answered.

"Understood. How do I go about making that deposit?" Lamar asked.

"I'll go ahead and draft those documents and email everything to you so that you can take care of that asap," Ms. Armand said as her hands moved across her keyboard.

"Sounds like a plan," Lamar began, "Is there anything else I need to be made aware of?"

"Yes, one last thing," Ms. Armand paused as she finished up the document she was working on. "I have a client I would like you to meet. Her name is Nicole, and she runs a property management company and I think the 2 of you would mesh very well," Ms. Armand said as she picked up her cell to glance at her calendar.

"I'm definitely game." Lamar smiled.

"I thought you'd say that, so I went ahead and set up brunch for next Monday at Beach Bar over in Sunny Isles at 1pm. I'll text you the details later on in the week just to remind you." Ms. Armand smiled.

"And before I forget..." Ms. Armand added, "I did a little digging about that property that you sent me. It's been listed for the last 15 years. I reached out to a colleague I know that's familiar with the area and I was told that the property is owned by a retired couple who have held out on selling the property due to concern for the surrounding neighborhoods."

Smiling, Lamar responded, "Well I was actually daydreaming earlier this morning and as my mind homed in on my apartment building, I began asking myself, as an entrepreneur, what other services can I provide? As I lay there, the word ownership popped up in my head, so I lay there some more, and I began thinking about what that could look like in the area where the land is, and what immediately came to mind was a plaza. I saw a wine and spirits shop along with a 16-pump gas station, a salon complete with pedicures and manicures, a barbershop, a few rental spaces, and I'm going to have to do some research but I was also thinking about a grocery store."

Smiling from ear to ear, Ms. Armand responded, "You truly never cease to amaze me." Ms. Armand paused to look, once more, at Lamar in admiration and respect, "I went ahead and informed my colleague about you and your vision and how you're moving in hopes of getting the conversation started so I will keep you posted on that."

"Yes, mam. Well, I'm waiting on getting those documents so that we can get that Earnest Deposit working," Lamar stated as he began to get up.

"Yes, sir, and thank you for not giving up on your vision," Ms. Armand said as she rounded her desk in order to walk Lamar to the door.

"The way things are set up nowadays, I couldn't if I tried. I'm really tired of the disrespect, disregard and the general feeling of just being tolerated. My thoughts are, if they don't want us at the table, we will build our own," Lamar responded as he moved to head towards the door.

"Amen to that!" Ms. Armand laughed.

"Honestly, the only time we seem to sit down together is politically, judicially, and at funerals, and that's not how it should be," Lamar said as he moved to open the door and exit Ms. Armand's office.

"Sad but true." Ms. Armand sighed.

"I'm just saying. I'm striving to do an old thing, a new way. You know? I did not invent the wheel but have recognized a few new ways to keep it going so that we may better navigate the spaces we occupy in this hour. And in this space, I'm no longer going to accept just being tolerated, especially knowing that it's painfully obvious that we were created with a lil extra seasoning," Lamar said as he moved in to embrace Ms. Armand.

"Yes sir. And that's why I say, just hold on a little while longer. Help is on the way," Ms. Armand began as she returned Lamar's embrace, "And you sir, are one of the ones that have been called forth during this time. Know that there are many standing with you, so even when it feels like you're alone, you aren't and will never be." Ms. Armand finished as she kissed Lamar on the cheek.

After again thanking Ms. Armand for her time and Ms. Sheila for her kindness, Lamar made his way towards the bank of elevators, where he waited for one to come. While waiting, his thoughts carried him away into a place where all men were equal and treated fairly. Where color was not a thing and mankind respected one another simply based on their character.

The dinging of the elevator door as it opened brought Lamar back from his thoughts. He stepped inside with a huge smile on his face because for the first time, he was really living out his dreams.

Chapter 30

It was 2pm by the time he got home from his meeting. On his way home, he'd stopped by the cleaners to grab his clothes from his night on the beach with Devon. He smiled as he got out of his car, clothes in hand, as he reflected over the sensuality of it all.

He made it into the house and put his clothing away, and then he made himself a small smoothie and headed towards the den where he kicked back in his recliner and turned on Netflix to some random show. He allowed himself to be immersed in his thoughts. He thought about his journey thus far and all his experiences, careful to skip through the ones that triggered him, and he honed in on the things that made him smile. His relationship now with his mom. His friendship with Julia. His business and all that had come along with it. Ms. Santi and all that she meant to him. And he finally landed on Devon.

As he lay back in his recliner, thinking about Devon, happiness spread through his chest at the fact that he not only had such an amazing man but also an amazing man with whom he could be himself and share his fruits. It felt really good to be in this space, and he was determined to enjoy it. As he pondered the wonderful things that were occurring for him, he eventually drifted off to sleep.

It was around 5:15pm when he began stirring from his rest. His mind immediately went back to the amazing news he'd received earlier today, and he took the time to sit in it.

Maybe there is something to manifesting after all, he thought to himself.

He recalled Ms. Santi feeding into him that he could do anything he wanted to do if he believed in himself and believed that the thing, he desired was possible. He recalled initially rejecting such thoughts because of the hell he'd experienced as a child, but those thoughts turned around when he was hired on at the lounge. Once there, he realized he'd found something that he was not only good at, but he excelled in. He'd sat under the previous owners and took note of everything that they taught him and made sure to ask questions just so he was clear on what he thought he understood. They were so gracious to him in the information and time they provided. They taught him how to effectively manage the lounge and how to hire and train staff. They also made sure to go over the handling of fiscal responsibility with him line by line so that he'd never run into any issues.

When all was said and done, his dream of ownership became a very real possibility and with new-found determination and the realization that his dream could become reality, he went to school. Once he'd completed his AS in Business Administration paired with an intense concentration on financial literacy, he began preparing for his own lounge, so the timing was perfect when the owners, where he worked, announced that they were retiring and wanted to offer him an opportunity to purchase. From there, life had been on a steady climb upwards and Lamar was here for all of it. He reminded himself that he'd survived through so much and while there was so much to do, he could take time to enjoy what he'd accomplished thus far although he rarely took time to sit in any of it.

His mind then drifted towards his acquisition of the apartment complex in what was known as Carol City. He was still in shock about it. Growing up, he'd known about the complex's reputation for drugs, violence and poverty. He'd also seen, first-hand, how the conditions of those apartments slowly declined, and it appalled him that people were forced to live that way. It saddened him even more when he'd hear conversations from others about how it must have been people's poor decisions that led them into those circumstances or their seeming lack of drive that kept them there. He'd hated those judgements, having grown up in those same environments. People would never understand the sting of trauma and the legacy of pain inherited from generation upon generations of woe. It was not as easy as folk wanted to make it out to be. Folks really needed help and it took him a long time, but he was finally in a position to provide it. He wanted his community to have a safe space where they were free to dream, thrive and prosper. He understood that in order for your imagination to really be uninhibited, you needed a safe foundation from which to launch.

"We here now," Lamar smiled to himself as he pulled himself up off of his chair. He made his way into the bathroom to relieve himself and rinse his mouth before washing his hands and heading back into the kitchen, where he stood in front of the fridge. He could not decide on what he wanted but he definitely knew that he did not want to cook so he decided to text Devon:

LAMAR: *What time do you need me so that I can be catered to?*

DEVON: ☺ *7pm would be perfect. Bring an overnight bag because you ain't going nowhere after.*

Smiling, Lamar sent him back a bunch of hearts and a kissy face emoji and then he decided on a small spinach, onion, cherry tomato and cheese salad just to hold him over. Once his salad was prepared, Lamar fixed himself a glass of water and made his way into his office. He sat everything down on his desk and powered up his PC. Checking the time, he saw that it was 5:35pm.

Once his PC was up, he checked his mail and saw that Ms. Armand had sent over the wiring instructions. Lamar printed them out and then reached out to Navy Federal, his Credit Union. They explained that for that amount of money to be wired, he would need to go into a branch to get that processed.

Lamar thanked them for their time, and he went ahead and filled in everything on the forms Ms. Armand sent over except his signature just in case it needed to be witnessed and then he made a note in his phone to head to Navy Federal first thing tomorrow morning to go ahead and get that wire working. He then sat back in silence and enjoyed his little meal and his water, and, upon finishing, headed back to the kitchen where he rinsed the dishes off and placed everything in the dishwasher, and started it up.

Lamar then made his way into his closet where he grabbed a teal linen short set along with some brown sandals. He then laid the items out on the bed before going back into his closet and grabbing a small duffel bag, which he then returned to his room and filled with socks, underwear, an undershirt, toiletries, and his charger.

Heading into the living room, he placed everything on the love seat near the front door and then headed back to his office to grab the paperwork he'd left on his desk and set it near the clothes. He then returned to the den and tuned into HGTV where Love it or List it was playing.

As he was getting into the show, he received a text message. It was from Ms. Santi.

MS. SANTI: *Are we still on for tomorrow?*

LAMAR: *Yes, mam. See you around 11am.*

MS. SANTI: *Looking forward to it. Love you and have a nice day.*

He then decided to call his mom. She answered on the 2nd ring and they chatted for a few minutes.

"I just wanted to hear your voice and make sure that you were ok, mum," Lamar said.

"Yeah, I'm doing ok."

"That's good to hear. Do you need anything?"

Lamar's mother softly laughed and replied, "No, I'm fine. I have every-thing I need."

"All right then. I'll leave you to it. Love you."

"Love you, son," Lamar's mother said then hung up. His next call was to Julia. She answered on the 4th ring. She sounded out of breath, which caused a bit of concern for Lamar.

"Hey Lady. Are you ok?" Lamar asked.

"Oh yeah. It-it's just me and Belinda at mom's house, cleaning and fixing dinner for mom," Julia said.

"How's everything going?" Lamar inquired.

"Everything's good."

"Nice. So, I'm headed to Devon's for the evening but let's catch up sometime later in the week."

"Yes, definitely," she agreed. They ended with I love you's and then Lamar got back into his show.

The next time Lamar looked up, it was 6 and Lamar figured it was time to go ahead and prepare to head over to Devon's, so he made it into his room and took a nice shower. Then he got out and oiled himself down and then threw on some fresh boxers, a wife beater and some basketball shorts and some socks and slides, and then he made sure that he had everything he needed before heading to the den to fold up his blanket and turn off the TV. Satisfied that he had everything, Lamar grabbed the things that he'd set by the front door and, after locking up, loaded up his car and made his way to his man's house.

Chapter 31

The night spent at Devon's was very chill. Devon didn't make it in until 7:30pm and Lamar quickly realized that there wouldn't be any cooking that evening as Devon had bags of food from Pollo Tropical. After eating their meal, they made their way upstairs to Devon's room, where he showered, and Lamar made himself comfortable in his bed. Once Devon came out of the bathroom, he slipped into bed and tuned into his recordings of Scandal, and then he wrapped Lamar up in his arms, and before long, the two of them drifted off to sleep.

It was around 8am when Lamar began stirring. He opened his eyes with a smile as he felt the comforting warmth of Devon's arms around him and his breath gently flowing across his neck. He reveled in this moment at the thought of the intimacy of it all. He really appreciated the care with which Devon handled him and in response, he snuggled in a bit deeper into Devon's embrace.

Lamar lay there quietly for a few more moments before begrudgingly gently removing himself from Devon's embrace. He quietly made his way into the bathroom—having grabbed his overnight bag from off the dresser near Devon's bathroom—and slightly closed the door so as to not wake Devon. He turned on the water, giving it a moment to get warm and then he splashed his face and stood there looking in the mirror, taking himself in. He didn't do it often, but he took the time to love himself at that moment. He appreciated himself and his hair and his skin and his smile. He took in the unevenness of his ears and softly giggled as his eyes washed over his body. He realized that what he was experiencing was appreciation. This had never been a thing in his life but with Devon, it was different. Devon made him feel like he was worth it and as if, for once, he was a prize.

Breaking away from his love affair with himself, he began brushing his teeth. Upon finishing that, he set his toothbrush to the side, washed his face, took out his body oil, and lightly oiled himself. As he was bent over oiling his legs and thighs, he let out a gasp as he felt Devon brush up against him. He hadn't even heard the door open. As he stood up straight, Devon turned him around and pulled him in close. He gripped his neck, turning his head up and to his left and began gently nipping at his ears while running his hands softly up and down Lamar's left side, causing Lamar to sigh in pleasure.

"Good morning my lil thickums." Devon growled as he released Lamar's neck and kissed him lightly on the lips.

"Good morning to you." Lamar lightly laughed as he threw his arms around Devon's neck and leaned up to provide his own kiss.

Positioning his hands to squeeze Lamar's cheeks, Devon pulled Lamar in even closer. "I'm sorry I got in late last night and wasn't able to cook. It was a super busy day, and I was so tired that I didn't even have the energy to make ya eyes roll back but I'mma make it up to you soon enough." Devon growled.

Laughing, Lamar replied, "It's ok. I appreciate simply being able to spend time with you."

At this, Devon picked Lamar up and placed him on the bathroom counter. He moved in and, upon tenderly lifting Lamar's face towards him, began kissing him. The kissing led to Devon squeezing Lamar's nipples, which caused Lamar to lift his legs and wrap them around Devon's waist in greedy desire.

Laughing, Devon pulled away. "Boy, you make it hard for me to focus," Devon began as he backed up to take in the view. "I'm not even gone do you like that this morning."

Lamar sucked his teeth in disappointment as his eyes ran over the length of Devon's beautifully sculpted, chocolate body, taking time to momentarily pause upon the source of his greed. It caused Lamar's body to involuntarily tremble as he became hypnotized by the length, girth, and curvature of Devon's manhood as it hung there, thick and seemingly ready for action. He wanted so badly to get on his knees and service Devon, but he kept his composure and brought his eyes back up to a smiling Devon's face.

"So, what's on your agenda today?" Devon asked as he crossed his arms across his chest.

"Well, since I can't get no lovin', I'm going to my Credit Union to take care of some business, and then I'm going to grab some food and head over to Ms. Santi's house to sit with her for a while. After that, I haven't planned anything," Lamar responded as he pulled himself off of the bathroom counter to pick up his oil and resume oiling his body. "How about yourself?"

"Another busy day but there is 1 thing I've changed my mind about," Devon responded. And with that, Devon again walked up behind Lamar and began kissing him on the back of his neck, which caused Lamar to let out a moan.

Devon then turned Lamar around and lifted him back onto the bathroom counter, raised Lamar's legs up and kneeled down before him and began biting at Lamar's cheeks before running his tongue across Lamar's wetness. Having had enough of teasing him, Devon drove his tongue into Lamar, which caused Lamar to cry out in pleasure. Between digging his tongue into Lamar and the amazing kisses he placed upon Lamar's secret space, Lamar felt the moisture running down his separation point.

There was a moment when Lamar felt nothing because his head was thrown back in sweet agony, and the next thing he knew, he was being filled up with Devon's pleasure principle. Devon entered him slowly, careful not to tear him. He then began slowly stroking Lamar while moving his left leg closer to his mouth so that he could simultaneously suck on his toes.

By the time Devon managed to slide all the way into Lamar, he felt Lamar's body beginning to quake, which caused him to speed up his stroke. Devon turned his attention to the sight of his meat slipping in and out of Lamar and the cream that suddenly appeared. This caused him to drive even deeper and faster while throwing Lamar's legs across his shoulders.

The deeper he drove, the louder Lamar cried out and pushed his hands against Devon's chest. In response, Devon scooped Lamar up and angled his body so that it was straight meat to cheeks. Lamar's body shook at the sheer force of Devon's digging. He tried to gain control of the situation by attempting to manage how much of Devon he received, but by this time, Devon had turned them around while simultaneously closing the door, and he went back to work on giving Lamar what, only a few moments before, he was crying for.

Shortly after Devon found his groove, he felt Lamar's body tense up and knew he was about to send him over. Not wanting to be left behind, he somehow pinned Lamar to the door and long stroked his hunger until Lamar's body finally erupted with him following suit. Devon's nostrils were flared by this time, and he decided he wasn't done. He walked them over to his bed, where he laid Lamar on the edge and went back to work.

Lamar weakly tried to push Devon off, but Devon was having none of it and positioned himself so that Lamar could not move. Then he pinned Lamar's arms down, and he went for what he wanted. As he stroked Lamar, he looked upon his face and it hardened him even more when he realized that in between the weak moans of pleasure, Lamar was actually shedding tears. He continued long stroking Lamar, totally caught up in the sounds their bodies were making. It wasn't long before Devon was again releasing, and this time, he paused until he was spent, and then he lay upon Lamar's chest, both breathing heavily.

"You happy now?" Devon groggily asked.

Lamar weakly laughed.

"You sure?" Devon asked as he softly slid in and out of Lamar with his still firm thickness.

Moaning and trembling, Lamar weakly responded, "Please..."

"You want me to stop?" Devon asked as he licked and nipped Lamar's neck.

"Umm..." Lamar moaned.

"Do you want me to stop?" Devon asked as his dick hardened a bit more.

"Ooh... Please..." Lamar cried out.

"Please what?" Devon asked as he continued his slow, torturous stroke of Lamar's wet grip.

"Ooh. Please..." Lamar cried out again.

"Oh, so you want more?" Devon growled. With that, he dove to Lamar's bottom, which caused Lamar to shake and cry out and throw his arms around Devon's neck while throwing it back to Devon.

"Oh, so now you with me." Devon smiled mischievously as he continued digging into Lamar.

As Lamar continued throwing it back, he let out this strange, continuous, low squeal. Devon looked upon him in humor and was about to laugh until he realized that Lamar was about to let go again. Devon decided to pick up the pace, and as he did, Lamar's squeal got louder and louder until his body began violently convulsing, which caused Devon to look down only to see Lamar's eyes rolled into the back of his head as his mouth flew open and he suddenly froze. Devon slid home one last time, and he, too, let go; this time, he was done.

Devon fell onto Lamar's chest and lay there for what seemed like forever before he finally pulled himself out of Lamar and then made his way towards the shower. He got the temp right and then came back into the room and helped Lamar up. Once he steadied his legs, he helped Lamar walk into the shower where they both washed. After, Devon dried Lamar off and took him into the room and sat him on the bed before heading back into the bathroom. He grabbed his towel, dried himself off and then returned to the room with Lamar's oil. He then lightly oiled Lamar down, and then he oiled himself down, and as he was moving around getting dressed for the day, Lamar finally got himself up and got dressed.

After they were both dressed and ready to go, Devon grabbed Lamar's overnight bag and followed Lamar downstairs into the kitchen, where Lamar grabbed a banana and a bottle of water and handed 1 of each to Devon. As they were sitting there, Devon burst out in laughter.

"What?" Lamar smiled.

"Boy, you hell," Devon replied.

"What did I do?" Lamar smiled coyly.

"Aiight." Devon laughed.

The 2 of them enjoyed their light breakfast and then made their way into the garage, where Devon opened the garage door. He walked Lamar to his driver's side door and embraced and kissed him before handing him his bag.

"Have a good day thickums and I'll check in with you a little later," Devon said as Lamar got into his car.

Lamar cranked up his car and waited for the AC to kick in. Then he backed out and blew the horn at Devon as he made his way into the city.

Chapter 32

Lamar was in pure bliss as he flowed across the Palmetto towards 95. There were no words this morning, only smiles and giggles. As much as he'd tried holding back, he found himself wide open for this guy who'd unexpectedly come into his life seemingly out of the blue. Everything was perfect, and Lamar was high off life.

This is what contentment feels like, Lamar thought to himself as he reveled in more happiness than he'd ever experienced. It seemed that it couldn't get any better and he allowed himself to just go with it. He didn't want anything disturbing his flow.

As he merged onto 95 South, his phone rang. Glancing over at his hands-free device, he saw that it was Ms. Armand and quickly answered.

"Good morning, lady!" Lamar smiled.

"Well, good morning, sweetheart!" Ms. Armand laughed. "You're extra bubbly this morning. To what do I owe the pleasure?"

To Devon's stroke game, honestly, Lamar thought but he replied with, "I'm just in a really great space. I'm actually headed down to my credit union to go ahead and get this wire processed."

"Look at you out here making power moves," Ms. Armand laughed, "So remember I told you how I reached out to my colleague about the land? Well, I have some potentially good news."

Lamar could have screamed at the excitement that immediately coursed through him, but he composed himself before eagerly asking, "What happened?"

"Well, he says that he was invited over to the property owners' home for dinner. They are Mr. and Mrs. Williams and they're retired and live in Miami Shores. Anyway, he informed me that he needed 10 minutes and that he would call me back. So, I sat around probably just as excited as you are right now and exactly 10 minutes later, my phone rang." Ms. Armand paused for dramatic effect.

"Please don't do me like this!" Lamar pleaded, barely able to maintain the volume of his voice.

Laughing, Ms. Armand continued, "He then tells me that he informed the Williams' about you and how he came to learn about you, and they've invited us over for dinner!"

For a moment, Lamar sat in silence as he processed what he'd just heard. The next moment, he hollered out "Yesss!" as he was no longer able to contain his excitement, but he caught himself because he was still driving.

Laughing at the sheer joy of the moment, Ms. Armand took a moment herself to gather herself. Having a servant's heart, it really blessed her to be able to help folks and position them so that they could help themselves, especially when their intentions were pure. "Now here's the thing, they want us at their place this evening at 6pm. Are you free?"

"If I wasn't, I would be." Lamar laughed in response.

"Amen to that!" Ms. Armand laughed before continuing, "The attire is casual, so be comfortable," Ms. Armand said.

"What should I bring?" Lamar inquired.

"A nice bottle of wine, Tequila and a Brandy just to cover all of your bases," Ms. Armand replied.

"Will do and I just want you to know that I really appreciate you and I'm again, so thankful for how you've stood with me," Lamar said as he fought down his emotions. In his life, it wasn't often that people were kind or had the best intentions for him but in this woman, he had no doubt.

"My love, I count it all joy. It's easy loving on you," Ms. Armand responded with a smile. "Now get off my line and I will see you later on this evening."

Laughing again, Lamar responded, "Yes, mam, and I'm looking forward to it."

The two of them hung up and Lamar pondered his current space. It was funny how all those lonely nights and long days grinding were finally paying off. The fact that he was finally living in his future, right now, brought a few tears to his eyes as an unknown sensation sparked up in his chest. He couldn't describe it but something warm and gentle seemed to overtake him and his tears began to flow so much that he had to exit 95 South at 103rd St and pull into a gas station to let them out. He couldn't put a finger on what it was but what he did know was that whatever it was, it was definitely not from a place of malice.

Lamar took about 5–10 minutes to let it all out and then he wiped his eyes with some napkins that he kept in the car. After checking the mirror to make sure he was again presentable, he hopped back on the expressway and continued towards downtown.

It was 9:45am when Lamar pulled into the parking lot of Brickell Plaza, where his Credit Union was housed. He grabbed the documents sent over from Ms. Armand and his phone, making sure to set it on do not disturb. Then he turned his car off and made his way inside.

Upon entering Navy Federal, Lamar did not have to wait long before he was sitting with a banker because it was so early in the morning. Lamar handed the documents over to Claudia, who was the banker assisting him at that moment and explained what was going on and what he needed just for clarity. She assured him that she would get him taken care of and she then went to work on her system. Shortly thereafter, she printed out some forms and had him sign off on them and she then notarized them and asked him to give her a few moments and stepped away.

After about 15 or so minutes, she returned with a few more documents. "These are records of everything that we've done today. The wire will be available in the escrow account no later than tomorrow morning since you made it in well before Navy's cut off point for processing." Claudia paused for a moment then added, "Is there anything else that I can do for you?"

"No," Lamar said and gathered up the documents and himself. "Thank you for your time."

She thanked him for his as well and then she walked him out into the lobby and led him towards the exit. Upon exiting, she thanked him again for his time and for choosing Navy Federal. He smiled at her and made his way back outside to his car.

Upon entering his car, he turned it on and just sat in a moment of silence as his AC kicked in and he reflected on the finality of what he'd just done. He broke out into a slow smile and allowed a few more tears to fall. He then gathered himself and sent Ms. Armand a text letting her know that the wire was done and then he looked up Liquors stores near him and decided on Brickell Wine Bank since it was closest so that he could go ahead and pick up the beverages suggested by Ms. Armand.

Lamar was in and out of the liquor store in 20 minutes and had even grabbed some Cuban's that the cashier informed him were hand rolled by a local artist by the name of Javier Ayala. Lamar thanked the cashier and asked if Javier had left some business cards with them, and the cashier ducked down for a moment and came up with one. Quickly glancing over the card, Lamar saw that Javier was also a painter, a singer and a chef. Lamar made sure to pocket the card, thanked the cashier again and then he navigated his way back to 95 where he headed North this time towards his brunch with Ms. Santi.

Chapter 33

Lamar was cruising 95 North when he decided, at the last minute, to take the airport expressway over towards the Palmetto in order to eventually merge on 75 North. He'd taken a moment as he merged into the northbound traffic on 95 to look for seafood restaurants near Ms. Santi and found one that was off of Pines Blvd so he decided instead of getting off on Ms. Santi's exit off 95, passing her house just to come back to it, he was going to make a nice little loop so that when he left Ms. Santi's, he could hop on 95 South and head home, in preparation of his dinner meeting with the Williams.

He rode in silence as his mind went over, for the thousandth time, how all the pieces were falling into place. He'd made a mental note to reach out to his brother once everything was finalized with the apartment complex so that his brother could come in with his crew and inspect the buildings and let him know what the bottom line would be. He then thought about his mom and decided to send her a quick voice memo letting her know that he loved her and was thinking of her.

Once the memo to his mom was sent, Lamar thought to himself, *ok, let me put on some music or something.* He opened his YouTube Music app and selected Erykah Badu radio which serenaded him all the way to the

Palmetto, 75 North and finally Pines Blvd, which is where he exited and made a right onto the busy street. As he headed East, he gradually made his way into the far-left lane. 10 minutes later, he was pulling into the parking lot in front of Mr. Shrimp which had not too long ago opened.

He didn't really feel like going in, placing the order and sitting down in there, so he placed his order online and received confirmation that his food would be ready in 20 minutes. He then tuned into YouTube and scrolled through some Breakfast Club interviews and clicked on one with Nate Parker.

As the breakfast crew began unpacking the gifts that Nate Parker shared with the world, Lamar received a text from Devon.

DEVON: *Made it to work. It's going well. Been in a meeting with some potential investors and that it was flowing decently. I'm excited about the growth of the organization and what that means for the communities we serve.*

LAMAR: *Congrats. So proud of you!*

DEVON: *How's your day going?*

LAMAR: *It's going well. I'm waiting on some food that I ordered enroute to Ms. Santi's.*

DEVON: *Cool beans. Well, I also wanted to share with you that I feel like a whole teenager out here in these streets. Lol.*

Lamar chuckled before texting back.

LAMAR: *Is that so?*

DEVON: *Facts. But anyway, I wanted to invite you to dinner tonight. There's something that I wanted to talk with you about.*

LAMAR: *What is it?*

DEVON: *Don't worry about it. I'll let you know tonight over dinner. But hey, I gotta run. Have a great day and I love you and I will see you later.*

Wait, what did he just say? Lamar thought to himself. He reread the message and concluded that he'd definitely said what he said.

So, it is mutual... Lamar thought to himself as fresh tears slowly rolled down his face. He was officially overwhelmed and not sure how to handle all of what was coming at him.

As Lamar sat there contemplating this latest revelation, he received notification that he had another message. He picked his phone back up and upon looking, realized that Devon had sent a photo. Lamar opened the message and immediately became bothered. In the photo, Devon had pulled his dick out of his pants, and it was hanging, to the left, down his leg. Focusing in on the photo, Lamar's mouth began watering and he wanted nothing more than to get under Devon's desk and take care of his issue.

Now laughing to himself, Lamar responded, "I love you too, daddy." He then realized that he actually couldn't make dinner with Devon that night because he had the meeting with the Williams. He quickly explained the situation to Devon and sat there waiting for a response.

As Lamar sat there, he finally realized what Devon meant when he said that he felt like a teenager. He was referring to how the two of them were humping like horny adolescents who'd just discovered the pleasure of release.

Devon called a few moments later. "No worries. Just be sure to hit me when you're heading home. And you better stop playing with me..."

"What? I ain't do nothing." Lamar laughed lightly.

"Aiight, act like you don't know," Devon answered.

"But what did I do?" Lamar playfully responded.

"Man, you got my dick thumpin right now and I'm so close to penciling you into my schedule because this shit crazy. I'm a grown ass man who can't leave his office because all I can think about is how your body responds to me, and how you be acting like you can't take it but always do and how it feels when I'm diving to your bottom," Devon responded.

"You need me to come see bout you?" Lamar asked in all seriousness.

"See, this the shit I'm talking bout. You want it just as much as I do an that fucks me up," Devon began. "As much as I don't want to, I'mma have to go dark for a lil while and hope my dick go down."

"Sir," Lamar began, "Thas my dick now."

"You ain't lyin bout that. I'm bout ready to beat my meat right here, right now. Damn you got my dick so hard," Devon breathed, as his voice lowered an octave.

"Yea daddy," Lamar teased in a much softer tone, "Imagine me gagging."

"I'mma fuck tha shit outta you tonight. Now get tha fuck off my phone before I come find you."

Lamar couldn't contain the laughter that came forth even though he knew Devon was dead serious.

"Love you and call me when you leave that meeting." Devon smiled and with that, he hung up.

Lamar sat there laughing to himself at the connection between the two of them. For the first time ever, he really felt as if he'd quite possibly found his one. They connected on so many levels and shared so many of the same interests. And even their work led them down so many of the same paths. It was as if it was almost too good to be true, and for a moment, a thought popped up in his mind asking, "what if it was?" But Lamar quickly dismissed it as fear of what could be and he then shifted his thoughts to the time. He then checked for his order and saw that they'd informed him that they needed another 5–10 minutes, which was perfect for Lamar as he too was thumping and wanted nothing more than to release. He tuned back into the Breakfast Club interview and re-focused in hopes of his member going down.

Lamar had been watching the interview for another 7 minutes when he received a notification that his order was ready. He paused the interview and was thankful that he wasn't aroused anymore and then he got out of the car, grabbed his phone and headed towards Mr. Shrimp.

A flood of cool air engulfed Lamar as he opened the door and entered Mr. Shrimp. The suddenness of the temperature change caused him to smile. As he made his way towards the counter, he took in the décor. Everything had been laid out in muted pastels, giving the place a very relaxed and comforting vibe.

Lamar was greeted as he approached the counter by someone coming out of the kitchen area. He greeted Lamar and asked how he could help him. Lamar explained that he'd ordered online and that he received a notification that his order was ready. The gentleman asked for the confirmation code and upon receiving it, stated that he'd be back in a few moments. Lamar then took the time to scroll through some articles on his phone before deciding on one that was about South Africa and in particular, Sandton. He'd been reading up on South Africa ever since he'd learned about Trevor Noah and while they also had their issues as well, he'd been impressed with the growth of the country and how blacks there had been working to establish their own supply and demand of goods and services. It was something Lamar was all too familiar with, and this news excited him.

As Lamar skimmed through the article, his senses were met with the most delicious scent of Garlic and Butter and Lemon and something else that he couldn't quite put a finger on, and it caused him to look up. Before he knew it, he couldn't help himself and smiled. Good food always lifted his spirit and the fragrance coming off of the pan before him was giving finger licking goodness.

The gentleman who brought him his pan of sea fare handed him a separate bag with dipping sauces, napkins, gloves, and bibs. He thanked him for his business and asked if there was anything else that he needed. Lamar smiled in return, took a 20 out of his pocket, placed it in the tip jar, gathered himself and his purchase, and made his way back outside.

After getting to his car, he situated everything and made sure that the pan was secure and then he hopped in the front and continued down Pines Blvd towards Ms. Santi's.

Chapter 34

It was 11:45am when Lamar pulled into Ms. Santi's driveway. He dialed her to let her know that he was outside. After hanging up, Lamar got out of the car and unloaded the food and the bag of extras. He locked his car and then made his way to the front door.

As he stepped up to the door, Ms. Santi opened the door, pulled it open further and welcomed him in. She gave him a quick kiss on the cheek, closed the door behind him and then led the way to the Lanai.

As Lamar stepped out onto the Lanai, he saw that she'd already set it up with paper plates, napkins and bottled waters. Lamar set everything down and then gave her a hug. It had been a few months since he last saw her, but they made sure to stay in touch at least twice a month.

"How you been?" Lamar began as he took his seat.

"I've been good baby. Been on vacation for the last 3 days now and I'm enjoying my time away," she responded. Ms. Santi was a behavioral therapist and not only worked with D.C.F.S. but she also volunteered with various organizations on the weekends. In addition, she was a wife, a mother, a caretaker and all-around anchor within her large family of nieces and nephews.

"How you been?" she inquired.

"I have been really good and am in a really amazing place!" Lamar beamed.

Laughing, she reached her hands out and upon him joining together, she led them in a quick prayer over the food. After she was done praying, she then responded, "Well that's what I like to hear," before unwrapping the food. She briefly closed her eyes and smiled as she inhaled the aroma of all this juiciness before them. Lamar had ordered shrimp, king crab legs, snow crab legs, oysters and beef sausage. The meal had come with corn, potatoes and eggs.

"Absolutely." Lamar laughed.

"So, are you dating?" she asked.

"I'm seeing someone," Lamar replied.

"Who is she?" She smiled knowing full well Lamar wasn't interested in women. Lamar chuckled as he thought about the many times, she'd told him that she prayed and asked God to send him a good woman. It wasn't that she rejected him or his choice of partners but rather that she really believed that he was missing out on a good thing.

Lamar had never taken offense at her admissions because he knew that her intentions never stemmed from a malicious space but rather from a place of love, as best she knew it, in addition to the fact that she didn't want to see him alone.

"That's another conversation for another day," Lamar replied with a smile as he began digging into the pan of goodies before him. Remembering that he had a dinner meeting later on this evening, he restricted himself to a king crab leg, a few shrimp, a few oysters and a small piece of corn.

"Umm huh," Ms. Santi replied as she sucked her teeth.

Laughing, Lamar responded, "I'm for real. It's super new and we've not even sat down to discuss what we are and how we want to handle it so I'm currently just enjoying the moment."

Ms. Santi obviously wanted to know more but seeing that Lamar was unwilling to share, she let it go.

Seeing that Lamar really wasn't digging into the food like she was, Ms. Santi's eyebrow arched as she looked over at him.

"I've got a dinner meeting this evening, so I didn't want to eat too much and be rude later on." Lamar shared.

"Gotcha. So, what's new with you? How's the family?" Ms. Santi continued.

"The family is good. We actually had brunch a few days ago." Lamar began, "And as far as what's up, you're not only looking at a lounge owner but I'm also Dade County's Newest Real Estate Mogul!"

Laughing, Ms. Santi replied with, "You better claim it!"

"Yes mam. I was able to complete the process of closing on a 65, I believe, unit apartment complex and I can't wait to get started on renovations."

Ms. Santi immediately grabbed Lamar's hand and squeezed in support.

"I'm so freakin' proud of you, Lamar!" Ms. Santi shared.

"I really appreciate that," Lamar replied.

Growing up, Lamar had often spent time with Ms. Santi and her family and was instructed many times on the complexities of life and how your choices were your own and that you never had to do anything that you didn't want to. Under her tutelage, he'd also discovered his knack for financial responsibility. Ms. Santi had introduced him to credit, investing and the importance of not only realizing your dream but how to remain steadfast about it. She'd really impressed upon him the notion of good stewarding and how you couldn't expect God to bless you with increase when you couldn't even maintain your current blessings. He really appreciated her views and outlook on life. He also appreciated how she'd played a pivotal role in restoring his relationship with his mom in his younger years due to her relentless nature of living life on God's terms.

In this current moment, he'd decided that as much as he wanted to, he was going to hold off on sharing any information about the potential land acquisition until the paperwork was signed so he instead shared his vision for his rental units. As he shared, she gave little tidbits of advice here and there, but she ultimately agreed that what he was doing was monumental and that he was truly on the cusp of becoming exactly what he believed himself to be: A Mogul.

The rest of their brunch was spent discussing their political views and the importance of representation and their views on religion and how it was no longer sufficient. They sat there and talked for what seemed like hours and upon checking his phone and realizing it was 1:30pm, Lamar made to excuse himself. He cleaned up his area and his mess and then he grabbed some of the wet wipes that were in the bag of goodies set off to the side. He was sure to clean his hands very well and then he gave Ms. Santi a really tight hug and let her know that it was time for him to run. He slid his phone into his pocket and then he beelined towards the bathroom that was just off the dining room. He washed his hands and dried them, After exiting the bathroom, Ms. Santi walked him out.

After opening the front door, Lamar turned and gave Ms. Santi a light hug and then made his way to his car. He sat for a moment with the windows down and the air blowing so that his car could cool down and then he let the windows back up, backed out of the driveway and began making his way back home.

Chapter 35

Lamar was 10 minutes out from his home when he decided to detour. Since he had some extra time, he decided to swing by the lounge to check on Angela and the staff. As he rerouted, the thought popped up that he'd forgotten to do something nice for his staff. He was still planning on sending Angela and her kids off to the Caribbean but since he needed to work out the details, he'd settled on sending her flowers and giving her a little extra money for the time being. With that thought in mind, he reached out to his point person, Sharon, with ADP, his payroll service, to see about blessing his employees.

Sharon picked up on the 3rd ring. "Hello Mr. Hicks," she began, "how can I help you today?"

"Hey Sharon," Lamar responded. "How are you today?"

"I'm well. And yourself?" she answered.

"I'm well," Lamar began. "So, question, when does my payroll finalize?"

"Just a moment here. Let me see," she replied as she opened up his account. "Ok, so I see that your payroll closes out on Sunday. What can I help you with?"

"Awesome sauce!" Lamar exclaimed as he realized that even though he'd forgotten, he still had time to bless his folks. "So, here's what I want to do. For everyone except Angela, I'd like to issue a 500.xx Employee Appreciation Bonus. And then for Angela, I want to issue 1000.xx Bonus for her hard work. Can we get that done in time?"

Laughing, Sharon responded, "We absolutely can, and I'll get everything set up for you right now. Give me a few moments."

As Lamar fell silent, he heard Sharon working her magic in the background. He thought over his conversation with Devon from earlier and became a little bothered and couldn't wait to link up with him again. As he was reflecting over their next encounter, Sharon came back on the line.

"Ok, Mr. Hicks. I've taken care of everything that you requested and just wanted to know if I have your permission to submit these requests to be adjusted on next week's payroll."

"Yes, mam, you do." Lamar smiled.

"Thank you so much, Mr. Hicks, for being a valued client of ADP. Is there anything else that I can do for you today?" Sharon inquired.

"You can have an amazing day and stop by the lounge and ask for me the next time you're in Miami," Lamar responded.

"Will do and I'm going to hold you to it sir." Sharon laughed.

"Yes, mam, and thank you again for your help, and you have a great day," Lamar replied.

As Lamar disconnected the call, he turned into the alley behind the restaurant and pulled into the employee parking lot. He parked, scrolled through his phone, found the number he was looking for, and hit dial.

The phone rang 5 times before someone answered. "Thank you for calling Estilita's Floral Arrangements. This is Marcia speaking. How can I help you?"

"Hey Marcia. This is Lamar. How are you?"

"Hey baby! How have you been?" Marcia responded.

Lamar had known Marcia for about 6 or 7 years now. He first met her when the original owners of the lounge were approaching retirement. He was searching around for flower shops to get them the biggest bouquet that he could possibly find, and Marcia really stood out in the arrangement. Since then, he'd used her often when he just wanted to say thank you and show his appreciation for the women in his life.

"I've been well, my love. How about yourself?" Lamar smiled.

"*Aye papi*. I've been wonderful. Business is good and the babies are getting so big."

Lamar could hear the customers in the background, and it made him smile to know that Marcia was thriving. "Yes mam. I'm glad to hear that." Lamar began. "I'm reaching out because I wanted to have a dozen purple roses put together with a thank you card for Angela."

"Ok. What do you want it to say?" Marcia asked as she readied herself with her pad.

"To an amazing woman, mother, friend, and manager, I really appreciate everything that you bring to the table, and this is one of many ways that I want to say Thank You," Lamar answered as he smiled at the vision of Angela receiving her card.

"*Ya lo tengo papi cualquier otra cosa por ti*?" Marcia asked.

"Nah. That's all. I didn't need anything else and thank you so much, mi amor." Lamar smiled.

"Ok papi. And when did you need them delivered?" Marcia inquired.

"Wednesday morning would be great, if possible," Lamar replied.

"*Ningun problema*. I can have them delivered by 11am," Marcia stated.

"Perfect. Well, that was all I needed. The card on file is still current. Go ahead and tip yourself 50.xx and again, thank you," Lamar responded.

"*De nada*, papi. Talk with you soon, mi amor." Marcia responded with a kiss and the two ended the call.

Pleased with the pending surprises for his staff, Lamar made his way into the lounge to check on Angela. As he passed through, he greeted everyone he encountered and inquired about their day. Everyone seemed to be in good spirits, and this made him smile because he genuinely cared for his folks. He recalled some of the things that a few of them had been through and trusted him with the information. He'd made sure they were taken care of as best he could and the fact that they showed up every day with a winning attitude caused him to want to give them the world.

He finally pulled up to Angela's office and tapped lightly on the wall a few times as he stuck his head in. She was busy on the phone with her eyes glued to her computer screen as usual. He gave her a few moments to wrap up her call as he stepped in and stood by the corner of her desk. Once she was off the phone, she got up and bear hugged him and invited him to sit down as she made her way back to her seat.

"How are you, my love?" Angela asked.

"I'm excited. I have a meeting this evening at 6 and then I'm getting together with some folks here on Saturday to pow wow and see what we can do together." Lamar began. "I did mention that to you, didn't I?"

"I do believe you mentioned it but refresh me," Angela answered as she took out her pad and pen.

"Well, I've invited 7 people but I'm planning for 12. I'd like to do some cocktails and a few tapas as we lay a blueprint for a potential future," Lamar responded.

"What kind of people are they?" Angela asked as she jotted down some notes.

"They're all working professionals and a few entrepreneurs who're already out here making moves. We had some interesting talks at the housewarming, and I just wanted to continue them because I really think this group has the potential to become something major," Lamar concluded.

"Gotcha. I'll make sure to take care of the drinks and food and will have a few servers available," Angela began. "But about the call I was on when you came in, that was the new Tequila company. We were talking about how well the Tequila has been doing and I've decided to up the order and we were just figuring out the logistics. I do believe that we're going to potentially become brand ambassadors for them as they work to establish themselves in this market. They were talking commercials and everything, so I'll keep you posted on the details."

Angela never ceased to amaze him with her prowess. Her attention to detail was second to none and he mentally marked a date on his calendar for next week so that he could really sit down and plan out her and her kid's trip.

"I love and appreciate you so much!" Lamar exclaimed.

"I know and that's why I go so hard." Angela smiled.

"Well, besides that, is there anything that you need?" Lamar asked.

"Not that I can think of, but you know, I'll reach out if that changes." Angela laughed.

"You better." Lamar laughed back. "Well, I didn't really want anything. I just wanted to check on you and see how things were going. I'm gonna leave you to ya work and go get ready for this meeting and as always, call me if you need me, which apparently, you never do." Lamar laughed as the two stood and Angela walked around her desk to embrace Lamar once more.

Lamar then made his way back through Ed's on his way to the parking lot and he made sure to bid everyone a great day and told them if they needed anything, to give Angela or him a call. With that, Lamar made his way back to his car and then navigated his way home to prepare for his dinner meeting that evening.

Chapter 36

It was around 4pm when Lamar began stirring. He hadn't even realized he'd taken a nap until he found himself waking up from his sleep. As he opened his eyes, he smiled. He smiled because life was finally falling into place, and it amazed him how he was literally watching his goals manifest. Before deciding to get up, he shot a quick message to his mom just to check on her and then pulled himself out of his recliner and made his way towards his bathroom where he stripped himself and turned on the shower. He was careful to put on his shower cap and then he stepped into the shower and stood there for a few moments, allowing the warm water to cascade over his body.

After standing under the cascading waterfall for a few moments, he finally began to wash himself. He took his time scrubbing and rubbing and rinsing. Once he was done, he got out of the shower, grabbed his towel and wrapped himself. He made his way to his sink where he flossed and brushed his teeth and then made his way back into his room where he removed the towel and lightly dried himself. He then selected an oil that he hadn't tried before and gently oiled himself down. After wiping off the excess oil from his hands, he then went into his closet and stood in the midst of it while looking around for what to wear. He decided on some boot cut, fitted, crimson-colored jeans along with a crimson-colored polo that had black accents. He then grabbed some black footies and a pair of low heeled, swede boots and laid everything across the bed. He then turned to his dresser where he opened and grabbed some burnt orange-colored boxers with a matching wife beater and he slid them on. He then checked the time and upon seeing the time, went ahead and began getting dressed.

Once he was fully dressed, he stood in front of his full-body length mirror and checked himself out from various angles and upon being pleased, took a selfie from the side. He then sent the selfie to Devon along with a winky eye emoji. He then made his way back into the den where he sat back in his recliner in order to gather his thoughts. He had no idea about who the Williams were nor what their demeanor would be, so he wanted to make sure that not only was he in a great mind space, but that he also had his presentation together.

After a few more moments of centering himself, he grabbed his keys, went into the kitchen and grabbed the bags with the liquor and cigars and then he made his way outside, after locking up his house. He then loaded his car up and turned on the engine to allow the car time to cool off. As he sat there, his phone rang. Seeing that it was Ms. Armand, he picked up with a smile.

"Hey love!" Lamar began. "How are ya?"

"I'm well, my love," Ms. Armand responded back.

"So, what's up?" Lamar inquired.

"Was just reaching out to let you know that I'm enroute now, and cause of traffic, wanted to make sure that you were working your way down as well."

"I'm actually sitting in my driveway about to pull off." Lamar smiled.

"Good. Did you get a chance to stop by the liquor store?" Ms. Armand asked.

"I did and have everything sitting right next to me," Lamar replied.

"Ok, well I'm texting you the address now and I'll meet you there." Ms. Armand smiled.

The two of them shared a quick laugh and then disconnected the call. Lamar went ahead and put his phone into his hands-free device and then opened the text from Ms. Armand and copy and pasted the address and then he put on his seatbelt and began navigating his way towards Miami Shores.

As he was making his way towards the Golden Glades Interchange, he received a text from Devon who'd sent a drooling mouth emoji which caused Lamar to laugh and squirm a bit due to the warmth he felt spreading through his body. He sent back a voice message telling Devon that he was on the way to his dinner meeting and that he couldn't wait until tonight. He also shared how he appreciated Devon's attentiveness and that he was definitely looking forward to that talk.

Once he sent the message, he refocused on everything that was before him and before long, he entered the interchange and made his way down 95 South in the midst of rush hour.

Chapter 37

As Lamar sailed down 95 South, he took in the impossibly beautiful day. There was not a cloud in sight and for some reason, he felt as if today, the vibrant colors of the city were even more so.

He soon came up on 79th St and exited to the right. He crossed over 82nd St, and shortly made a left onto 79th St and headed towards Biscayne Blvd. As he made his way down 79th St, he took note of all the growth and development that was occurring and immediately thought about the effect that these things must have had on the community here. He shook his head in slight disgust at the thought of how long time homeowners in the area were being forced out of their neighborhood.

I'm so thankful to be moving in the direction that I am. This has got to stop, Lamar thought to himself.

As Lamar neared Biscayne Blvd., Lamar made a left onto NE 5th Ave, which wound him through a little shopping plaza in order to make a left onto Biscayne Blvd. As Lamar sat at the light waiting his turn, he was notified that he'd received a text message. Looking at his screen, he saw that it was from his mom. She'd responded letting him know that she was ok and feeling much better and would talk with him later.

Lamar took a quick second to send a voice message telling his mom that he was happy to hear that she was feeling better and that he would reach out later on. As he sent the voice message out, the light turned green, and he made a left onto Biscayne and headed towards Miami Shores.

Once Lamar reached 96th St, he made a right and was immediately immersed in the lush beauty that was Miami Shores. He took his time heading towards N. Bayshore Dr. in order to take in the well-kept homes and lawns. As he approached the intersection of 96th and N. Bayshore Dr., he smiled at the sight before him. The waters of Biscayne Bay shone brightly under the Miami sun. As he sat there taking it all in, he let his windows down and inhaled deeply before making the right and locating the address.

Not seeing Ms. Armand's Volvo XC90, Lamar pulled into a space alongside the barrier that separated the neighborhood from the bay waters. He turned his car off and allowed his thoughts to flow along with the gentle breeze that caressed his face.

He didn't realize it, but he'd drifted off and was brought back to reality by the sound of someone tapping lightly on his car. He looked around and then finally out his window and into the face of a smiling Ms. Armand. He smiled and then let his windows up and got out of the car. He gave Ms. Armand a quick hug and then grabbed his phone, keys and the bag of gifts and then followed Ms. Armand over to the Williams's home.

"Beautiful huh?" Ms. Armand observed as she took in the neighborhood and the water and finally the house that sat before them.

"It absolutely is, and I could sit out here all day." Lamar smiled.

"I see Bryce beat us here." Ms. Armand observed as she nodded towards the dark, champagne-colored convertible Bentley. As the two of them walked up to the door, they were enveloped by the aroma of something beautiful being moved around on the stove and they turned to each other and smiled.

"Ready to get this property?" Ms. Armand asked as she grabbed Lamar's right hand and squeezed.

"I'm ready," Lamar replied as he squeezed back.

Ms. Armand then rang the doorbell. It wasn't long before they were greeted by a tall, handsome, light-skinned guy with hazel eyes, a chiseled body and a fresh Caesar. Upon seeing Ms. Armand, his eyes brightened, and he embraced her in a loving hug before pulling back.

"Thank you both for coming." He turned towards Lamar. "I'm Bryce and it's such a pleasure having you here. Come on in. The Williams are out on the Lanai and waiting for us." He led them through a lavishly styled home filled with all sorts of black art. Unique statues and abstract paintings adorned the space but the one that stood out to Lamar was the family portrait over the fireplace. In it, you could see how proud Mr. Williams was as he towered over his wife and 3 kids. The portrait touched Lamar and caused his heart to smile as he continued his journey towards the Lanai.

As Lamar finally stepped out onto the Lanai, he was immediately at peace. Before them, sat the handsome and humble older couple that he'd seen in the portrait. The couple looked to be in their late 60's, possibly early 70's and Lamar was taken to them immediately. Mr. Williams gave off *pop pop* vibes and Lamar realized in that moment how much his life had been affected by not having his dad in his life. He was regal in his humility and exuded a wisdom that only life could provide you.

"Welcome," Mr. Williams offered as he stood at the head of the table to receive his guests. "Please, come and have a seat." He finished as he waved towards the right side of the table.

Before heading to his seat, Lamar fell in line with Ms. Armand as they made their way around the left side of the table to shake the hands of the people before them. After hugging and kissing Ms. Williams on the cheek, Ms. Armand and Lamar then shook Mr. Williams' hand and then seated themselves to his right.

"Thank you so much for having us today," Lamar began, "I'm Lamar and this is my attorney, Ms. Armand."

"Pleased to meet the two of you and sitting across from you is my beautiful wife, Betty," Mr. Williams said as he too took his seat. "And you've already met Bryce."

"It's a pleasure meeting the two of you and again, thank you for your time," Lamar replied with a smile.

"The pleasure is all ours." Mrs. Williams smiled.

As they settled into their seats, Bryce asked Lamar if he could take his bag to which Lamar agreed.

Bryce then took the bag from Lamar and made his way back into the house and just as soon as he entered, a small, brown-skinned woman emerged from the house with a cart that contained multiple trays set up on it. Lamar learned that her name was Sarah and he watched her as she made her way towards the opposite end of the table to arrange them. As she set up the trays, Bryce returned with a bucket of ice, 5 glasses and a pitcher which he set in the middle of the group. He then returned with the bottle of Tequila Lamar had purchased alongside a container of Mango Nectar and some limes. As he set about fixing everyone a drink, Lamar took in the scenery.

The Williams's pool and pool house were next level and came complete with a grill station and a rock hewn waterfall arrangement that gently recycled the water from the pool in a wide fan of overflow. Lamar also took note of the beautiful china pattern that he recognized as having the colors of the Haitian flag adorned in the edges.

"Ah, so you like our china?" Mrs. Williams asked as Lamar looked up with a smile.

"I do. They're beautiful. Where'd you get them?"

"Well, my family specializes in fine china, fabrics and furnishings," Mrs. Williams began, "And my sister made these." She adjusted herself in her seat, before continuing. "It's the reason why my family even migrated to

Miami from Haiti, and I keep them, amongst other things, to remind myself of where I've come from."

"Your sister is really gifted," Lamar responded as he took in the detail put into the china.

"That she is. In fact, it's honestly a gift that my family has, and it was decided that we'd done so well in Haiti, that it was time to explore new territory, so we moved here in 1965 and opened our first shop in Liberty City off of 62nd St and NW 7th. The store did so well that several years later, we opened our second store in Broward up off Oakland Park Blvd. and with that store's success, a few years after, we opened up our last shop in Palm Beach off W Atlantic Ave."

As Mrs. Williams shared stories about a few of her clients, Lamar took the time to appreciate the wisdom of this beautiful, brown skin woman. She possessed flawless skin, a radiant smile and an air of feminine grace that made him think of his grandmother.

As Mrs. Williams concluded her story telling, Mr. Williams picked right on up. "And that's actually how I met this young woman here," he began as his eyes lit up. "I'm a contractor by trade and picked those skills up from my dad who'd relocated us to Miami back in 1966 from Tifton, Ga when I was 19." Mr. Williams paused as he took a sip of water.

"The year was 1972 and I was told about a job that we'd landed to build a store front along Oakland Park Blvd. The first day on site, we met with the owners to go over the vision and discuss costs. As my dad and her dad were talking, she and her sister walked up with a little dog and upon laying eyes on her, I knew right then that I had to have her." Mr. Williams paused again as he gazed lovingly upon his wife. "Yea man, she was standing there all sweet and kind and smelling like a spring day in Atlanta, and it was over for me."

Lamar smiled at their love and wondered about all they'd endured during those years and what kept them together. He'd heard stories from older folks in his family about how life was during those times and had to learn to control his anger in response to it, so he was always curious about the perspectives of those who'd not only lived through it but came out on the other side of it successful.

"But I pursued her for 3 months before she shared her name with me and 7 months before she allowed me to take her out on a date and we've been stuck with each other ever since." Mr. Williams laughed softly as he recalled that very first day they met.

By this time, Bryce had finished mixing the drinks and began passing out their glasses. Once everyone had their drink in hand, Bryce raised his glass and said, "To new ventures and the continued elevation of our people."

"Here here!" Everyone responded as they clinked their glasses and then took a sip. As Lamar sat back in a moment of reflection at the possibility before him, the small, brown-skinned woman who'd set up the trays at the end of the table began fixing plates and passing them around. Once everyone had their plates, she covered up the food again and excused herself from the Lanai. Bryce finally took a seat next to Mrs. Williams who extended her hands. Everyone grasped a hold of each other's hands, and they bowed their heads as Mrs. Williams led them in a beautiful prayer of purpose, passion, truth, humility and guidance. When she finished, everyone responded with Amen, and they began digging into their food.

Lamar took a moment to appreciate the meal before him and had to catch himself as he felt himself on the verge of drooling in front of everyone. He laughed quietly to himself and then picked up his fork and dug in. He was instantly in heaven. His plate consisted of callaloo, pigeon peas and rice (with a brown gravy), fried plantains (creole style) and a perfectly grilled piece of stuffed salmon and he enjoyed every bite.

In between bites of food, Lamar alternated between his Tequila and water. Conversation was minimal as everyone savored their meal. As the food disappeared and plates were slid to the side, Bryce pulled himself up from the table and grabbed the pitcher of beverage he'd mixed earlier. He topped everyone's glass and placed the pitcher back where it was and then he took his seat.

For a few moments, the group sat in silence as they slowly sipped their drinks and pondered their thoughts. As they entertained the chats within their minds, Sarah returned to attend to the group. She asked if anyone was interested in dessert to which everyone resounded with a hearty no. At their collective response, everyone, including Sarah, shared a nice laugh. As everyone passed their plates to Sarah, she thanked them and made her way back into the house.

"So, Lamar, I hear you're interested in purchasing that parcel of land off of 199th?" Mr. Williams inquired as he finally got down to the meat of this union.

"Yes sir," Lamar replied as he adjusted himself in his seat.

"Well, let me tell you a little story," Mr. Williams began as he took a sip from his drink. "I'm sure you're aware of the history of colored folks in this country, right?"

"Yes sir. I'm familiar," Lamar replied.

"So then, Betty and I were married about 2 years at this point. We're happy with no kids yet and we're living in an apartment in N. Miami Beach. Her family's business was thriving as was my family's." Mr. Williams paused as he took a sip of water before continuing.

"The time came when we were ready to purchase a home as we were eager to get our family started. Naturally we wanted to remain in N. Miami Beach but to our dismay, nobody would sell to us and to add injury to insult, we weren't even allowed to purchase land in order to build our own home. Of course, I was pissed but Betty here encouraged me to remain steadfast as she reminded me that what was for us was for us." Mr. Williams paused as he looked over at Mrs. Williams and squeezed her hand. Lamar's heart melted a little more at the adoration that shone in Mrs. Williams's eyes.

"Anyway, this lit a fire in me. I searched and I searched, and I searched some more until I learned that there were acres upon acres of land available in the area we now know as Carol City. See, back then, it was mostly farmland, but the majority of the farmers had either sold or were in the process of selling to developers who were presenting them with offers they couldn't turn down." Mr. Williams paused to clear his throat.

"Once I verified for myself that all of this undeveloped land was available, I began digging into public records until I was able to locate one of the owners. And let me tell you, I don't think I'd ever been so relieved in my life. I found out that a Mr. Arthur Levy was one of the multiple owners of this swath of land. Now here's where the tide began changing for us. 4 years prior, me, my pops and our team landed a contract with him where we built several detached homes and a few 20-unit apartment buildings over in Miami Beach, so we'd already had an amazing working relationship. So, I did not hesitate to reach out and wouldn't you know it, he was in the office that day. His secretary sent me right on through." Mr. Williams paused again but this time it was to smile that regal smile of his as he thought over the favor he'd experienced in spite of the pain of the day.

"We arranged a lunch meeting for the following day. The next day, me and my wife met him down at Bayfront Park where we all gathered on the steps facing the bay. Mr. Levy had already gone ahead and ordered a few sandwiches and some cokes, and we enjoyed the light meal while looking out over the water. Once we were done with our sandwiches, I dove right in and asked him how many available acres he had for sale in Carol City. He replied that different sections of the area had different amounts available and then he asked me how many acres I was interested in. Now mind you, I've always been ambitious, so I said 700 and he didn't even blink. Instead, he pulled out some paperwork from a small briefcase I hadn't noticed earlier along with a calculator and after flipping through several pages, he began calculating. After 3 or so minutes of tabulating, he reached into his blazer and pulled out a small piece of paper along with a pen and he wrote down a number and he handed it to me." Mr. Williams paused to take another sip of his drink and then he continued.

"For a moment, me and my wife sat there stunned. We honestly found it difficult to receive what we were looking at. There was no way that number could have been correct and as if he'd read our minds, he lightly laughed and said to us that he would consider it an honor to sell the land to us." Mr. Williams paused to gather himself as he'd gotten a bit emotional. It was difficult for Lamar to watch because, in some ways, he understood how Mr. Williams felt. All his life, all Lamar had ever wanted was a break, but it seemed that there was no rest for him and if he wanted to sit down and kick his feet up, he was going to have to be the one who built the chair and the stool.

"I'm sorry," Mr. Williams began.

"Mr. Williams, you have absolutely nothing to be sorry about. I'm actually filled with joy for you in this moment because someone gave you an opportunity." Lamar gently replied as he patiently waited for Mr. Williams to compose himself.

It didn't take long for Mr. Williams to recover, and he continued his story, "Mr. Levy then said to me, you and your dad have always been good to me, and your work has always been exceptional. This is the least that me and my partners can do for you as a formal way to say thank you. He then put away his documents and said that he would have his attorney reach out to me within the next 7 days with the paperwork. We shook hands and parted ways, and sure enough, on the 5th day, I received a call from his attorney asking when I was free to meet with him and replied that we could meet him the following day, so he set the meeting for 1pm. We reached out to our family attorney and informed him of the pending transaction, and he agreed to meet us there. The next day, we got there about 15 minutes beforehand and when we all finally sat down, the attorneys went over the paperwork together and then had us review the documents as well, being sure to answer any questions. Once we were satisfied, we signed the documents and were then told that he would do his best to expedite the deeds over to us and then we shook hands. 30 days later, we were the owners of 700 acres." Mr. Williams paused for effect, and he definitely got it. Everyone burst out into laughter and shouts of victory.

When everyone had contained their excitement, Mr. Williams continued, "From there, we constructed our first home and then brainstormed about a way to ensure that as many people as possible could avoid the frustrations that we did in their search for a home. So, we formulated a plan to sell homes to qualified black and brown folks. We made sure to get our LLC set up and we sat with our attorney and began the process of assisting our people to get a piece of the American Dream." Mr. Williams paused as he took another sip of his drink.

"So how did you qualify the folks that eventually purchased the homes?" Lamar inquired. He was on 10 right now at all the wisdom that was being shared.

Laughing because he realized that he'd stoked a fire in Lamar, Mr. Williams replied, "Well, we had to sit down and really talk this thing through because we also understood the times that we were living in and had heard many stories where qualified folks were being denied home loans. So, initially, most folks came in as renters but for the ones that were deemed qualified enough to possibly get approved, we would connect them with a team of financial specialists introduced to us by Mr. Levy as he vowed to do everything he could to assist us in our venture. Once we sent them to his team, most of them were able to get qualified for an actual mortgage and from there, they became official homeowners." Mr. Williams took another sip before going on.

"As more and more homes went up, we sat back in gratitude that we were able to help so many recognize the dream that was before them in addition to those who were well on their way to eventual ownership. It was amazing to watch how these families thrived knowing that they had a place to call their own that could never be taken from them as long as they did what they needed to do. So this process went on until we were left with 10 acres and I just couldn't bring myself to let it go as I wanted to ensure that whoever I decided to sell to would love it just as much as we did and not purchase it just to become something else that we don't either have access to or is not serving the community which brings me to you." Mr. Williams paused as he picked up one of the cigars Bryce had previously set near him.

"Why is it that you desire this land?" Mr. Williams finished as he sat back and crossed his leg and lit the cigar.

Talk about the right place at the right time, Lamar thought to himself as he took a moment to gather himself.

"First of all, I want to thank you for encouraging and inspiring me. I can't even begin to imagine growing up in a time like that and I really appreciate and sit in awe at how the two of you persevered and then made it a priority to reach back and help. That does my heart good." Lamar paused as he felt his emotion rising at the honor of sitting before such Black Excellence.

"So now, let me share a little about myself." Lamar started.

He went on to share how he'd moved to Miami when he was 10 with his mom and siblings due to his mom desiring to kick her habit. He explained that as his mom worked her way through her journey, he'd met Ms. Santi and how she'd challenged him to dare defy his circumstances. He told them how he'd pursued credit and financial management along with investing and how to live on a budget. He shared his journey to becoming owner of his lounge and how it was thriving and how he'd be honored to show them a good time should they come visit sometime. He also shared his love for his employees and how he did as much community outreach as he was able to do. He shared how entrepreneurship had been a lifelong goal and with his thriving business, he was now moving into the next phase of his evolution with the recently acquired apartment complex. He described how he had a vision for renovating and re-presenting the apartment community as an affordable community in order to alleviate some of the burdens of life. He then went on to share how the reason the land even ended up on his radar was his interest in ownership and how it was necessary to build a foundation that stood to ultimately reroute the black dollar by recirculating it through black and brown communities first before making its way elsewhere. He explained to them his vision for the land was to build a grocery store as an anchor and then he wanted to place a liquor store there along with a restaurant, hair store and a corner store with 16 pumps along with several spaces for local artists and entrepreneurs alike. He also shared how he planned to help those that had actually done the work and could produce a sound business plan get their idea off of paper and into reality. He then went on to share that not only would the businesses be black and brown owned, but that every one of the employees would be given livable wages with the option of purchasing stock in the holding company that would be created in order to assist in wealth building. He lastly shared how he'd met some wonderful folks through a friend and come to find out, they were on the same type of time as he was with their Community Center, affordable condo tower and community outreach and how they were meeting that Saturday to discuss how they could have the biggest impact and how the parcel of land in question was central to that pending conversation.

Lamar, having now wrapped up his vision and goals, sat back and sipped slowly on his drink as he watched Mr. Williams. Mr. Williams sat back with a grin on his face as he slowly pulled on his cigar.

After about 5 minutes of silent thought, Mr. Williams finally spoke. "Young man, I respect you and I like the way your mind challenges an issue until it is no more." Mr. Williams paused as he put his cigar down on the ashtray that seemed to have appeared out of nowhere. Then he picked up his drink and took a nice long sip before continuing.

"If you can assure me that you will honor your vision and not allow yourself to be moved by the greed that sweeps through this nation, I can have my attorney draw up the paperwork and have it ready for you by Friday." Mr. Williams smiled as he quieted for a response.

Lamar sat there with his heart feeling as if it was about to jump out of his chest. He took a deep breath to calm himself and finally answered, "Mr. Williams I can and will. My dream and purpose in life is to ensure that we are set up properly and cared for with love and consideration. It's my mission to leave a legacy of sustainable help so that when I'm gone, if folks will stick to the blueprint, and I will have documents drafted to ensure my standards are upheld, we here in Miami will always have a home, a job and a support system."

Mr. Williams then set his cup down, slowly got up, adjusted his clothing and extended his hand and said simply, "Deal."

As Lamar got up, his emotions, this time, couldn't be contained and the handshake ended up in a hug from a father to a son. After releasing each other from the embrace, Mrs. Williams made her way slowly and carefully around the table to stand before Lamar as he stood there still weeping. She grabbed a napkin and wiped his face and gently said to him, "I'm proud of you son and I want you to know that God is all over you. You don't understand it all right now, but you will and know that you will become even stronger because of it." And with that, she embraced him and pulled his head down towards her and gave him a kiss on the forehead and she then squeezed his hand and made her way back to her seat.

Once she returned to her seat, Lamar took a moment to look around and he saw that Ms. Armand had an impossibly large smile on her face as she too dabbed at her tears and the two shared a smile between themselves and then he looked over towards Bryce who stood there like the big brother he never had, and he nodded in respect.

"I thank you, young man. Now my mind can rest as I know we gone be all right as much as we're willing to be," Mr. Williams said as a single tear rolled down his face.

The rest of their time at the Williams's was spent sitting on the front porch with the 5 of them now seated in folding chairs overlooking Biscayne Bay as the sun continued its path across the sky and lights began coming on.

They sat out for another hour or so, as they finished off the last of their glasses. Lamar, sensing it was about that time, made sure to exchange information, He assured them that he would keep them updated on everything he had going on and that he really hoped to wait on them at Ed's and how they were going to be given the royal treatment at the grand opening of the plaza that he'd envisioned in his mind. They all then hugged, shook hands and bid each other good evening.

As Bryce escorted the Williams back into their home, Ms. Armand and Lamar walked arm in arm towards their vehicles where they stood for a few moments in silence as they gazed over the gently rolling waters.

"It's time, young whipper snapper." Ms. Armand smiled, still gazing out upon the waters.

"Yes, it is and it's crazy because it's happening right in front of me and I still can't believe it," Lamar replied.

"We can then confirm that you wouldn't believe it if I showed you." Ms. Armand laughed lightly as she turned to face Lamar. "I am beyond thrilled about the direction of your life, Lamar. I want you to know that I will always be here for you so understand that you are never alone and receive that no matter what you face in life, you are stronger than you know, and we won't let you fall nor fail." Ms. Armand finished as she kissed him on the cheek and said she was going to head home so that she could get a start on his paperwork for the holding company and check on the process of the transfer of the deed to the apartment complex.

Smiling, Lamar just stood there soaking it all in as he watched Ms. Armand get into her vehicle. She cranked her SUV and blew a kiss at him as she passed by on her way to her home. Lamar again turned towards the water and, this time, looked up into the sky and just smiled before finally getting into his car and pulling off the curb to make his way home.

Chapter 38

Lamar pulled into his driveway at 9pm. He was beyond thrilled after the dinner this evening. The stories, the persistence, the patience, the favor, the wisdom... he'd walked away full of hope, drive and ambition.

The aligning of it all, he thought to himself as he turned his car off and sat there for a few moments in reflection. As he was about to get out of the car, a thought hit him, and he placed a quick call to Ms. Armand.

"Hey, babes. What's up?" Ms. Armand asked.

Lamar could hear the slight rush of the wind and he was happy that he'd caught her in motion. "So I was thinking about Saturday's meeting and while I'm probably going to be covering quite a few topics, I'd love for you to create an official offer about the development of a plaza on the land to present to the attendees."

"Funny you should say that," Ms. Armand answered with a soft smile, "I actually recorded a voice memo maybe 10 minutes ago about this exact thing."

"Look at you knowing your client!" Lamar laughed in response.

"I better for what I charge," Ms. Armand replied back as the two of them engaged in laughter.

After their brief moment of laughter, Ms. Armand asked Lamar if there was anything else. He thought for a second before responding that he was good. The two then bid each other a good night and ended the call. Lamar then gathered his things, got out of his car and headed towards his front door, making sure to lock his car along the way.

Once inside, he set his things down on the kitchen island and went into his room where he kicked off his shoes and stripped down to his boxers, undershirt and socks. He then laid his clothing across his bed and made his way back into the kitchen where he ended up standing in front of the fridge. He wasn't really hungry due to the beautiful meal that he'd previously had but he definitely wanted something to snack on, so he ended up grabbing some plain vanilla yogurt along with some blueberries and some granola. He closed the door with his foot and then set everything on the counter next to the fridge and then he took out a bowl and a spoon and made himself a quick parfait. Once he was satisfied with his snack, he put the leftover items back in the fridge, grabbed his phone and his bowl and headed to his den where he got comfy in his recliner.

As he sat there enjoying the series Scandal and his parfait, his phone rang. He looked and saw that it was Devon. Smiling, he answered, "Hey bae. How are you?"

"Better now that I'm finally hearing your voice." Devon smiled.

Lamar felt heat spreading throughout his body as he mulled over Devon's words. "How was your day?" Lamar asked.

"That's actually why I was calling you. How'd the meeting go?" Devon countered.

Lamar took a moment to compose his thoughts and then gave Devon a summary of everything that had occurred earlier that evening. He ended with the meeting that was going to happen this Saturday and how he was excited to be getting together with everyone to pow wow and figure out ways to create sustainable ownership.

"Congratulations bae!" Devon replied enthused. "I'm really happy for you and I'm also looking forward to Saturday."

"It's going to be a great time," Lamar responded.

"You sound a little tired." Devon inquired.

"I am but what's up?" Lamar asked.

"You feel like a little company?" Devon asked as he lowered his voice a bit.

Laughing, Lamar replied, "I'm always down to kick it with you."

"Good cause I was already in my truck and backing out of my driveway." Devon laughed.

"A little anxious there, my guy." Lamar laughed.

"You already know what it is," Devon replied.

"True..." Lamar laughed. "So, check it, I'm going to unlock my side gate and leave the kitchen door unlocked. I'm hopping in the shower."

"Make sure to prolong it for me." Devon growled.

Still laughing, Lamar replied, "Boy get off my phone."

Laughing as well, Devon responded, "See you soon," before disconnecting the call.

Still smiling, Lamar finished the rest of his parfait and then got up and went out his kitchen door, unlocked the gate. After unlocking the kitchen door, he hopped into the shower.

It was around 25 or so minutes later when Devon pulled up to Lamar's house. He came in through the side, being careful to lock the gate behind him and then he made his way in through the kitchen, also being careful to lock it as well. He kicked off his shoes at the door and then walked them to the front door while announcing to Lamar that he was there. Once he placed his shoes down, he walked into Lamar's room, where Lamar had just finished throwing on some boxers, socks, and a tee shirt. Devon walked over to him and placed his hands around Lamar's lower back and pulled him in to gaze upon him for a moment before kissing him.

After a few moments of rubbing Lamar's back and squeezing his cheeks, Devon pulled away and said, "I'm glad to see you."

Lamar then grabbed another blanket out of the closet along with a pillow and handed it to Devon and then followed him into the den where Devon made up the couch and stripped down to his boxers and socks. It took everything Lamar had not to fall to his knees as Devon's thickness swung seductively backwards and forwards. Lamar found himself about to drool but swallowed before it crossed his lips and then he resumed watching Scandal and the two of them laid up together.

They spent the remainder of their evening laughing and talking about the meeting with the Williams and the meeting on Saturday in addition to the things that were going on with the Community Center and other projects that Devon had an interest in. Before long, the two of them were fast asleep with Lamar wrapped up in Devon's warm embrace. They stayed that way until the sun roused them from their slumber.

Chapter 39

It was 11am Thursday morning when Lamar finally rolled out of bed. The night before with Devon had been special in that they simply enjoyed each other's company. They'd fixed a quick drink and then eventually fell asleep watching Netflix.

Devon had gotten up around 8:30am to get ready for work and Lamar vaguely remembered giving him his house key after telling him to make himself a copy. Lamar had also noticed that Devon's mind seemed to have been occupied. He'd asked if everything was all right to which Devon replied that he was good but Lamar knew something was going on, but he let it go having made a decision to revisit it at a later time.

Lamar decided to spend the day taking care of his house. He was excited about the arrival of the bulk of the items he'd ordered for his home that afternoon. He also made a mental note to reach out to his mom and siblings to check on them and share the good news.

He went through his morning routine, minus breakfast because he wanted to get in a work out. His work out took him into 12:30pm, after which he showered and ate a light lunch. He then checked his emails and was notified that some of his items were to arrive between 2pm and 3pm so he then decided to make his calls.

First, he reached out to his siblings via 3way and shared the latest developments as an entrepreneur. He made sure to set up a time with his brother for a walkthrough of the apartment complex to gauge the work needed to bring the units up to his standards. They both agreed on the following Thursday at 1pm, and the three of them chatted a few moments more before ending the call with well wishes and plans for dinner the following Saturday.

He then called his mom to see how she was doing. After answering on the 3rd ring, she informed him that she was ok, just tired. He quickly shared the good news and let her know that he would stop by on Saturday to sit with her. They shared their love and well wishes for each other and then ended their call.

Lamar then spent the next hour or so watching TV until his doorbell rang. Upon approaching the door, Lamar saw that it was the delivery man with his items. He excitedly opened the door, greeted the driver, signed for his things and then gathered everything inside his home.

It was around 5pm when Lamar was able to finally relax. He sat back in his living room and took it all in. He was very pleased with the end result of the additional items. He then got up and took his time appreciating the splashes of color, depth and texture the pieces brought into his space.

After appreciating his choices, he gave Devon a call. The two of them talked for about 20 minutes or so with them both deciding on dinner from Boston Market and Devon again staying over. After the call, Lamar ordered their food online and texted Devon the info so that he could pick their order up on the way over. Lamar then made his way into his office and again woke up his PC and began looking over photos of the apartment building.

It's a little dusty right now, Lamar thought as he scrolled through the pics. *But when I finish with it, baabay!! It's going to be very welcoming and homey.* He finished scrolling through the photos, feeling his pride swell with each slide of the screen.

He had such an amazing vision for this property and was excited to get started. He looked over the tenant list and was relieved to see that it was only 15% occupied. This meant he was free to move around how he wanted to.

After spending another 45 minutes going over the property details, Lamar pulled himself away from his PC. As he relocated himself to his den, he heard Devon opening the front door. He got up to go see if he needed any help but realized after a quick kiss that Devon was good.

As the two made their way to the kitchen, Devon stopped for a moment to appreciate the newly placed décor.

"Ok. I see you..." he smiled in appreciation. He then resumed his walk towards the kitchen where he placed everything on the island while Lamar set about readying their plates, cups and silverware.

After everything was set up, Devon walked into Lamar's room and showered. He returned shortly thereafter with a tee shirt and boxers on. Lamar then briefly reheated everything and then fixed their plates before sitting down and enjoying a nice, fairly quiet dinner.

After wrapping dinner up, the two set about straightening everything up and then the rest of the evening was spent doing more of what they'd done the previous night, which was watch Netflix and enjoy each other's company.

As Devon lay there holding Lamar, he thought about that talk that he said he wanted to have with him but decided that he was just going to live in the moment since they were in such a good space. He figured that he'd give it a bit more time before sitting Lamar down and laying a few things on the table.

The two of them watched a few movies and shared comments here and there until around midnight. Devon dozed off with Lamar laying there in silence as he took comfort in the presence of Devon and his embrace. He didn't have anything in particular on his mind nor did he have the words to describe the peace he felt snuggled up in Devon's arms, so he just smiled and snuggled even closer.

Chapter 40

Friday proved to be a really great day. The two of them stirred around 11am, with Devon practically leaping off the couch until he realized that he was off today. They both shared a laugh and began their day together.

They sat down and had a light breakfast, and while enjoying their selections of fruit and oatmeal, they discussed what they wanted to do for the day. Lamar shared that he wanted to head to the beach for a while. Devon was game with it, so they packed up a cooler with some ice, waters and a few turkey sandwiches before piling into Devon's truck and making their way to Haulover beach.

Between the beautiful day, the inviting waters and that constant, cooling breeze, the two of them had a blast. They swam, splashed each other and floated, hand in hand, before making their way back to their spot right near the shore where they talked for what seemed like hours.

They finally called it a day around 3pm. As they made their way back towards the parking lot, they made sure to stop off at the outdoor showers to rinse all of the sand off of them before continuing to the parking lot. After arriving at Devon's truck, Devon opened the back where he piled everything into the cargo area and then they hopped in the truck and pulled off, headed towards Lamar's house.

Before leaving the beaches, Lamar asked, "Could we stop by Publix so that I can grab a few things to snack on?"

"Sure," Devon said.

"Do you want anything specific from there?"

"Nah, whatever you grab for me is cool."

They made their way to Miami Beach and pulled into the parking lot. Devon found a spot with shade and Lamar got out and made his way into the store.

Upon entering, Lamar grabbed a little hand basket and then began his browsing. He grabbed some chocolate covered almonds, yogurt covered raisins, some mangos and decided to place an order for some steamed crab legs.

As he stood there waiting on his crab legs, he had the entire shit scared out of him as a familiar voice whispered in his ear, "You ain't got no weapons now."

Lamar froze as fear washed over him. He quickly turned around and upon seeing Tee, took a few steps back. He hadn't seen Tee since their fight and desperately wished he had his phone to call Devon, but he left it in the truck.

"Don't get scared now pussy nigga," Tee began as he slowly moved closer to Lamar. "You already know what it is."

Lamar's mouth had gone dry as he again took several steps back. "Look," Lamar began, stuttering, "I don't want no problems. That was a long time ago and you were beating the shit out of me, and I didn't know what else to do. Please just let me go."

"An' I still want my one fuck nigga." Tee snarled as he began moving in again. "An ain't nobody here to stop me."

Lamar wished the store was more packed. As it stood, his items were still being steamed and the clerk was at the back preparing his order of crab legs. At this point, he panicked and began trembling with fear of what was about to come. He had never been a fighter and had learned from previous experience that his blows had no effect on Tee. As Tee moved in those last few feet with his hand balled up, Lamar dropped his basket and turned to run. As he was mid-step, Tee caught him by his shirt. What happened next, though, caused Lamar to cry out.

As Tee went to pummel Lamar, all Lamar saw was a blur of brown fly by. He didn't know what happened, but he did realize he wasn't hit. He turned and saw that Devon had rushed Tee and knocked him on the ground. Tee jumped up immediately with shock and confusion in his eyes as he squared up, but before he could get his hands up, Devon hit him with a left so vicious that not only was there an audible crack, but blood flew out of Tee's mouth as he crumbled to the ground.

"Come on," Devon said as he grabbed Lamar's hand and guided him out of the store.

The two of them rushed out of Publix, hurried to Devon's truck and quickly pulled out into traffic on the way back to Lamar's house. As they rode in silence, Lamar had to force himself to breathe cause his heart was beating so hard. Devon, upon noticing that Lamar was still trembling, grabbed his hand and held it tight as he navigated his way closer to Carol City.

Devon ended up stopping at Wendy's off 79th and Biscayne and threw the truck in park. "Babe, it's ok. You can calm down. I'm here," Devon said as he rubbed Lamar's arm.

Lamar, still in a bit of panic, finally realized that he was safe and that nothing had happened. He took a few more deep breaths and then, with tears in his eyes, said to Devon, "Thank you."

"Babe, I told you I gotchu," Devon said as he kissed Lamar's hand. "Who was that though?" Devon inquired.

"That was Tee..." Lamar began after taking a moment to respond. "He's the guy I dated until he beat the crap out of me."

"I wish I would have known that. I would have kicked his fucking face in." Devon snarled.

Grabbing Devon by the forearm, Lamar interjected, "Baby, it's ok. You broke that man's jaw and laid him to rest for a bit. You did enough."

When Devon heard that, He paused his flaring anger and began laughing. "I did, didn't I?" Devon reflected as he pulled Lamar in to kiss him.

After passionately kissing Lamar for a few moments, Devon said to him, "I love you man and I'm here." Devon finished as he again kissed Lamar's hand.

The two of them finally pulled out of Wendy's parking lot and began heading North on Biscayne. As they traveled, Lamar asked Devon what he had a taste for, to which Devon responded that he had a taste for Haitian food. Lamar concurred and the two continued North on Biscayne until it split off onto NE 6th Ave, which took them into N Miami where they eventually made a slight right onto West Dixie and, shortly thereafter, the parking lot of Chef Creole.

As Devon placed his truck into park, he turned to face Lamar and said, "This time, I'll go in," to which they both laughed as Lamar lightly pushed him. Devon got out of the truck and made his way into Chef Creole, leaving Lamar behind with his thoughts.

Lamar's thoughts immediately went to Tee and how he now felt uncomfortable that next time he encountered him, he might not be so lucky. He mulled over what he could do to ensure his protection and sadly, came down to him really considering getting himself a gun. He'd always hated guns, not because of the guns themselves, but because of the assumed invisibility and false bravado it gave people. The thought of purchasing one actually made him nervous, but the only other thing was to get some heavy duty pepper spray but that only temporarily avoided the issue and, at this point, he realized that it was obvious that Tee was going to come for him and he needed to protect himself. As he sat there and weighed backwards and forwards on what to do, he put a reminder on his phone to do some research and speak with some folks about his concern.

Having gotten comfortable with his decision, he leaned his seat back, locked the doors and closed his eyes in an attempt to clear his mind. As he was getting into his peace and quiet, he heard a tap on the driver's side window. Opening his eyes, he saw it was Devon. He unlocked the doors and grabbed the bags from Devon and his mouth started watering immediately as he set them on the floor near his feet. He couldn't wait until he was back at the house so he could dig into these dishes.

Devon, after getting situated, pulled back out onto West Dixie and resumed navigating towards Carol City. Once they arrived at the house, they both set about emptying Devon's truck and then they situated all the food on the counter. They took a shower together and then put on some boxers and a tee shirt and then they fixed themselves a plate and sat in front of the TV together. After finishing the food, Lamar cleared their plates and after rinsing the dishes, placing them into the dish washer and making his way back into the den, Lamar was very pleased with what he saw before him.

Devon had stripped down and was sitting there flip flopping his semi hard dick. His flip flopping turned into the most sensual, pleasurable and fulfilling love making yet. It was so good in fact that as soon as they were done, Lamar instantly fell asleep to which Devon laughed. He made sure to clean them both up and then he got behind Lamar, pulled him into his embrace, kissed him on the back of his neck and he too drifted off while thinking to himself, *Thas mine right there.*

Chapter 41

It was Saturday morning around 7:45am when Lamar stirred. He recalled having another strange dream but couldn't remember exactly what it was. But once he felt Devon's arms around him, he didn't even care anymore.

Half smiling, he lightly kissed Devon's forearm. As he made to slowly get up, so as to not disturb Devon, he gasped in pleasure. Last night had been incredible and this morning, he was a bit swollen so certain movements caused Lamar to feel as if Devon were still inside him.

Considering his movements, he carefully pulled himself up and just as he was almost off of the couch, Devon reached up and pulled him back down. At Devon's unexpected grip, Lamar let out a little yelp, which turned to shared laughter.

"Good morning, babe," Devon said huskily as his hot breath flowed over the back of Lamar's neck, causing his throat to dry.

It don't make no sense how much this man affects me, Lamar thought to himself as Devon began slowly grinding up against him while slowly sucking on the back and sides of Lamar's neck.

Lamar tried responding but between the way Devon pressed up against him every few seconds coupled with the pleasure surging through his body from Devon's lips and caresses, Lamar could do no more than moan and gasp with pleasure.

As Devon was about to enter Lamar, Lamar jumped and ended up falling off the couch and rolling on the floor. Laughing, Devon got up to help Lamar up.

Once he'd helped him up, Devon asked, "What's wrong?"

"This," Lamar responded as he gripped Devon's rock-hard dick, "Sir, last night left me swollen and there's no way that I can handle you."

"Swollen?" Devon inquired. "I can fix that." He continued as he began kissing Lamar again.

Laughing, Lamar pushed away from Devon. "The hell you say."

"So, you gone make me chase you?" Devon asked as he slowly made his way towards a fully aroused Lamar.

"Bae please. I can't right now. I need time to recover," Lamar pleaded as Devon again approached him and wrapped his big arms around him, pulling him in close.

Tenderly kissing Lamar, Devon finally relented. "Ok. I'll give you a rest but what about that mouth though?" Devon asked as his dick jumped against Lamar's leg.

Laughing, Lamar slowly walked Devon back towards the couch and pushed him back so that Devon sat down with his legs open. Lamar kneeled in front of him and proceeded to tease and pleasure Devon until he couldn't take it anymore and released all that pent up energy.

After swallowing the last of Devon's protein shake, Lamar looked up and asked, "You ok now?"

Breathing heavily, Devon managed a thumbs up. Lamar then got up and pulled Devon up and guided him to the shower.

After showering and brushing their teeth, they ate a light breakfast. As they sat there eating, it occurred to Lamar that Devon had stepped in just in the nick of time.

He wanted to know how Devon had known that he was in trouble, so he asked, "Bae, yesterday, how did you know to come into the store? That I needed you," Lamar asked as he cocked his head to the side.

Smiling, Devon replied, "Well, I was sitting there in the truck and I went to call you and tell you to grab me some M&M's but when I dialed you, your phone rang and I realized that you'd left it in the truck so I made my way in." Devon paused as he took a sip of juice. "As soon as I made it into the store, something to the right caught my attention and once I turned to follow it, I saw you and saw how terrified you were. When I saw ol boy step into the picture from the other side of the aisle, I just reacted."

Lamar reflected on how perfect his timing was and had never been so thankful for Devon's sweet tooth in his life. Changing the conversation, the two of them began talking about the brunch scheduled for today, which reminded him that he needed to reach out to Angela.

They finished breakfast together, cleaned up and Devon went back into the den while Lamar went into his office, where he'd left his phone. Upon picking it up, he saw that he'd had a few missed calls and text messages. He opened the text messages first.

ANGELA: *Thank you for the bouquet! I LOVE YOU!* ☺

LAMAR: *Well, and a good mornin to you too. Those are to show you how much I appreciate you and I'm thankful you are in my life. Side note: is everything a go for today?*

The next message was from Julia.

JULIA: *I was thinking about you and thought I'd check in real quick.*

LAMAR: ☺ *I'm good best fren'. Can't wait to see you at the brunch.*

Seeing that there were no more text messages, he then checked his call logs. He saw that his vendors had reached out to him yesterday. He marked his calendar to call them back on Monday and then headed back towards the den.

As he stepped into the den, his phone rang. Looking down and seeing that it was Angela, he answered.

"Hey lady!" He quipped.

"Hey yourself, you wonderful man!" Angela exclaimed as they both broke out in laughter. "How are you?"

"I'm super excited this morning!" Lamar shared as he sat to Devon's left on the couch and threw his leg across Devon's.

"You should be. You're making major moves out here in these streets," Angela replied.

"I'm trying." Lamar chuckled.

"You're doing more than trying, sir. You're accomplishing," Angela began. " I just wanted you to know that everything is a go for today. You guys will be having your choice of Chicken and Waffles or Shrimp and Grits served with garnished French Toast, Turkey Sausage and Bottomless Mimosas."

"See, now I'm hungry." Lamar laughed in appreciation.

"Well, all right then. I'll see you soon," Angela responded.

The two of them bid each other well wishes and then disconnected. Lamar and Devon then watched TV until around 10am, which was when they began to get ready for the upcoming brunch. It was about 10:45am when they were finally ready and walking out of the house.

They piled into Devon's truck and were making their way towards Ed's when Lamar's phone rang. It was his attorney, Ms. Armand.

"Good morning counselor." Lamar smiled.

Laughing, Ms. Armand replied, "Hey there sir. I just wanted you to know that I'm enroute to Ed's with some good news."

What is up with all this goodness flowing my way? Lamar thought to himself.

"I'm living it and find it still hard to believe all of this is happening." Lamar finally answered.

"He said that he would pour out such a blessing that you wouldn't be able to receive it, so just stand in it and trust him," Ms. Armand replied.

"Yea, but I ain't even been in contact with him like that to be honest. Why would he be doing all of this?" Lamar asked as he truly couldn't fathom the literal reset he was experiencing.

"Well baby, in my experience, God rarely chooses the qualified. He qualifies those whom he calls, even when they have no idea that they actually belong to him," Ms. Armand countered.

"Well, he sure got a sense of humor about it." Lamar finally laughed.

"That he does my dear," Ms. Armand began. "You'd be amazed at the number of folks who, even though they've read the bible backwards and forwards, have no idea what's in it. For instance, the super religious often look down their noses at folks due to their decisions and they will shun them. In the bible that I read, Jesus was almost always found with the sinners and outcasts and shunned from society. He was amongst the whores and the thieves and the liars and the swindlers and the doubters and he loved them. It was them religious folk that not only did he not have much to do with, but they were the ones who actually had him killed."

"Come on preacher!" Lamar declared as he felt a surge of excitement run through him.

Laughing, Ms. Armand continued, "My whole thing is get to know God for yourself. You will find he is not traditional nor is he stuffy and judgmental like us humans down here. All he wants from us is to develop a relationship with us personally and that requires work and even though you may not see it and may not even be ready, he still loves you and has many more blessings for you. But enough of that, I am looking forward to our meeting today and I will be seeing you soon!" Ms. Armand blew a few kisses over the phone and then the two of them disconnected the call.

The rest of the ride to Ed's was spent in silence as the two of them sat there in their thoughts. In Lamar's mind, Ms. Armand's message continued to cycle through. He'd been briefly taught about God when he was younger and even tried praying but when life started happening and he began experiencing the hurt and pain that was his childhood and even into his teenage years, he recalled when he stopped inquiring and stopped talking to. He couldn't wrap his mind around how a loving, all knowing, kind and gentle God could allow all of the terrible things that happened to him happen. Because of those hurts and disappointments, he pulled back from anything to do with God.

On the other side of those things, he thought about how he'd thrown himself into his work and focus and saw how his life began to turn around. He then wondered, *was that God or was that me?*

It was hard to say because he'd really disciplined himself and he really went hard at it so he could easily take the credit but there was something gnawing at him that refused to receive it. This same thing caused him to look over the kindness of the previous owners of the lounge. The fact that his mom had worked hard at overcoming her addiction. The introduction to Ms. Santi and what she meant to his life. The love of Julia. The fact that he'd been able to obtain a whole apartment complex and most recently, he believed, several acres of land in Miami Gardens. These were the questions that swirled around his mind as they navigated their way towards Ed's.

The remainder of the ride was uneventful. As they drove through downtown Opa-Locka, they passed by the front of Ed's and Lamar's excitement kicked in at the cars that were parked in front of the lounge with waiting passengers.

Lamar directed Devon to the service road, and they entered through the employee parking lot. Devon turned off the truck and looked upon Lamar. He pulled him in for a quick kiss and squeezed his hand. They got out and made their way into the lounge to get the party started.

Chapter 42

It was 10:50am when Lamar and Devon stepped into the main seating area at Ed's. Lamar was immediately impressed. Angela had really done her thing with the layout but the first thing that Lamar noticed was the fragrance. She'd set up 8 tables in a semi-circle and had replaced the usual tablecloths with a variety of earth tones with contrasting floral arrangements. Now the floral arrangements were lovely but once Lamar and Devon made it to the table that was furthest to the left, Lamar's smile became even bigger when he recognized the source of the scent. Scented candles had been centered within the arrangements. Lamar took a moment to inhale deeply and was briefly transported to a place of bliss.

Angela had also made sure to set every table up with covered pitchers full of ice water and 2 glasses per table. And not to be outdone, she'd put on Miles Davis's Bitches Brew, which was playing softly in the background. Lamar was really pleased with her attention to detail and was overcome with a sense of contentment at the meeting before him as he set his phone and keys down on the table.

"And just when I thought it couldn't get any better…" Devon exclaimed as he smiled down at the envelope in his hand. Lamar hadn't noticed them earlier but on every table were 2 envelopes that flowed with the color scheme. Lamar took a moment to open the one that Devon had picked up and chuckled softly upon seeing that Angela had taken it upon herself to provide everyone with a 50.xx gift in addition to a personalized Thank You note.

As they stood there in respect of the time Angela had put into the entire affair, they were met by the sound of Angela's heels coming down the hall from her office. They both turned towards the direction of her heels and shortly thereafter, she appeared with the most beautiful smile. She'd chosen to keep it simple with a nice, little form-fitting deep maroon skirt with a blazer and some mid heeled black shoes. She'd thrown her hair into a bun and had kept the makeup to a minimum. As she drew closer, Lamar was the first to meet her with open arms and kisses on the cheek. Devon was next in line.

"Good morning, loves!" Angela began, taking a step back to take them both in. "So, what do you think?" she asked, waving her hand around the section.

"I think you did that!" Lamar answered.

Laughing, Angela then replied, "I'm happy to know that my work is appreciated. So, we've got all of the food prepared and we have the servers ready to go. There is a full bar and we've got more than enough of everything if they desire a second plate or want one to go. I figured that you would welcome everyone in, thank them for coming and begin introductions. Once those are out of the way, the servers will come out and take their food and drink orders, and from there, ya'll just do what ya'll came to do." Angela paused to confirm with Lamar. Upon his nodding, she continued, "Now, are we ready for this crowd?" Angela asked.

"We are." Lamar smiled.

"Ok, Devon, you go ahead and have a seat and get comfy. Lamar, come with me." And with that, Angela looped her arm through Lamar's and the two of them walked towards the entrance to open and allow the waiting crowd to enter into what Lamar hoped was their future.

Chapter 43

As the doors opened to welcome in the special guests, Lamar was a bit overwhelmed at the weight and significance of the meeting. He thought of the lives that had already been affected and the lives that stood in queue and it made him a bit emotional, but he was sure to contain himself.

As the people filed in, he greeted them all with hugs and handshakes. He also noticed that there was only one person there that he was unfamiliar with. Once everyone was in and seated, Lamar made his way to the stage area where he stood, momentarily taking it all in before speaking. Finally ready to get things started, he began.

"Good morning and welcome." Lamar opened as everyone smiled and said good morning back. "I am Lamar and welcome to Ed's."

"How's everyone doing today?" Lamar inquired as he gave the crowd a moment to respond.

"Well, I'm grateful you guys thought enough to consider getting out of your beds to come and see what was up with this business," Lamar said as everyone laughed lightly in response.

"So, before we get started, we're going to introduce ourselves, what we do and why we decided to come out today. Once we get those introductions out of the way, the servers will come around with the food and drink selections and then we will dig into the meat of it all." Lamar paused to allow it to sink in. "Cool?"

"Cool." Everyone replied in unison.

"So what I'm going to do is start from the right side of the room, work around to the left, and then end with myself," Lamar said as he unhinged the mic from its stand. "Is everyone good with that?"

The crowd all replied that it was well, so Lamar made his way off of the stage and headed towards the right side of the room. Ms. Armand and Julia were sitting at the first table. Julia decided that she would go ahead and start everything off.

"Good morning everyone. My name is Julia and I'm the head Charge Nurse over the ER at Jackson Memorial. I came out today because me and Lamar not only grew up together, but he is my best friend. We've spent plenty nights in my backyard dreaming and sharing thoughts and goals so for me to see where he is now and where he desires to go in the future was enough to get me up early this morning to figure out what role I can play in his vision." Julia then thanked the crowd and passed the mic to Ms. Armand.

"Good morning everyone. My name is Christine Armand, and I am a Corporate Attorney with a focus on Real Estate Law and Business Law. I met Lamar when he was about 20 or 21 and was just a worker here at this very lounge. I watched him struggle, grind, sacrifice and ultimately obtain his goal, which was ownership. I am so very proud of the man that he has become, and I whole heartedly stand with his vision of not just local unity but national and international unity and not only do I believe he's going to see it through, but I'm also here to make sure that the transition is as smooth as possible." Ms. Armand thanked the crowd and passed the mic to the person at the next table, which was Deena.

"Good morning everyone. I'm Deena and I am a Licensed Psychologist. I am here because growing up in rural South Ga, I often observed the pain and trauma left on our people. It hurt my heart to see families struggle just to make ends meet only to be told that it still wasn't good enough. As I grew older and experienced personal pain, I began to recognize the mental anguish many of us colored folk were faced with yet were never acknowledged and I vowed to make a difference. I am here because I met Lamar a few weeks back and the first thing that drew me was his passion and conviction. I saw in him a fire and I really respect how he is moving to satiate that passion and fire and I would love to know what more he has in mind so that I can better understand how to lend my services." As Deena sat down, the guest who Lamar did not recognize stood up.

"Good morning everyone. My name is Elle and I'm an investment banker. Deena is a really close friend of mine so when she shared with me the opportunity to come and pow wow with other folks who were driven to make a change, I couldn't miss out and after hearing how amazing Lamar is, I knew that I was in the right place. I believe that it is time now to prepare for the future and I am offering my support and resources unconditionally." As Elle took her seat, the mic was passed to the next guest.

"Good morning all. I'm Carlos and I am a pediatrician. I am here this morning because quite frankly, we are in a state of emergency. Our communities are suffering, resources are scarce, and our leaders seem to turn a deaf ear to us and our needs until they need our votes. I want more than that for us and I realize that we must unite, those of us that will and can, and take control of our narrative and our future." As Carlos took his seat, the crowd burst out into loud applause and whistles. The next to stand was Joseline.

"Good day, everybody," she began, "How do you follow that?" she asked as she laughed along with the crowd. "So, my name is Joseline and I'm an immigration attorney. Every day I deal with anger, frustration and hopelessness. I generally serve people from the Caribbean but typically deal with folks from Haiti and D.R. who've left their countries, often with nothing, and come here and don't have any family or network to help them get acclimated to life in America. I showed up today because I feel their pain as I, too, immigrated here at a young age from the D.R with my mom and even younger brother. We grew up in the trenches and while my mom did her best, we were in Scott Projects until me and my brother were able to take her out. I became an Attorney, and my brother opened a small corner store where he was able to give back in the way of jobs. I believe that Lamar's vision ties all of us together and I'm eager to see what's on the other side." As Joseline sat down, there was light clapping. As the mic was passed to the next person, the room again fell silent.

"Morning family. How are ya?" the guest began. "My name is Richard and I'm a burgeoning Real Estate Mogul. I grew up in Liberty City off 69th and 17th and it was rough. You heard and saw the violence every day and all you could do was pray, tuck your chin, and keep it moving. On top of that, I saw how drug addiction led to many of my classmates being put out of their homes because their mom couldn't maintain the rent. It really did something to me, and it always stuck with me and spoke to me that when I was able to do so, in spite of the circumstance with the parent—or parents if they were lucky—the children would at least have a stable environment. So, I put myself through Real Estate School, worked really hard and once I was in a comfortable enough space, I began purchasing properties in The City and other areas, wholesale, and I renovated them and placed them on Section 8. This way, if the parents were unable to afford their portion, at least I wouldn't have a total loss. Now, I know that it comes off as enabling, but my concern was truly in making sure those kids had stability so that they could at least not have that to be worried about. Anyway, this also positioned me to be able to go through and check on the families to make sure they had food and things needed for school. So, I am here because I believe that the only thing missing with us are folks who are willing to step outside of themselves and be in it, not just for the money but rather the progression of the people."

As Richard took his seat, the crowd erupted again in applause and whistles. Lamar then stood back as the mic was passed to the last guest, Devon, and he observed this beautiful stature of a man as Devon's words began to flow.

"Well, hello everyone. I'm, first of all, super excited to be here sharing energy with all of you. My name is Devon and I'm a licensed Social Worker. I'm here today because I've had the privilege of having a few conversations with Lamar and I love where his heart and mind are. He is truly an artist whose canvas is the world and his tools are passion, diligence, vision and leadership. I believe in him and believe that what he ultimately sees, he will soon carry out and our community will be the better because of it." As Devon took his seat, everyone clapped it up. As Lamar made his way back to the stage, the crowd continued their clapping until Lamar was once again standing in front of the mic with it being lodged into the stand.

He stood there for a moment, taking it all in. His 29 years of living had come to this moment, and he was overcome with emotion so much so that tears began flowing. Angela rushed to the stage with a tissue and a firm hug with whispers that it was ok. Once he finally composed himself, he spoke up as Angela returned to her seat.

"This is all so surreal," Lamar began. "I recall not all that many years ago of this simply being a dream and a seemingly impossible feat. And now here we are today. I've been able to obtain an apartment complex and just recently closed a deal on 10 acres in Carol City and I am honored to stand here before all of you today with what I believe to be the keys to our success as a people." Lamar paused as he allowed time for the weight of his statement to sink in. He then continued, "So before we get too heavy, we're going to go ahead and get those meals moving and drinks flowing. Your servers are on their way to go ahead and take care of you so with that said, please enjoy and let's get our mingle on!" Lamar smiled as he left the stage and Angela tuned the speakers into Earth Wind and Fire.

True to expectation, the servers came out ready to serve all of the guests. Once orders were placed, everyone engaged each other, and laughter rolled through the building. Shortly after the orders were placed, the servers returned with everyone's drink orders. As everyone continued fellowshipping, the food began arriving. Everyone enjoyed their food and drinks, in between sharing pictures, stories and mingling.

Once they were all done with their food, everyone had their drinks refreshed and they continued their chats. In the midst of everyone getting more familiar with each other, Ms. Armand broke away from the crowd and made her way over towards Lamar and asked if she could speak with him for a moment. Lamar excused himself and the two of them made their way over to the furthest part of the room to have a little privacy.

"First of all, I wanted to share that this is really nice and I look forward to your presentation." Ms. Armand waited long enough for Lamar to give his thanks and express how excited he was to share his vision as well before she continued. "So the reason why I pulled you to the side is because Bryce reached out to me late in the evening yesterday. The paperwork for the transfer of the property is complete and I'm picking it up once I leave here."

Lamar let out a big whoop and then quickly composed himself as he drew Ms. Armand into a bear hug. "I don't even know what to say."

"You don't have to say anything. This is your season and your time. Receive it and own it." Ms. Armand smiled as she hugged him back.

"This is all too much. I mean, even down to the reasons why my guests are here. It's like they were speaking from my heart." Lamar smiled as his eyes glanced over the crowd of guests who had come to hear his ideas.

"What you don't realize, my love, is that God has a calling on your life and even though you've never gone out of your way to get to know Him, He absolutely loves you as you are and where you are. He only wants to take you higher. And the day you begin seeking Him out, will be the day you begin to understand that He's been there all the time. But enough about that, let's get back to this meeting," Ms. Armand said as she looped her arm into Lamar's.

Lamar had never been into religion. In fact, he'd come to despise it having had a few instances as a kid that soured him. He could remember being laughed at for not speaking in tongues. He remembered being singled out for being gay. And he could never forget the loneliness he felt whenever he would get stares and sneers from those who claimed they loved the Lord. And don't get him started on all the pastors who were either secretly sleeping with the women of the congregation or sleeping with the men. He'd grown tired of hearing about a new pastor every other week who'd robbed the church.

What sickened him even more was seeing these pastors live in their lavishly kept homes and vehicles while many in their congregations didn't even know where their next meal was coming from. Yeah, he'd definitely taken a stance against organized religion with all of its rules and regulations that seemed to only ever apply in times and circumstances of convenience. He'd come to the conclusion that if they were a reflection of God, he wanted nothing to do with them or their God. And don't even get him started on slavery and the weaponization of the bible against slaves in the justification of the horrendous treatment that they'd received at the hands of those who attended service faithfully.

As they began moving back towards the guests, Ms. Armand stopped and said, "Oh, I knew there was something else to tell you. So, the process for the complex is moving along a bit faster than I thought it would be and it looks like you will be receiving your paperwork week after next."

Lamar stood there for a moment and just looked at Ms. Armand. He finally gave her a tight squeeze, and a few tears rolled down his face. As he let her go, he was fueled with new energy and ready to get to the point of the invitation to this brunch. He wiped his tears away and made his way back to the stage.

Chapter 44

As Lamar stood behind the mic, he leaned to the left to pick up the glass of water Angela had set on a small table next to the mic stand. He took a sip and slowly swallowed as he gathered his mind and emotions.

Setting the glass down, Lamar began speaking, "I want to first of all thank you again for your time, effort and passion. In you all, I've found my tribe and I am humbled." Lamar paused as the crowd clapped and cheered in response. Once they quieted, Lamar picked back up. "Really quick, the folders that are about to come around now are the reason for this meeting," Lamar said as Ms. Armand got up and removed a stack of navy blue legal folders from her attaché and began passing them around before making her way back to her seat. Lamar picked back up, "I invited you all here today because today is the time for change. Not tomorrow and not next week. Today." Lamar paused at the snaps of a few folks. "It's been over 400 years and what exactly do we have besides more reason to cry, scream and cuss? I, for one, am done. I've decided that it's time to do something about it. You see, I thought back on our ancestors and how any and everything that they had, they had to build and work for it only to be taken and so the cycle continued with many of them growing tired of being beat down and having no protection and so many more just fell in line and seemingly accepted their lot in life. But in 2017, we are gathered to do a new thing in homage to our yesterday." Lamar paused at the sound of everyone's clapping and whistling.

"My vision began manifesting after I took over ownership of Ed's. It was in those moments that I realized the possibilities before me and have worked diligently towards them every single day since."

"So, you are already aware that the facility that we're in is mine and we've seen nothing but growth over the last 3 years. In addition to this, I've recently purchased a 65-unit apartment building that's being closed on within the next few weeks and a few days ago, was also able to seal a deal on a 10-acre parcel of land up in Carol City, which is the focal point of this meeting."

"Ownership. This word means everything to me and without it, we're all no more than resounding gongs in this massive sea of humanity. Now with control comes structure and with structure comes foundation and I'd like your help in establishing that foundation." Lamar took a moment as the crowd again cheered and whistled their approval.

"I found it absolutely astonishing that for the last few years, our purchasing power as black and brown folks has steadily increased from billions to now trillions of dollars. I want you to reflect on that. And when you're done reflecting, I want you to think of our communities and their current state. We've got poorly maintained roads and sidewalks. A broken education system that does not invest in our students, leaving our educators having to scrap together whatever means they can to educate our babies. The lack of affordable housing in our city as prices surge and then the biggest insult, in my personal opinion, is how leaders in our city allow developers to come into our communities and neighbors buying up property only to turn around and price out people that look like me. Like why should any of us have to seriously consider moving to another city or town simply because we can no longer afford to be here?"

"As I thought about these things, I had to allow my anger not only to rise, but finally crest before slipping into sadness at the reality." Lamar paused to grab a sip of water before continuing, "And then I considered my story. A mother who was a drug addict. A broken family that refused to heal. A dad whose face I can't even begin to imagine and within my heart surged hope. Hope at the fact that my mother overcame. At the fact that she raised 3 children and not only did she raise them but all three of us are business owners and financially sound. We'd been able to make it out. And finally, that hope crescendoed into my ambition."

"It is with these thoughts that I present to you the things I'd like to see happen on this parcel of land. The first thing I wanted to do was carve out a space for our own grocery store. I believe this to be vital to not only our community but also the many black farmers across this state and others that I've researched. We need to be able to access fresh, affordable and regional goods and products. We also need a gas station. Then I imagined a top tier, multi leveled plaza with ample parking in the way of a parking garage that contained a credit union, a liquor store, a beauty supply store, barbershop, salon, a spa, a variety of professional services and a few boutique stores ranging from things such as clothing to shoes onto accessories and various crafts and electronics."

"You see, the objective is to recycle as much of those trillions through our communities as possible. I believe now is the time for us to stand up for each other and not only that, but to also support each other and operate in such a way as to become not only a standard but the norm. It is my hope that this vision will not only spark similar mind shifts in South Florida, but also the state, the region and the nation. I see nothing limiting us as all of us in this room are well-to-do and have put in the work and have proven that we are on the tides of change and we're riding hard."

"I can't stress enough the importance of the village. You see, while there's a necessity in marching, protesting and speaking out publicly for the equality, I believe that we're also tasked with living in the spaces that we belong. It's got to be real now and you must own it in order for it to be a real thing. You must realize it and then receive it. That is the foundation of a seed."

Lamar paused to take a sip of water as the crowd stood on their feet in applause. Lamar took a moment to let it all soak in before motioning for the crowd to sit. He smiled before moving on, "I know this is some good stuff but it's more than that, it's a viable glimpse of the future if we move to act. And let us not forget, we need representation so in addition to developing lobbyists, I also believe it's necessary to rear up our own politicians and senators and governors and judges and attorneys and doctors and CEO's and stand behind them to push them and make sure that they're capable and present because as we all know, we're over the whole democrat/republican thing. I believe we should push to create an alternate party as it is my belief that there are more people who desire decency, transparency and truth than anyone else. There are many folks out there who simply desire those that will care for this country and whip it up into its greatest potential because I don't think that it's ever been reached and we're now in possession of the reigns of change."

"The time is now that we and those who look like us take our rightful seat at the table to represent our needs, thoughts, desires and interests, no longer begging and pleading with those who don't like us and could care less about what's best for us. It's up to us and I need you all to help me help us help our community in order that these things be more than fire that burns in the pits of everyone who's ever dreamed of equality and justice. I sincerely believe in us and it is time to act on the things that we can get to right now."

The crowd again stood to cheer and clap and Lamar noticed even a few tears of pride as they stood together in solidarity. He allowed them a few more moments to cheer before quieting the crowd.

"So folks, that is the reason why I brought you here today and I'm going to step down in a few moments but I wanted to let you all know that everything that I touched on, you will find in the folders handed out earlier. I'm not asking for any commitments today as this was just to whet your appetites, however, I am asking that you take your time and go through those documents. I want you to truly understand where it is we're standing in time and when you've had your time reviewing the documents, get back to let me know what we doin'. Again, I really appreciate you and thank you so much for allowing me to speak with you. And with that, please continue to eat, drink and let's do it big!!" Lamar stepped back from the mic as the crowd roared their approval. He even joined in on the clapping and cheering before leaving the stage to rejoin Devon at their table.

The rest of the time spent at Ed's was particularly pleasant. There was a lightness present that Lamar had never experienced before and it brought a certain calm to him, and he welcomed it with a smile as he looked upon everyone. They seemed to all be on fire with joy and an eagerness to really move and that brought a tear to Lamar's eyes to bear witness to such beauty.

Now this is what life is about, Lamar thought to himself as he sat back, taking it all in. He realized that without verbal confirmation from anyone, the value of blackness had just increased, and it took everything within him to remain seated and not run around the room screaming. Laughing at himself, he lifted his glass slightly to get the server's attention and he poked around his plate as excitement replaced his appetite.

As his drink was refreshed, everyone decided to move their chairs around his table, and they then dug into everything that he'd gone over. It was exhilarating the types of questions that he received and observations that were shared but what lifted his heart even more was the fact that all shared a commonality that the vision was possible. Lamar reveled in these facts and for the next hour, this groups of Freedom Fighters sat there and concocted their plan.

The brunch finally wrapped around 1:30pm with hugs, handshakes and a few cheek kisses as everyone promised to keep in touch. After everyone was gone, Lamar thanked Angela, the servers, the bartender and the cook for everything and then he and Devon made their way, hand in hand, back to Devon's truck. It had been a great day and all Lamar wanted to do now was kick his feet up and soak in the beauty that had become his life.

Chapter 45

The rest of Lamar's Saturday was slow motion. He and Devon made it back to his house around 2:15pm after stopping by the meat store off 167th and NW 27th to grab some snow crab legs, king crab legs and some oysters and shrimp to cook later on that evening.

Once all of the food was unloaded and placed into the freezer, Devon turned to Lamar.

"Hey, I need to make a run to my house real quick to grab some things."

"Ok. I'll be here. Chillin'."

Devon kissed him on his forehead. "I'll be right back."

Lamar, after locking the door behind Devon, stripped down to his underwear and white tee. He fixed himself a glass of grape juice, grabbed a bottle of water and made his way into the den where he turned on the TV. He clicked on Netflix and tuned into The Royal Hibiscus Hotel.

As he got into the movie, he found himself slowly unwinding. It was funny because he hadn't even realized that he'd been tense until now.

As the movie played, he began losing himself in his thoughts. He replayed the meeting from earlier and could not contain the smile that spread across his face. He thought about how easily things flowed into place for him and how he'd reached out looking for investors and walked away with a family.

He couldn't have asked for a better crew of people to have linked up with and his mind was still blown at how he didn't even have to convince anyone. His vision stood on its own and with each introduction. It was as if yet another piece was added to the puzzle, which in turn, produced an amazingly vivid and concise image that he couldn't wait for the world to see.

Yea, in this space, Lamar was content. He was thrilled at the unlimited potential with this newly formed collective vision of a people, for a people.

As Lamar thought about all the beauty of what he'd been privileged to take part in, sleep began tugging at the edges of his sight and it wasn't long before he'd drifted off into a light nap. When he woke up, it was around 4pm. His phone rang when he was stretching after getting up. He looked and smiled upon seeing that it was Devon. Devon let him know that he was pulling into the driveway, so Lamar made his way to the front door, unlocked it and made his way into the den to grab his empty glass and empty bottle of water. He headed to the kitchen to place his glass and bottle in the sink.

As Lamar grabbed another bottle of water, Devon made his way into the house with additional clothing and bottles of liquor. Lamar greeted him with a kiss and helped him unload some of the bags. He smiled at the kebab sticks and assortment of fruits and veggies that Devon had brought over along with a few very specific seasonings.

As Devon took his clothing and other personal effects into the bedroom, Lamar set about taking the purchases from earlier out of the fridge. He went ahead and rinsed everything off and then went about seasoning the meats and setting the kabobs up. As he was finishing up the kabob sticks, Devon again entered the kitchen and made his way out onto the patio where he prepared the grill.

Once the grill was ready to go, the two of them moved everything outside and set it up on the counters that had been built into the patio area. As Devon set about prioritizing what was going to go on the grill, Lamar made his way back into the house and created a pitcher of beverage with the Tequila that Devon had brought over along with some fruit and peach liquor that he rarely used. Once he was satisfied with his mixture, he added a bit of ice to the pitcher, grabbed two glasses and took everything outside.

Once he'd fixed their cups, he sat back and let Devon do his thing. As Devon was moving about, he realized that they were missing music, so he made his way into his den where he grabbed the portable Bluetooth speaker. From his phone, he placed the music on Frankie Beverly radio and he adjusted the volume on the speaker. Then he sat back down to enjoy his drink, smiling as Devon began 2 stepping in time with 'Before I Let Go'.

As Devon maneuvered between monitoring the food and sipping his drink, Lamar slid up behind him and hugged him. Devon set his cup down, turned around and embraced Lamar with a deep and passionate kiss as the two of them slowly rocked together. Lamar eventually let Devon go so that he could continue on with the food.

As Devon grilled, Lamar went about setting up the patio table for them to eat outside by wiping it down with Windex. He then set out the plates, napkins, and utensils and sat back down.

It wasn't too long before the food began coming off the grill and into the trays that Devon had grabbed in between flipping the food and sipping from his drink. Once everything was on the table, Devon fixed their plates.

The rest of the evening was spent with them enjoying the deliciousness of Devon's culinary skills and the tunes that serenaded them into the evening. They reveled in one another's company, and before the end of the night, Lamar found himself straddling across Devon's lap as the music comforted their view of the stars.

Chapter 46

Sunday found the two of them again wrapped up in each other's arms, on the couch, in the den. It was around 1pm when Lamar stirred. The two of them had drank, laughed, talked and eventually sang until the wee hours of the morning.

Lamar lay there for a few moments, comforted by Devon's steady breathing, before slowly getting up. He made his way to the bathroom, relieved himself and then washed up and brushed his teeth.

Lamar then made his way back to the kitchen to explore his fridge for breakfast options. After searching through the available items, he decided to make French toast along with Turkey sausage and egg whites. He set everything up and as he set about preparing everything, he felt Devon slide up behind him. As Devon's hands slid around Lamar's waist, Lamar allowed himself to fall slightly back into Devon's embrace. As Devon nipped and licked at Lamar's neck, Lamar giggled and then let out an involuntary moan as he felt Devon's hardness pressed up against him.

Being that everything was practically done, Lamar turned everything down on low and then turned to face this beautiful man. They began kissing slowly and tenderly which led to Devon slowly stripping Lamar off his clothing before undressing himself. As Devon pivoted Lamar towards the counter, he lifted him up onto it and immediately lifted Lamar's legs and began feasting before he slowly slid inside Lamar.

The two of them made agonizingly slow and passionate love which left Lamar trembling, speechless and gasping for breath. After many strokes, tears and cries of pleasure, the two of them released together with Devon collapsing onto Lamar's chest where they lay for a few moments before Devon removed Lamar carefully from the counter, careful not to spill any of their juices. They then hurried to the bathroom where they showered and teased each other while cleaning. Once they'd finished showering, they dried, oiled and changed clothes and made their way back into the kitchen where Lamar set about wiping the counter down and fixing their plates.

Once they'd finished eating and cleaning up the dishes, they made their way back into the den. Netflix was still on from last night, so he decided to tune into Stranger Things. Lamar remembered that Julia had invited them over for dinner, so he made sure to set his alarm for 4:50pm so as to not be late. They then snuggled together and almost instantly; Lamar was out.

Lamar next stirred at around 5pm. He yawned and then stretched a bit before getting up to get his phone and turn off the alarm clock. He looked at the time on his phone and stepped out of the den to call Julia.

"Hey there rockstar!" Julia began as she answered. "How are ya?"

Laughing, Lamar replied, "Hey best friend. And I'm well rested and still excited from yesterday."

"And with good reason," Julia responded.

"So, I was hitting you up to find out about those dinner plans. Did you need anything?" Lamar inquired as he stood in the kitchen, looking at the grey clouds outside.

"Nah. I got it but I'm glad you called," Julia said as she moved around in her kitchen. "Everything will be ready by 6:30pm so make sure you and Devon are on time."

"Gotcha," Lamar responded as he made his way to the fridge to grab a bottle of water.

"All right. I'll see you guys soon," Julia replied.

She and Lamar said their goodbyes and he drifted into his room to pick out what he was going to wear. As he poked around in his closet, he heard Devon making his way into the bathroom.

He decided on some baby blue cotton shorts, a white polo with baby blue highlights, and some baby blue slides. As he laid everything out on his bed, Devon came out of the bathroom and made his way around the bed to embrace Lamar with a kiss.

"How'd you sleep?" Lamar inquired as he rested his head on Devon's shoulder.

"Very good actually," Devon responded as he placed a kiss on Lamar's forehead. "But then that's the effect you have on me."

Laughing, Lamar replied, "Tell me anything."

The two of them laughed a bit more and then Devon headed to his things, which he had placed in Lamar's closet. He emerged with some black basketball shorts, a D Wade jersey and some black slides.

They then decided to sit outside on the patio and have a drink. The first thing they noticed was how dark it had gotten. As they sat down, the wind kicked up. They relaxed as the wind caused the palm trees to sway back and forth as the storm moved in. Before long, it was storming, and the ensuing breeze had both of them almost comatose.

They sat there in silence as the rain came down around them. After about 30 or so minutes, they decided to go ahead and get dressed and began making their way towards Julia's.

They quickly dressed, and Lamar grabbed his extra-wide umbrella. After locking up, they made their way outside towards Devon's truck. Once inside Devon's truck, he cranked it up and adjusted the thermostat, and then he navigated his way towards Julia's.

With the weather going on, it took them about 15 minutes to get to Julia's. Once they pulled into the driveway, Devon grabbed the umbrella, and after turning the truck off, got out and hurried around to Lamar's side and opened the door. They then made it to the front door together where they rang the doorbell.

"Hey there!" Julia smiled as she stepped back to let them in. "How are my two favorite people?"

They hugged and removed their slides before Julia led them into her dining room. Lamar was instantly hungry because of the scent in the air. His senses were further assailed at the spread before them. She'd prepared collard greens, baked leg quarters, Spanish rice, cornbread and yams.

"Ok cuz! I see ya!" Devon exclaimed at the beauty before them.

They all quickly took their place around the table, with Julia sitting at the head. Smiling, Julia extended her hands, clasped each one, and Julia led them in prayer. "Father God, we thank you for life, freedom, love, and each other. We're honored that you've chosen us to move through and I ask that you lead us and guide us down this path. We trust you and we're grateful for the opportunity to serve. We ask for your continued protection, peace and mercy as we walk on this tedious journey, and we love you. We also thank you for this meal and may it hit the spot, especially after I done slaved over that hot stove cooking it." Julia paused as everyone burst out into laughter. "But seriously, Lord, we thank you for the opportunity, and we do these things in Jesus' name, Amen." She finished.

"Amen." Lamar and Devon responded in unison.

The three of them then dug in. They shared laughter, love and compliments on the wonderfulness of the meal. They followed the meal up with drinks and thoughts on the future as they sat on Julia's patio watching the rain fall.

At around 9:30pm, they all called it a night and after hugs, kisses and well wishes, Devon and Lamar headed back to Lamar's house.

Once they were situated at Lamar's house, they decided on a few more drinks and then put on 'All About The Benjamins'. The two of them were sleep almost immediately afterwards.

Chapter 47

Monday seemed to take its time showing up, at least according to Lamar as he stirred from his sleep. As he opened his eyes, he realized two things: he was definitely hung over and that Devon was not behind him. He picked his phone up off the floor next to the couch and realized that it was 9am.

As he sat up, he had to pause midway as his head swam. Once he gathered himself, he made his way into the kitchen where he fixed himself some tomato juice. He downed the drink rather quickly and then made his way into the bathroom where he splashed water on his face and popped two aspirin. He then took a cool shower and took his time grooming himself.

As he made his way back into his room, he jumped as Devon entered the room.

Laughing, Devon asked, "You, ok?"

"Yeah. You startled me, didn't think anyone was here. Where were you?"

"I was in your office, taking calls. I'm about to head on out. Got to be in the office at 10am."

The two of them kissed and then Lamar walked him to the door where he locked up after Devon was gone. He then made his way back into his room where he got himself dressed in boxers and a tee shirt before heading back into the den where he sat down and picked his phone back up to go through and see if he'd had any messages or emails. He saw that he'd received a text from Ms. Armand.

MS. ARMAND: *Hey you. Brunch coming up at 1pm. Here's the address. Can't wait to see you there.*

He then saw that his mom had texted him.

MOM: *Love you, son. Speak soon.*

He then checked his email and saw that Angela had sent over the numbers from over the weekend. After going through a few more, Lamar decided to go ahead and take a nap just to gather himself.

When Lamar next woke up, it was 11:45am and he vaguely recalled someone calling for help. As the clouds cleared, he realized that he was that someone. He couldn't remember exactly what had occurred in his dream but he recalled the darkness and not being alone in it. He sat up and gripped the couch trying to make sense of it. But before he could dig too much into it, he realized that he needed to go ahead and get ready for his meeting, so he headed to his room, where he quickly chose floral print shorts along with a floral print button up tee with a white undershirt. He also picked out some teal-colored loafers and teal-colored socks and then got dressed. After being satisfied with his selection, Lamar then left out, locked up, hopped in his car and made his way over to Sunny Isles.

The ride over was uneventful and the weather was still cloudy and super humid from yesterday. As he crossed over the intercoastal using 163rd St, his mind drifted over his dream, and he mulled over the reason why he continued having these dreams that made no sense. He was in a great place and things were going exceptionally well and he could not understand what the point of these visions was, why they were so vivid and why he was left shaken and disturbed after each occasion.

As he drew nearer to his destination, he shook those thoughts free from his mind and navigated to Beach Bar's parking lot, where he paid the valet and made his way inside. He approached the host and let them know who he was meeting with, and was led to a table on the patio overlooking the ocean. He looked down at his phone and saw that it was 12:40pm and he was the first one there, so he took time to take in the view. Even though the day was overcast, the contrasting Azure-colored waters took his breath away. As he gazed out upon the waters, his thoughts were stilled by each roll of the waves. He was so caught up in his thoughts that he didn't hear the server nor the other two guests who'd arrived shortly after him.

Laughing, he stood up and hugged Ms. Armand and shook the hand of the individual that Ms. Armand wanted him to meet. Before they got to their introductions, they all ordered their drinks, dishes and water.

After their order was taken, Ms. Armand began the meeting. "So, Mr. Hicks, this is the woman I was telling you about." The woman was a beautifully, cocoa-colored, curvy, middle aged sistah with grey eyes. She wore bantu knots, lip gloss and a bronze-colored sundress that perfectly adorned her voluptuous figure. She introduced herself as Nicole.

"It's a pleasure meeting you hun. Christine here has shared so many amazing things about you so I count it an honor to get to know ya," Nicole began. "I want to begin by saying I truly respect how you're out here representing for our ancestors and when I heard about what you were doing and wanting to do, I was immediately on board with anything I could do to help."

"Well, thank you so much. I appreciate that more than you know," Lamar began with a smile. "So, tell me about yourself and your background."

"I started my career as a Real Estate Agent with REMAX about 15 years ago. While my sales were solid, I realized rather quickly that I gravitated more towards the Property Management side. Once I mastered all that I could master, I decided to set up a Brokerage where I oversee a small Boutique Firm with 12 employees where we sell and manage properties that our clients acquire. I'd also like to note that as of today, we manage 10 properties between here and Broward." Nicole paused for a moment as she took a sip of her water. "I've been overseeing our Boutique Firm for the last 7 years now and we're very picky about the types of clients we take on because we realize that not everyone is a fit for us." Nicole paused as the server returned with everyone's drinks.

"Now Christine provided me with the address of the property you just purchased and again, after sharing what she shared with me, I decided that I absolutely had to meet with you because I am all about helping our folks. In fact, my firm sponsors several charity events in the N. Miami area where we do holiday drives, school drives and summer events for the youth and older folk. So, tell me, what is your vision with this property?"

"Well, I'm going to be getting together Wednesday, I believe, with my brother, who's a contractor, and we're going to first walk the property and assess its condition, and what all needs to be done. Once we have that, I plan on bringing the property up to my standards and then we're going to not only provide affordable housing for the community but I'm also going to be looking into partnering together with some of my folks to get some financial literacy classes going so that we can also assist those interested in home ownership. In addition, I only want folks who gross 50,000 or less. I also want to ensure that at least 40% of the units are set aside for section 8 because growing up how I did, I recognized that most folk on section 8 are just trying to make it and need a hand in getting to where they want to be in life."

"I'm here for that!" Nicole exclaimed as she clasped her hands together in pleasure. "So, then I tell you what, once you do your assessment, I'd love to then do a tour of the property and if allowed, make suggestions, if any, on things that can further enhance the property and make it safe for the residents."

"Absolutely. Just as soon as I get a run down from my brother, I will then reach out to you to get a time set so that we can do that walkthrough." Lamar paused as he took a sip of his beverage. "Now what about your fees because we believe in solid business round these parts."

Laughing, Nicole began, "I will forward all of that information over to your attorney here. Now while I do urge you to research and compare rates, I do believe you will find mine to be some of the most affordable in the county."

Smiling, Lamar replied, "Will do and thank you for your display of integrity."

"Without it, I would not be where I am," Nicole replied with a smile.

"Yes mam. That's what I'm looking for because I think it is imperative to develop relationships with our tenants that go beyond renting so as to assure them that we are in it for the long haul," Lamar replied.

"I can see that my decision to assist is a wise one and I look forward to providing all of the help and support that I can. And just note, we are a one stop shop. We make sure that not only is rent handled, but we also have quite a few vendors that we partner with in the way of maintenance requests. That's in addition to handling background checks on the residents and making sure the property is in compliance with the city at all times," Nicole responded.

"That's what I'm talking about!" Lamar smiled as he raised his glass to cheer.

"So it appears that we're going to do good business together..." Nicole began as she took another sip of her beverage. "Our job is to ensure that the property flows as smoothly as possible and that essentially all you're doing is signing off on permissions for this and that and ultimately collecting a check."

"Sounds like a winner to me, and I do look forward to doing business with your firm," Lamar said as he extended his hand across the table to embrace Nicole's hand. The rest of the brunch was spent indulging in the flavorful seafood and talking about the future of South Florida under Lamar's care and eventual expansion into Jacksonville, Tampa, and Atlanta.

All in all, it was another successful meeting. Lamar was super confident in his acquisition of the apartment complex in addition to the renovation and eventual management of it.

It was around 3pm when they all decided to part ways. There were hugs and kisses and Lamar and Nicole exchanged numbers. Ms. Armand advised Lamar that she would have comparisons for him tomorrow and upon his decision, would also go ahead and draw up the paperwork within the next 3 days should he decide to go with Nicole's firm.

As Lamar made his way back to the valet and waited on his vehicle, his mom popped into his head. He decided against calling her and instead decided to pull up on her. He wasn't sure why she was so heavily on his mind, but he needed to ease his concern, so as soon as he hopped into his vehicle, he made his way towards her house.

Chapter 48

It was around 3:45pm when Lamar pulled into his mom's driveway. He sat in his car for a moment before turning it off as he gathered his thoughts. He was really not one to worry about his mom so he told himself that she was fine and that he was probably just tripping. After convincing himself he'd be ok once he laid eyes on her, he turned his car off and made his way up to the front door.

He knocked a few times, and after not getting an answer, he used his key to unlock the door, and he entered his mom's house. "Hello?" he stated as he crossed the threshold into her living room. Still not getting a response and noting how quiet it was, his heartbeat sped up as he quickly searched through the house, where he found his mom lying peacefully in her bed. He stood and watched for a few moments, comforted by the gentle rise and fall of her chest.

After a few moments watching her, he heard her tired voice ask, "Boy what chu doing, stalking me?"

He laughed softly and answered, "You were on my mind, so I wanted to see you. How are you?"

Laughing weakly, his mom gestured to the chair that was at the foot of her bed. Lamar made his way to it and sat down and gazed upon her.

"I'm ok. I've just been really tired lately. I appreciate you checking on me though. How you doing?"

Lamar paused for a moment then went on to share with her everything that had occurred in his life up until that moment except Devon. He wasn't ready for that conversation just yet.

"I'm so proud of you! Proud of the man you've become. I know your childhood wasn't easy but I did my best..."

"You absolutely did! You pulled us through it. I can't thank you enough."

Her next question knocked him off center a bit when she asked, "Aside from all of your accomplishments and stuff, when you are alone with just your thoughts, how are you really doing?"

Taking a moment, Lamar sat back in the chair and really considered her question. He thought about the sense of darkness that frequently invaded his dreams and his waking thoughts. He considered how his life was taking off and how he'd formed all of these amazing relationships and how, in spite of these things, he often felt lonely and empty. He thought of the anxiety that sometimes reared its head and how hard he fought to keep it in check while in real time, no one even knew he struggled in this way. He reflected on these things for a few moments before finally responding.

"Well honestly, I've never sat down and allowed myself to think about it. I usually just focus on something else to do or another goal to reach and the journey usually keeps me so busy that I don't have to think about it."

Weakly reaching for her eldest son's hand, his mom answered, "Son, ain't nothing wrong with success but you can't use it as a cover up or you'll never truly enjoy it." She paused as she asked him for the water on the nightstand next to her bed. After taking a few sips, she began again, "I asked if you were ok because lately, I've been in this house thinking on my past and how many mistakes I've made and how I could have done better by you." She paused as tears began to flow. Lamar's eyes welled up and his began to flow as well. "I just want you to know that I've always loved you and am so proud of you and am so sorry for the pain I caused you." She finished as she weakly squeezed his hand.

Lamar was floored with emotion as he sat there for what seemed like ever and wept along with his mom as he held her hand. Sure, things early on had been rough between them but he'd long ago accepted that she'd done her best and had learned, through Ms. Santi, to forgive his mom because in spite of the trauma she never shared and pain that she'd lived through, she did her best to try to work through her adversity and provide a better life for her children. He'd also learned not to engage when they were at odds because that was always going to be his momma and that he would only ever have one. In those talks, he'd learned about forgiveness and had learned to move on in spite of the hurt he felt. Seeing the pain that she was in crushed him and he wanted nothing more but to soothe her. He also realized in this moment that he'd also hurt her by pulling away and cutting communications off with her for a time and while he'd eventually come around, he could never get the years he'd spent distancing himself. That broke him even more as he realized that he'd been petty and spiteful.

He now realized that over the years, his mom had concluded that she was partially responsible for their broken relationship and that she'd lived with that guilt for years. He wanted nothing more than to take away the pain and fix it, but he realized that he could not get that back. Sure, they'd developed an amazing relationship over the last 7 years but at the memory of so many times that they could have spent mending their lives together, Lamar could do nothing but hold his head in his hands and sob.

He finally looked up at his mom, smiling down upon him. "You're a good kid, and I never realized how sensitive you were, but I learned how forgiving you were. For that, I appreciate you because I understand it was difficult for you, and I am so sorry for the hurt I brought upon you." She smiled as tears flowed down her face.

"Mommy, I forgave you long ago and it hurts to know that you still walked around with all of that on your chest. You are my mom and I love you more than you will ever know, and I am proud of you and am grateful to have had you in my life. You taught me how to stand, how to fight and how to pray and I will never forget the lessons I learned. I know it may have felt like it but even when I was away, I never gave up on you and I never stopped praying for you. The happiest day in my life was when I saw the change for myself. I've never been prouder. I also realized that you had your own issues that you were battling, and I wish I could have helped you through them but the day that you made the decision to fight for your kids, helped me more than you will ever know. I want you to know that even though you've lived with these feelings of guilt, you didn't have to. You loved us the best you could, and I think you did an amazing job. I want you to know that I will never hold anything against you because even in the dark times, there were still lessons to be learned. I'm honored to have you as my mom, and I hope that you can forgive yourself."

His mom smiled and squeezed his hand again. "You sure you're ok?" Lamar asked as he got up to grab some napkins to wipe his mom's tears and then his own.

"Yea baby, I'm just more tired than usual."

"You sure you don't need me to come over and sleep on your couch or take you to your doctor?"

Weakly laughing, she replied, "I'm fine but if I'm not feeling any better by tomorrow, I will go to the hospital."

"All right now cause you know I will call the emergency wagon."

At this, they both laughed. The rest of the time was spent with them going over Lamar's vision for the future and everything he had in store. His mom lay there taking it all in as she smiled. He eventually fixed her some soup and then helped her to the bathroom. Then made sure she was comfortably tucked into her bed with her remote and her phone was charging by her side just in case she needed to reach out for anything.

Around 6pm, his mom had drifted off to sleep so Lamar adjusted the TV volume and turned on the closet light in her room and he made sure everything was locked up and then he left and made his way home.

When he finally got there, Devon's truck was in the driveway. It was odd but, in the moment, Lamar was unable to be excited because seeing his mom still weighed so heavily on his mind. He sat in his car for a moment before going into the house.

Finally dragging himself out of his car, he made his way into the house, and he was instantly reminded that he'd not eaten anything. He found Devon in the den who was chowing down on Salmon, jasmine rice and asparagus. He smiled at him and then made his way into the kitchen, where he fixed himself a plate and made his way back into the den, kicked off his shoes, and sat next to Devon who leaned over for a quick peck on the cheek before returning to his meal.

Devon didn't know exactly what it was, but he knew something was bothering Lamar, but rather than press him about it, he just decided to be there. He knew that when Lamar was ready, he would talk about it.

After the two of them finished their meal, Devon washed the dishes and put everything away. He then made it back into the den where he observed Lamar absently staring at the TV. Devon got comfortable on the couch and drew Lamar into his arms. After gently kissing him on the back of his neck, Devon drew Lamar into an even tighter embrace and just held him until the two of them drifted off to sleep.

Chapter 49

Tuesday found Lamar wrapped up in Devon's arms. He lay there with his eyes wide open just staring at the wall as Devon slept soundly behind him. Normally, this would comfort him but this morning, it did nothing for him as his mind was elsewhere. He could not help the worry he felt about his mom and it would not let him go as much as he tried to shake it.

Seeing that he was not going back to sleep, he quietly got up and hit the bathroom before heading into his gym area and working out in silence. He really pushed himself until he just about collapsed on the floor. He cooled down and then made his way towards the bathroom. As he stripped himself and got into the shower, he heard Devon enter the bathroom as well and shortly thereafter, Devon was in the shower.

Devon sensed that something was still bothering Lamar so the two of them showered in silence and then got out and after drying off, Devon got ready. Before leaving, Devon gave him a tight hug and let him know that he was there if he needed him and then he kissed him on the cheek and left for work shortly after.

Lamar wandered into the kitchen and realized that he had no appetite, settled on some orange juice and then made it back into the den where he just sat silently. He remembered that he had his meeting at 1pm with his attorney but that was some hours from now and he just wanted to sit and be still. The more he sat there, the more anxious and frustrated he became and before he knew it, he was doing something he hadn't done since he was 7. He prayed.

"Lord God, it's me. I know I have not talked with you since I was a kid and with everything that I'd experienced in my life, I felt I was right to do so and honestly, I feel weird talking to you now but I'm asking that you help my mom because I don't know what's wrong and I ask that you help me because I am not sure what's going on with me either. I'm here before you because I feel heavy and I'm feeling empty, and I don't like it and I don't know what to do. Again, I know it's been forever but if you love me like you say you love me, please help." Lamar paused as he recollected how folks had always said that when asked anything of God, to ask in Jesus' name and it would be done. "In Jesus' name I pray. Amen."

Lamar wasn't sure what he was supposed to be experiencing but he honestly did feel a bit lighter so with that little bit of relief, he decided to go hang out at Haul Over Marina and watch the boats come in and out. He dressed in some blue basketball shorts and a white tee shirt and blue slides. He grabbed some bottles of water, hopped in his car and made his way over to the beach.

He made it to the parking lot of the marina around 10:30am. He found a spot, got out and locked his car. He went towards his favorite bench that was under a tree and sat there, mere feet from the water and just gazed out upon it. There were no people walking around just yet and it seemed as if he'd missed the boats going out so he attempted to enjoy the water. But before he knew it, he felt something bubbling in his chest and next he was bent over crying.

He felt as if some long-forgotten crypt had been opened for all the world to view its hidden secrets and knowledge. Things were falling out of it faster than he could process, and this scared him. So he ran to his car, turned it on and sat there in agony as the tears flowed and he screamed and beat his dashboard.

He sat there, like that, in his car for about 20 minutes before he was able to bring himself to some type of neutral space where his eyes, emotions and heart could rest. Amazingly enough, as he got his breathing under control, he felt so much better. It was as if the weight from yesterday was fleeting.

At the realization that he was literally shedding the pain and emotion of yesterday, he offered up a quick "thank you" to God and vowed to speak with him more. Looking down at his phone, he saw that it was now 11:20am. He then decided to go sit back near the water since he had an hour or so before he was to meet Ms. Armand.

This time, once he sat down, not only did he feel lighter, but he also actually smiled. A gentle breeze blew through the leaves of the tree as he did, causing the sunshine to dance across the ground before him but what caused him to smile even harder was the fact that the breeze seemed to gently caress his face. At this, Lamar closed his eyes and held his head up as the breeze increased a bit. The beauty of the moment caused tears to slowly fall from his eyes but what shocked him was that they seemed to be attached to something foreign. A sensation that he'd never experienced before. He couldn't really say what it was but he knew that it made his heart smile and caused him to exhale in a way he'd never done before.

He wasn't sure how long he'd sat like that but suddenly the sound of splashing caught his attention, and he looked out over the water and didn't see anything. Odd, he thought until the next time he saw a pretty sizable fish jumping out of the water as 3 dorsal fins swiftly pursued it. He smiled at the pleasure he took in seeing this play out before him.

He looked down at his phone and, seeing that it was now 12pm, he decided to go ahead and make his way towards his attorney's office. He downed the water bottle that he had with him, tossed it in the garbage, and then made his way back to his car and, after cranking it up, slowly

merged into afternoon rush hour traffic as he made his way towards N
Miami Beach.

Chapter 50

Lamar pulled into the parking lot of his attorney's office around 12:35pm. He sat in his car for a few moments, reflecting on his day thus far, and he felt content. After about 10 or so minutes of sitting there in silence with his eyes closed, he finally readied himself to head upstairs for his meeting.

As usual, he was greeted by Ms. Sheila as he stepped off the elevator. As he was making his way towards the waiting area, Ms. Sheila redirected him to Ms. Armand's office, stating that "she's been waiting for you." Lamar thanked her and made his way into the office.

"Good afternoon, my young visionary." Ms. Armand began as she stood with an extended hand.

Laughing softly, Lamar took her extended hand and responded, "Good afternoon."

After they both took their seats, Ms. Armand produced two folders. "Today is going to be short and sweet. This first folder is for your LLC. It's been completed and you can take it with you so that you have copies of it," she said as she handed him a navy blue folder.

"This next folder contains the title to the complex and you walk out of here today the official owner!" She smiled in pride as she handed him the next folder.

Lamar looked from one folder to the next in silence. Here it was and so it began. He smiled and then got up and made his way around her desk and gave her a huge hug as tears flowed down both their faces.

When they finally let each other go, Lamar sat back down in his seat. Ms. Armand got herself together and then she handed him four sheets of paper that were stapled together before she began. "These are the other property management companies that I told you I'd research just so you can get a feel for how they operate, how long they've been in business, the properties they manage and their fees. I also went a step further and included BBB reviews and customer reviews from actual tenants and just to be fair, I did the same for Nicole's firm. Go ahead and take a few moments to look over them and let me know what you think," she said as she refocused her attention on her PC.

Lamar took his time reading through all of the information, paying close attention to the listed conditions of the properties per recent city inspections. He then honed in on the fees and services offered and then lastly, he reflected over the reviews. From here, he broke it down to his top 3. After comparing the numbers, he decided that Nicole's firm slightly edged out the other 2.

"Ms. Armand," Lamar interrupted his attorney who was in the middle of replying to an email. "I'd like to move forward with Nicole's firm."

"Excellent. I'll draw up the forms and get them to you on Friday. Now, about the brunch... I haven't heard anything back yet but that's ok. Once I do hear from them, we will have to arrange another meeting, which I will set up with an accounting firm that I use so that we can begin to consult about the potential cash structure. From there, we would then begin to finalize those plans and then we would reach out to a few developers in order to get some renderings and bids. Otherwise, Mr. Hicks, we are done for the day. Any questions?" Ms. Armand smiled.

"None at all. Thank you so much!" Lamar smiled.

"It's always my pleasure." Ms. Armand smiled as she got up out of her seat, hugged Lamar, and then walked him out to the lobby. He thanked her again for her time, thanked Ms. Sheila as well, and bid them both a good day.

He then hopped on the elevator and made his way back down to his car, where he sat inside with the engine running for a few moments, looking between the two folders.

This is really happening, he thought to himself.

Smiling, he decided to call Julia. When she didn't answer, it occurred to him to check on his mom. He was planning on going by later on but since he was free in the moment and bubbling with great news, he decided to give her a buzz.

"Hey lady." Lamar smiled as his mom answered.

"Hey baby." His mom began. "I'm in the hospital just so you know. Please don't worry about me. The doctors are running some tests, but I wanted you to know that I'm going to be ok. I'm going to get my rest and I'm going to be fine."

Lamar's first instinct was to go into panic mode but there was something that held him back. "I'm on my way." Lamar finally managed.

"No, you're not. You're going to go on with your day. If I need you, I will call you and just so you know, I told Peirre and Sharena the same thing. Ya'll don't need to worry about me. I'm going to be fine." His mom smiled.

"You sure?" Lamar asked.

"Yes. Now enjoy your day and I love you. Call me later." His mom smiled.

"I will and please call me if you need anything," Lamar answered.

Lamar then decided against doing or going anything or anywhere else and beelined home. He rushed in the house and went to his patio where he sat down, and he began praying. He prayed for his mom. He prayed for his siblings. He prayed for his family and friends and employees. He prayed for his attorney and his tribe. He prayed for Devon. He prayed for those that were hurting and hopeless. He prayed for peace and whatever joy was. He prayed for strength to deal with the battles to come and for help with the residue of yesterday's wars. And then lastly, he prayed for himself and then he just sat there in silence looking off into the distance, not really focused on anything but awaiting his answers.

Once he'd had enough of sitting in silence, he made his way back inside where he stripped down to his underwear and hopped on the couch. After wrapping up in his comforter, he cruised through his cable channels. Finding nothing as usual, he logged into Hulu and put on Scandal. As he got into the events surrounding Frankie Vargas's death, he drifted off to sleep.

Chapter 51

Lamar woke up around 5pm, and his first thought was to call his mom. He leaned over the couch, picked up his phone, and dialed her number. He let the phone ring several times before disconnecting. He then decided to get up, get dressed, and pop up on his mom. As he was about to walk out of the den, his phone alerted him to a text message.

He turned around and picked the phone up off the couch and saw that it was from his mom. She let him know that she was ok and that she was just tired, and she didn't feel like talking. He texted her back that he understood and to call if she needed anything.

The remainder of the evening was spent relaxing to soothing sounds and great cuisine as Devon stopped by Fogo de Chao and picked up a variety of items. He'd also stopped by a beverage store and picked up some pairing wines.

The two of them enjoyed the meal, music and each other well into the evening before either of them called it a night. They showered together and for the first time, actually slept in Lamar's bed where they were serenaded by 50's Jazz.

Wednesday came and went without a hitch. Lamar had a chance to speak with Peirre and they set up a time for the following Monday to walk the property and assess the repairs but other than that, there was nothing eventful that happened. He decided not to bother his mom thinking she would reach out when she was ready to talk.

For dinner that night, he chose to eat at Ed's and called Angela to see if there was a VIP booth available. She said that there was, and she took his food and drink orders and said that everything would be ready when he arrived.

Lamar and Devon arrived at Ed's around 7pm. Angela led them to their booth and true to her word, she had everything set up. They both thanked her and took their time enjoying the selections Lamar had chosen. By the time they were ready to go, it was 9pm. They made it back to Lamar's house, where they showered together and again slept in Lamar's bed with Devon holding Lamar tight.

Now, Thursday morning rolled around and it started off pretty typical. Lamar and Devon woke up around 8:30pm and Lamar was the one who decided that Devon needed a quickie before work. He eagerly provided Devon with a slow and tender piece of mouth and then hopped on top where he rode Devon for dear life. The pleasure was so intense that when Lamar finally dismounted, he found himself still trembling. Devon laughed while squeezing Lamar's cheeks. The two then showered and upon getting out and drying off, Lamar, still naked, made Devon a little breakfast while Devon got ready for work.

After giving Devon his neatly packaged breakfast sandwich and coffee, Lamar and Devon kissed at the front door before Devon made his way outside and off to work. As Lamar locked the front door and headed to his room to grab a robe and underwear, his phone rang. Seeing that it was his sister, he answered.

"Hey lady," Lamar said as he slid into his underwear.

"Hey. You need to come to the hospital. It's mommy," she said bluntly.

Lamar immediately began crying asking her what was wrong with his momma. She replied, "Just come" before hanging up.

Lamar tried to keep himself calm but he could not control the nervousness. He quickly threw on the first clothes and slides he laid his hands on. Not trusting himself to drive, he called an Uber.

As he waited, he texted Ms. Armand, Julia, Ms. Santi, Angela, Devon and his aunts Christine and Elaine that his mom was in the hospital, and something was wrong. He let them know which hospital and then he went back to the uber app and upon seeing that it was 5 minutes away, grabbed his keys, wallet, phone and then he locked up and stood outside waiting on his Uber.

About 20 or so minutes later, he was dropped off in front of Jackson North. He rushed into the doors and beelined towards the receptionist's desk. He told her who he was and who he was here to see and was given her room number and floor. He then dashed to the elevator where he waited maybe a minute before the next cab became available. He stepped inside and hit the button for the 7th floor.

As he came out of the elevator, he looked around for signage. Finally locating what he was looking for, he made his way quickly to his mom's room. He was met there by his brother, his sister, Nicky, and all the kids. He stepped into the room and the tears immediately flowed as everyone stood around his mom's bed.

His heart was broken and his spirit crushed as he looked upon her lying there, restrained in that bed. As sad as he was, he couldn't help but notice that she didn't appear to be there with them. I mean, yea she was breathing, and he could still feel the warmth of who she was, but it was as if this woman who lay before him was merely her representative here for this very moment and that the woman who he knew her to be had already begun her transition. She was staring off into the distance, fixated on something that nobody else could see. She didn't seem to be in pain or sad but rather calm and at peace, even though she never spoke another word.

They stood there over her crying for about 30 minutes before they heard a gentle knocking on the door. It was the doctor who was attending to her.

Her name was Dr. Tamika Johnson. She asked if she could see them for a moment. Nicky told them to go, and she would see about the kids. So then Dr. Johnson led Linda's 3 children to a small room where she closed the door after they were seated.

"I hate to be the bearer of this news, but your mom's cancer has spread throughout her body and has been attacking her organs for some time now. There's nothing more we can do except place her in hospice."

"What are you saying?" Lamar asked, eyes full of tears.

"What I'm saying is that the cancer has spread so swiftly that her insides are being ate away and we can't do anything to stop it."

"But cancer?" Peirre asked as his tears flowed.

"Yes. You didn't know?" Dr. Johnson asked as her heart went out to the three of them.

"No, we didn't," Sharena responded as she wiped away her tears.

The three of them sat there in stunned silence. Years ago, their mom had shared that she had battled and beaten breast cancer so they thought nothing more of it and knew that she was keeping her doctor's appointments and doing everything that she could so they were floored at the suddenness of this onslaught.

Composing herself, Dr. Johnson continued, "She never told you? I'm so sorry that you all had to find out this way." She looked upon them in compassion at the pain their mother must have experienced to not share this news with her children and in awe at the bravery she exhibited so as to not have her children suffering with her.

"I'm so sorry," Dr. Johnson began, "I want to tell you that the best we can do is give her morphine to keep her comfortable in easing her pain. We don't recommend moving her. In addition, we need to know whether or not you want us to resuscitate should we lose her but keep in mind that her bones are so brittle that the pressure from the compressions may very well break her bones."

"Resuscitate," Peirre answered.

"No, we're not doing that. Did you hear what she said about her bones?" Lamar responded understanding fully the pain his brother was experiencing.

"So you gone just let her die?" Peirre responded with tears in his eyes.

"Bra, she's already gone. Did you see her?" Lamar replied with tears flowing down his face.

Looking at Dr. Johnson, Lamar answered her question. "Do not resuscitate."

The remainder of Thursday was spent with the three of them sitting by her side in silence.

It was around 10pm when they all started filing out. Lamar was the last one there. He looked down upon his mom and smiled with tears in his eyes. He told her that he was proud of her and that he loved her and then he left.

As he walked down the hallway, he pulled out his phone. He saw that he had 15 missed calls. He'd received calls from Julia, Devon, Ms. Santi, Ms. Armand, Angela, and his aunts Christine and Elaine. He turned his phone off after deciding that he was not in the mood to talk to anyone.

He finally made his way outside and upon seeing several taxis, flagged one down and made his way home. He sat in silence the whole way there as his life with his mom flashed before his eyes. The tire swing they'd made when he was younger. The peanut butter cookies he and his siblings had made his mom one evening. The bike she'd bought him when he was 12. The big wheel she'd bought his sister when she was 5 and how she'd driven head on into the bushes. How his brother had climbed to the top of a tree that was in their yard and they'd had to call the police as they stood on the ground watching and looking to catch him if need be. The boxes of books she often sent to him when he'd moved out. All of the times she'd bbq'd at Silver Lake when they lived in Bristol. How she'd taught him how to read, write and do math and supported his love for books from early on.

He recalled so many things and as he finally got out of the taxi in front of his house, he stood there and just cried. He cried because he selfishly allowed so much time to pass when he could have done more to fix the relationship with his mom. He could have been more patient and not so stubborn. He could not have let his emotions lead him as much. He could have stuck around and tried a little harder but there was nothing he could do about any of it now because she was gone.

His proud and broken Queen was gone.